I0637745

WEST of
WESTPORT

ALAN E. CRAVEN

MILFORD
HOUSE
an imprint of Sunbury Press, Inc.
Mechanicsburg, PA USA

MILFORD HOUSE

an imprint of Sunbury Press, Inc.
Mechanicsburg, PA USA

NOTE: This is a work of fiction. Names, characters, places, and incidents either are the product of the author's imagination or are used fictitiously. While, as in all fiction, the literary perceptions and insights are shaped by experiences, any resemblance to actual persons, living or dead, events, or locales is entirely coincidental.

Copyright © 2025 by Alan E. Craven.
Cover Copyright © 2025 by Sunbury Press, Inc.

Sunbury Press supports copyright. Copyright fuels creativity, encourages diverse voices, promotes free speech, and creates a vibrant culture. Thank you for buying an authorized edition of this book and for complying with copyright laws. Except for the quotation of short passages for the purpose of criticism and review, no part of this publication may be reproduced, scanned, or distributed in any form without permission. You are supporting writers and allowing Sunbury Press to continue to publish books for every reader. For information contact Sunbury Press, Inc., Subsidiary Rights Dept., PO Box 548, Boiling Springs, PA 17007 USA or legal@sunburypress.com.

For information about special discounts for bulk purchases, please contact Sunbury Press Orders Dept. at (855) 338-8359 or orders@sunburypress.com.

To request one of our authors for speaking engagements or book signings, please contact Sunbury Press Publicity Dept. at publicity@sunburypress.com.

FIRST MILFORD HOUSE PRESS EDITION: December 2025

Set in Adobe Garamond Pro | Interior design by Crystal Devine | Cover by Lawrence Knorr | Edited by Leah Brennsteiner.

Publisher's Cataloging-in-Publication Data
Names: Craven, Alan E., author.
Title: West of Westport / Alan E. Craven.
Description: First trade paperback edition. | Mechanicsburg, PA : Milford House Press, 2025.
Summary: Lee's Army surrenders and five days later President Lincoln is dead by an assassin's bullet. In Lawrence, Ezra Middleton watches Kansas as the new state grows westward along the railroads, and the Indians are pushed out of the best land. In Missouri, he faces Rebels and robbers like Frank and Jesse James and works with Colonel Benjamin Maypole of the Missouri Militia to pursue the last of the Bushwhackers.
Identifiers: ISBN : 979-8-88819-359-4 (paperback).
Subjects: HISTORY / United States / State & Local / Midwest (IA, IL, IN, KS, MI, MN, MO, ND, NE, OH, SD, WI) | HISTORY / United States / State & Local / Middle Atlantic (DC, DE, MD, NJ, NY, PA| HISTORY / United States / Civil War Period (1850-1877).

Designed in the USA
0 1 1 2 3 5 8 13 21 34 55

For the Love of Books!

For Janice

CHAPTER ONE

IN THE STILLNESS of the night came the pounding on the door, a boy calling my name, and the dogs—Caesar and the younger one, Brutus—sounding an alarm that other dogs were answering across the town. "Mist' Middleton! Mist' Middleton! President's been shot!" he shouted. "Not likely to survive."

In my nightshirt, instantly awake, I ran to the door, throwing it open to reveal the boy, his face yellowed by the lantern he carried. "Lincoln," he stammered, gasping for breath. "Father sent me. Stopped at the papers . . . then came right here." His neck was wrapped in a scarf, and he shivered in the April damp, incomprehension and fear in his face.

"What happened, boy?" I asked as we faced each other, boy and man, sharing a moment of shock. "The President shot? Just as the war has ended?" There were questions I wanted him to answer: "Are you certain of the message? Who shot him?"

"Dunno," he replied to my queries, still breathing heavily. "Father said you . . . could come to the office. He's watching the wire."

"Thanks, Young Orville," I answered, touching him on the shoulder. "I'll get on some clothes and head right over there." He was ashen-faced and trembling, alarmed by the news or perhaps just chilled. Glancing up at me, he gave an enigmatic nod and took off across the lawn like a rabbit, his lantern bouncing as he ran, eager to return to a place of safety. Turning, I saw Hannah holding a candlestick, a shawl over her shoulders, face attenuated by shadows; in the candlelight, her hair shone like sparks from iron beaten at the forge.

"President's been shot," I pronounced the words distinctly to be certain she understood. "Orville sent the boy over." One hand flew to her mouth as though she might be sick, but she held the candle steady in the other. "I'm afraid he won't survive, Hannah. I am sorry."

"But there's peace now," she averred, watching me, her eyes wide with shock. "The war's *over*!" There was confusion in her eyes—and sadness, of course, since she admired Lincoln above all others. Still, she did not weep or tremble. I had pulled on my trousers, suspenders over my shoulders, and stuck my bare feet in my boots. Luckily, the knocking had not awakened the children.

Holding Hannah, I answered. "Well, Lee's army surrendered in Virginia, but there could be a plot in Washington, or just some lunatic there. Maybe Orville can tell us. Just keep the door locked 'til I return."

Pulling on my coat, off I went, trotting through the early morning dew, still stunned by the news. The double-quick trot I had mastered in the militia—less exhausting than running—and I could trot for miles as I had done at Westport. Odd I should think of that now with the war being over. The half-moon, cold and distant, hung high in the sky, and I could see well without a lantern. Silence had returned to Lawrence. Turning the corner onto Massachusetts, the main street, I saw that all the buildings were dark save one; lights burned in the telegraph office.

A few people were gathered there, and I leapt to the wooden sidewalk and pulled open the door. At his instrument beneath a kerosene lamp, bending over the tablet on which, click by click, word by word, recording the messages with a pencil, sat the telegrapher, Orville Roden. Around him in the circle of lamplight stood John Speer, editor of the *Kansas Tribune*, his bald head shining, Hovey Lowman of the *Kansas Journal*, in a fur hat, and Young Orville Roden, scarf still around his neck, blowing on his hands to warm them. Both editors were Republicans, their papers replacing Free-State ones destroyed by Quantrill.

The editors nodded to me, fearing to speak lest Orville be bothered or perhaps—the telegraph having so recently come to Lawrence—reluctant to shatter the spell spun out by the electrical magic. Although four chairs stood along the wall, both men were content to stand, eyeing the machine warily as though it were a coiled rattlesnake signaling its intention to strike. An unlit stove occupied the corner, although lighting it would have removed the chill and damp from the room. This was, of course, a death watch—as though the President might be lying in the next room, not fifteen hundred miles away in Washington.

"How could this happen?" Speer asked in a whisper, glaring at us, his eyes narrowing. He was a florid man, bewhiskered, now inclining to plumpness. "Isn't Washington chock-full of soldiers? Can't they protect one goddamned man?" He jerked his head and turned away in anger. A supporter of the ambitious U.S. Senator James Lane, Speer had been a sociable, ebullient man before Quantrill's Raid, during which two of his three young sons had been murdered by the Confederate guerrillas; now he had become preoccupied and taciturn, with little time for jokes.

"A tragedy, I say!" Lowman added, trying to adjust his collar, as the instrument suddenly chattered again, and everyone looked at it. Orville raised his left hand as he recorded the words he deciphered from the electronic language. He nodded as he wrote, as though reassuring the machine that he understood its message. Seeing some of the words written on the page, I took a deep breath, reading "conspiracy," and then "Seward."

As the machine went silent again, Orville looked around at us, his brow furrowed as he spoke. "Nothing new about Lincoln, but Secretary of State Seward was attacked at his home." He stopped for a moment and then continued. "Roads out of Washington have been closed. The word used was *conspiracy*. But what does that mean? And where is Vice President Johnson? Has he been killed too?"

"After it fell, Lincoln wanted to see Richmond," Lowman asserted. "You read those stories of his bravery? Didn't you, Ezra?" I nodded because, as a correspondent for the *St. Louis Globe Democrat*, I continued to receive communication from the editor, Russell Downing. Now, however, the West—Nebraska, Kansas, and Missouri—was quiet, after Price's Confederate invaders were soundly defeated at Westport in Missouri and again at Mine Creek in Kansas, and so I had little noteworthy information to report to him.

Lowman now had everyone's attention. His uncombed hair stuck out from under his hat, and his unbuttoned collar and clothing in disarray suggested that, like the rest of us, he too had been roused from sleep and had dressed hastily. "Yes, Lincoln went to Richmond to tour the Secesh capital," Lowman shouted, waving his arms. "On the fourth of April, wasn't it, Ezra?"

"Two days after the Confederate army and officials fled the city—or what was left of it," I answered.

Of course, Lowman's audience already knew the story. Who did not? I thought I saw what Lowman was building toward. "Lincoln went on a barge rowed by twelve sailors who, on land, carried naval carbines. That was all! And Admiral Porter and Lincoln's son, Tad, too. Going to inspect the ruined Confederate capital."

"Heard the whole town turned out to see him! Some whites, but many hundreds of Blacks. Got down on their knees to him, didn't they?" Roden added, also caught up in the excitement of the story. "Like some emperor or king!"

"My point is . . . Lincoln was in extreme peril then, so how in Christ's name could somebody shoot him *in Washington?* And in a *theater?*" Hovey Lowman asked. It was the first I had heard of where the shooting took place. Now he seemed ready to answer his own questions. "Yes! Conspiracy! Treachery! Betrayal!" In my mind's eye, I could see the words like headlines in his newspaper. Surprised by the outburst, everyone was suddenly quiet.

Although the *Kansas Tribune* and the *Kansas Journal* competed against each other, both had been staunchly Unionist and abolitionist despite supporting rival factions of the Republican Party. The *Globe Democrat,* my former paper—for I had written nothing for it since Lincoln's reelection in November of 1864, the interest of the nation turning away from the Border to Lee's surrender at Appomattox and the end of the war— had followed the lead of Lincoln and made the survival of the Union its great cause, the key to which was keeping Missouri and Kentucky, both slave-holding states, in the Union. I was, therefore, not surprised to see Speer nodding in agreement.

Although a great weariness now possessed my body, I knew I would not sleep that night, but because I needed to share my grief with Hannah, who waited at home for me, I bid my companions good night, except for Young Orville, who, wrapped in a blanket, now snored in the welcome oblivion of youth.

I did not trot home but walked slowly, ruminating on the morrow, sunrise still five hours away. The news of Lincoln's death had come with the force of a violent flood, scouring out all life before it and leaving behind only bare stone. Kansas, now four years a state in the Union, was regarded as among the most patriotic of all the states, always reaching its quota of army volunteers, among the first to send Negro troops into combat, and long associated with John Brown, the abolitionist martyr, whose execution in '59 had ignited antislavery sentiment across the North. Downing, I believed, would want a report for the *Globe Democrat* about the Kansas response to the assassination. Since hearing of Lincoln's wounds—"not likely to survive," the boy had said—the nation's problems seemed insurmountable to me: several million freed slaves, ruined cities in the South, railroads and cropland destroyed on a wide scale, and, in the West, Missouri bushwhackers, armed and angry Confederate Indian soldiers in the Indian Territory, and lawlessness in Texas. A dreadful future, all this without the one, the only man, with the moral stature and intelligence to lead an exhausted and still-divided nation where so many had already died.

Oh, I was acquainted with Death. My dear friend, Henry Sonnet, had been brutally murdered here in Lawrence by the Confederate guerrilla band of William Quantrill, and Zeke Skinner, my old neighbor, had his face blown away as he stepped from his door. Young Judge Carpenter was shot down by long-barreled pistols while his wife and sister begged for his life, and a dozen or so recruits, unarmed, still in nightshirts, were butchered at dawn, coming from their ripped and flattened tents. With only a few men left alive to help, I picked up bodies, men and boys slaughtered in Lawrence, some so badly burned that we could not tell white men from Negro. For two days, we collected them, wrapped them like bundles of laundry since there were no coffins, and buried them, many in a common grave on Hogback Ridge (now called Mount Oread), horseflies buzzing around us in the sweltering heat.

Then, a year later at the Battle of Westport, Dan Cornish, who commanded the Kansas Militia Regiment in which I served, had died in combat along with a boy from Lawrence whom I had promised to protect. There, on the Missouri prairie, I saw men that I knew shot, bayonetted, slashed, hacked, and blown to pieces by artillery. Nevertheless, Lincoln's death, which was imminent, seemed crueler than those of men who had perished in that terrible war. Only five days since Lee's surrender, the man who saved the Union was about to die without knowing of the love and gratitude of the nation he had preserved.

CHAPTER TWO

IN TIMES OF turmoil, many people turn to The Bible for solace; I, on the other hand, am more inclined to seek peace in the words of William Shakespeare. Because my mother had died when I was young, my brothers and I were reared by my father, an eminent attorney in St. Louis who loved Shakespeare. In my mind, I can still hear him pronounce, "Shakespeare holds the mirror up to Nature, Ezra." My two brothers, several years older than I, were indifferent to literature, but I must have seen in the Bard's plays and poems a way to please a father whose attention I desperately sought.

After college in the East, I studied for my law diploma with my father and every night at dinner—my brothers having entered his law firm and marrying—my father and I regularly discussed Shakespeare until I decided to migrate to Kansas to practice the law there and, almost by accident, also became a correspondent for the *Globe Democrat*, reporting on news as the Territory moved toward and gained statehood in the year Lincoln was inaugurated and the Civil War began—1861. In Kansas, we were as likely to call it the War of the Rebellion.

Moreover, in addition to providing me endless reading pleasure, it was to Shakespeare—or rather to a phrase from Shakespeare—that I owe the greatest happiness of my life, for on a return visit to St. Louis after six months in Kansas Territory I met a young woman, quite beautiful but scornful, who after some shrewish comments, described herself in a whisper to me as "a maiden never bold," a phrase I recognized as from *Othello*. Identifying it, I responded with a line about Cordelia in *King Lear*, and the scornful lady countered with one from *Much Ado*, where

Benedick and Beatrice, the Bard's wittiest lovers, exchange insults that hide a deep but sudden mutual passion.

When I laughed, she responded with a sudden effulgent smile. Although our meeting lasted a mere ten minutes, I was immediately smitten with love for the *bold* Hannah Waterhouse. On my return to St. Louis a year later, after the exchange of many letters, I asked for her hand in marriage, and we were wed in April 1858, the sixteenth, the anniversary now only a day away.

On the morning of April fifteenth, Hannah and I dressed in silence. After a sleepless night, we were in no hurry to learn more about the act of murder and the identity of the assassins—for there was already evidence of a plot. That information would not salve our pain. Lincoln had died in a house across from Ford's Theatre in Washington at 7:22 in the morning, my friend Eli Foster told us. Eli, who had served with me in the Kansas State Militia, had been the first to knock at our door. Since Eli, now courting the new schoolteacher, Prudence Franklin, was still a bachelor, Hannah assumed he would need a proper breakfast and could be prevailed upon to eat flapjacks and bacon with us, our children, sleepyheads, still in bed.

"Just one flapjack, Hannah," he said. "Not much appetite this morning, you see." He took a sip from his mug of black coffee and winced. "Hot!" he exclaimed, putting his hand to his mouth as though in pain. That was Eli, winking and smiling at every pretty woman who came into his bank, and Hannah was no exception.

"Papers out on the street yet?" I asked, and Eli nodded, brushing carelessly at his thick blond hair. I knew all the papers would have the same story: whatever words the telegraph fed us. Each editor across Kansas would be cranking out what outrage he could muster up to accompany the grim headlines that screamed from the front page: *HORROR! HORROR!*

"Be ready for questions," he warned with a laugh. "People think you know more than the local papers. As though you have a direct telegraph wire from St. Louis." He chuckled again. "Or maybe a direct wire from God," he said, rising from the table to thank Hannah with a wink.

Hannah was accustomed to Eli's joshing, but this morning was not one for banter, so she replied only with, "Most welcome, Eli," and a weak smile.

As Eli and I walked silently across our lawn in the fragile morning sunshine, I began to notice the rich smell of newly plowed fields and animal dung, the welcome smell of life in death. On Massachusetts Street, people were gathered in knots as if for a holiday—except for their faces, drawn, hollow-eyed, or red from weeping. Friends and neighbors did not call out or wave, sharing with us only a silent nod of sorrow.

In the balmy time of April, it seemed to me the deepest December. Leaving Eli behind, I turned down Massachusetts and walked toward the telegraph office. Through the front window, I could see Skeeter Duncan, the other telegrapher, sitting at his post, surrounded by the curious. Near the door, I met Hovey Lowman, who, after getting his papers on the street, had come back to the office, still wearing the wrinkled clothes he had worn the previous night, still waiting for the latest accounts from Washington. He was running his hand through his tousled hair. Tragedy always sells papers.

Some words of Shakespeare's moved through my memory, the obvious ones, the line about the noble Brutus at the end of *Julius Caesar*, or Horatio's praise of the dead Hamlet, but what I sought were sentiments of more substance or guidance in this bitter hour, both for myself and for our country.

Then a phrase began to worm its way into my brain, not a eulogy for a tragic hero, but words spoken by a minor villain in *The Tempest*: "What's past is prologue." Those who read Shakespeare know that villains often get the best lines. I took these words to mean that everything in our lives can be seen as the beginning of a still-unfolding action. At this moment, the gnomic phrase *did* console me, as did the sun now shining above the buildings in the commercial district.

"They know who the killer is," Lowman said to me, leaning close. "Booth . . . John Wilkes, an actor, apparently with Southern sympathies." Yes, I knew of the Booths, the most famous Shakespearean acting family in America. In fact, I had seen Edwin, brother of the murderer, on stage in Boston, but I could not remember the play.

"I know about the Booths," I replied to Lowman. "Have they caught John Wilkes yet?"

"Some accounts say he escaped but broke his leg jumping from Lincoln's box to the stage." Lowman appeared exhausted, but he could not leave, needing to stay close to the wire. At the *Globe Democrat* in St. Louis, Russell Downing would be seeing the news on the telegraph. What he might want from me, I surmised, was a response to the assassination from the frontier state of Kansas.

Since the *Globe Democrat* was a weekly that competed with the dailies, Downing wanted strong writing: no florid or purple prose and no bombast. Many papers used appellations added to or replacing an actual name: *Honest Abe* or *The Rail Splitter* for Lincoln, *The Little Giant* for the diminutive Stephen A. Douglas of Illinois, *The Grim Chieftain* for James Henry Lane, a rabblerousing senator from Kansas. Downing wanted writing as clear as a windowpane. Although I doubted that weekly papers would long survive the telegraph, I knew I would write for him as long as he wanted me and if my legal practice allowed me to do it. My law practice filled our bellies, but writing nourished some inner need.

As I pushed past Lowman, he thrust a copy of his paper into my hand. "This is the latest from Washington, Ezra," he said grimly, "so now we wait until the federals catch Booth and his friends—and we know more."

Bad news travels fast, the proverb says, and it was spreading through Lawrence; many people were already in mourning black. Then, on the board sidewalk, there was someone I could not avoid: Big Ears King, a follower of Senator Jim Lane, whom I knew to be in Washington. Big Ears, loud and jovial, ran a livery stable and watched over the senator's interests when Lane was in Washington. His face was freckled like a quail's egg. King's ears, in fact, were not larger than normal, but they stuck out from his head at an impossible angle; it was said, when drunk, that he could even wiggle them, but that seemed questionable to me.

"Anything from the senator?" I asked as King turned toward me, a chew of tobacco in his cheek. He spit tobacco juice into the street before he answered, wiping his mouth on his sleeve.

"Terrible day, Ezra! Guess the senator was attending to the President, loyal to the end. All of those damned Southerners need to be strung up, uh, straight-away! No! Put 'em in a pit of snakes . . . your copperheads . . . your water moccasins . . . your diamondback rattlers . . . a den of 'em . . . of vipers!" Of course, *copperhead* was a derogatory term for a Southern sympathizer in the North, but King apparently had in mind actual snakes waiting to deliver a painful death to traitors. No metaphors for Big Ears.

"Probably no snake pit big enough for those who wished ill to the President." I paused and rephrased my question. "You heard from the senator today?" King blinked and shook his head.

Jim Lane was an energetic demagogue, someone I had followed to mine his wealth of solecism, patriotic bombast, and ribaldry for Downing and the *Globe Democrat*, but despite his outlandish speeches, Lane was no fool. Rather, he was a cunning opportunist, mercurial and shrewd, and usually at odds with the state's first governor, Dr. Charles Robinson, whom I admired. But to give Lane his due, his military experience contributed to the defense of Lawrence in Territorial Days, and I credited him for training Negro troops and using them in battle in 1862, perhaps the first state to do so. So, in my reports to Downing, I described him as able but flawed—and that was also how the paper presented him. This, Lane seemed not to mind, since we helped make him one of the best-known politicians on the Western Border.

"Been looking for you, Ezra," Ed Whitman called out, reining in his gray mule and sliding from the saddle. I bid King goodbye and jumped off the sidewalk and ran into the street. It was at the Whitman house that I saw John Brown in the winter before the Harpers Ferry raid of 1859, when Ed, a committed abolitionist, and I were horrified at Brown's bloody plan for a war on slave owners in Virginia.

Brown's raid failed, of course, but in death, he was remembered, causing abolitionism to sweep through the North like a wind-blown prairie fire. Then, with Lincoln's election, the South seceded state by state, and when war came, it was worse than anything Ed and I foresaw. "Heard the news as I rode into town," Whitman exclaimed as he tied up his horse at the rail in front of the bakery and shook my hand. "How could it happen?" I handed him the copy of the *Kansas Journal* Lowman had given me moments before.

"You can have this," I said. "We know now that Johnson wasn't harmed . . . oh, the assassin's name was John Wilkes Booth, an actor. Lincoln died this morning, and Johnson's been sworn in. That's about all I know."

"Some kind of Secesh plot, I reckon," Whitman speculated. "Even though they lost the war." Putting his hand to his weathered face, he seemed moved by passion. "Though I never laid eyes on him, Lincoln seemed like a dear personal friend." He looked away and swallowed hard. "Now we got Johnson." I felt sorry for this amiable man with his grizzled beard and his tattered, wide-brimmed hat.

"Well, Johnson'll have to do," I replied. "He's all we got."

"Not much consolation, Ezra," my friend said with a grim smile. Ed and I were tied together by a hatred of slavery, admiration for Lincoln and John Brown, and my affection for the youngest of his boys, Jeremiah, whom I had tried to watch over during the Westport campaign against the Confederate army of Sterling Price; not all of the Lawrence boys came back, but the clever, wise-cracking Jeremiah did, and Ed, believing I had kept him alive, thereafter treated me like a brother.

"There's life in death," I replied. "I've been thinking about that today. The Easter message."

"Don't seem to help much right now, though. Maybe it will tomorrow." Big Ears King watched us from his spot in the sun and, although he probably couldn't hear our words, nodded.

Up the wide dirt street toward us slowly came Larby Jones in the mule-drawn mail wagon of Sonnet Freight and Wholesale, now operated by Henry's widow, Leona. Larby had been wounded in the Westport campaign, where he lost his left leg below the knee. When he returned to work, on a wooden leg which he knocked for good luck, his first words to me were: "Tell the eager widows, Ezra, Larby's got something now that's big and stiff and always useful!" Then he guffawed and knocked his wooden appendage three times.

"Lincoln died this morning, Larby," I said as Whitman reached up to shake Larby's outstretched hand, and then, moving so the mules couldn't kick him, patted the haunches of one of the mules.

"As expected, I guess," Larby answered, sitting contentedly in the mule wagon like a Byzantine potentate, gently grinding his teeth. 'Heard people say this morning, his death was just like Jesus. God sent him here for a purpose and now has called him home."

"Ain't sure about that," Whitman answered and looked at me. "*Do* know a thing or two about mules, though." He chuckled and hitched up his pants.

"Lincoln's gone. 'What's past is prologue,'" I said softly, but no one seemed to hear my words.

CHAPTER THREE

MY FIRST DAY in Lawrence—May the twenty-first, 1856—I shall not forget. After riding in Henry Sonnet's mule-drawn wagon from Westport into Kansas Territory, it is the smells I remember: animal dung and burned wood. The latter scent from the Free State Hotel, a fortress-like building with a thick concrete exterior and gun ports, destroyed by Missouri Border Ruffians hours earlier in the day in what newspapers called "the sack of Lawrence." Although, except for the hotel and a print office, the only damage done in the town was a few broken windows and smashed doors and the theft of several bottles of whiskey, a few cigars, and a hat or two. Now it is the heavy perfume of May lilacs that greets visitors, bushes planted after Quantrill's Raid of August 1863, when approximately five hundred Confederate guerrillas on horseback burned down much of the commercial district and murdered two hundred unarmed men and boys.

On this May morning, as Hannah and I walked in our garden, songbirds called to one another like choristers in church. The lots in Lawrence, laid out by surveyors from the New England Emigrant Aid Society, were sizable enough for each to contain a large kitchen garden besides a house, outhouse, and barn. These buildings on our lot were spared when Quantrill's guerrillas came, owing to the bravery of my quick-witted wife, who burned a tubful of rags to make it appear the house was already afire.

Beans, lettuce, and carrots in rows, newly sprouted, and pumpkin, squash, and potatoes in hills, all shared space with roses which Hannah cared for, while blooming lilacs planted near the house masked the odor from our barn and chicken coop. Although I shall welcome the testament of lilacs each spring, I wonder if, henceforth, their fragrance will be associated with death. Two days had passed since our President was buried in Springfield, Illinois, on the first of May, and we spoke of him less often, remembering him as he appeared in copper-plate engravings in newspapers and periodicals and through his widely printed speeches.

A sound in front of the house announced the arrival of visitors, Maude Cornish, driven by a man I knew as her cousin, Oswald. Our dogs, in a pen by the barn, had responded to their arrival with furious barking. By the time I reached the street, she had been helped from the trap buggy. "I hope all is well with you," I uttered, taking her gloved hand. Her hair was pulled back, giving a severe look to her lined and wan, but still attractive face. She continued to wear funereal black for her dead husband, like many widows in mourning.

"A terrible time, Ezra," she exclaimed as I took her arm to lead her to the door. When Hannah joined us, Maude's eyes filled with tears, and as she and Hannah embraced, she began to sob. "One of our farm hands was killed . . . two nights ago in a frightful accident." Maude's late husband, Dan Cornish, was my friend and my client as well. He had been a captain in our militia regiment, a tall and handsome New Englander—in fact, as handsome a man as I had ever known, in his blue Union jacket, sitting astride his great bay gelding, tragically a prime target for a Secesh marksman. At Westport, only the militia officers wore Union blue; the rest of us, in our dirty overcoats, were partially obscured by the yellow smoke, rail fences, scrub oak, and cornstalks. Now seeing the grief of Maude, I again keenly felt the loss of my friend. In handling his wife's legal affairs after his death, I had come to know the well-meaning young Oswald, who arrived from Boston to help his widowed cousin.

Hannah and I took Maude to my office, one of the rooms I added to our house as our family grew with the birth of Samantha and then Henley. It was a pleasant room with book-filled shelves and windows that admitted morning light.

"Let me make some tea," Hannah suggested as Maude, who now seemed to have a rein on her emotions, nodded and thanked her in a weak voice.

"The second death I've had to face," she said, swallowing and wiping her dark eyes with her handkerchief. "In addition to that of our President, of course," she added with a touch of embarrassment. She examined her handkerchief as if uncertain what to do with it.

"Please tell me what happened, Maude," I said. "Then we shall look at what needs attending to." She sighed wearily.

"Well, Oswald and two hands from our farm went into Lawrence, my cousin on horseback . . . the others in a wagon. As young men do, they drank too much whiskey, Oswald especially, it seems," she explained, speaking slowly and carefully. "Drinking toasts to our dead President, perhaps. So, when it came time to return, Oswald was too drunk to sit his horse, so he was put in the wagon . . . uh, Frank Kittleston, an excellent rider, took the horse."

Hannah's return to the office seemed to encourage Maude. She smiled and continued her story. "We were eating supper when the dogs began making a terrible commotion, and we ran into the barn lot to see my cousin's horse," Maude paused, "a body, his foot in the stirrup . . . dragged with clothes pulled up over his head so no one could tell who it was in the dim light from the kitchen door. But we *thought* it was Oswald." As she talked, she addressed Hannah, who took her hand. Then her eyes returned to my face.

"We were filled with *both* horror and relief," Maude said. "The dead man was *not* Cousin Oswald but poor Frank Kittleston, terribly bloody and bruised." She swallowed, shook her head, and spoke, "Never seen such a sight." Tears returned to her eyes, and she began to sob.

"Must have been a shock, Maude, but I'm happy Oswald's safe," I said in a futile attempt to comfort her, but I understood immediately why Maude was so distressed. Kittleston was the foreman and Dan's most trusted and knowledgeable worker, the only person who knew horses the way my deceased friend Henry Sonnet or Ed Whitman knew mules. The Cornish farm bred and raised the finest horses in Douglas County; unfortunately, neither Maude nor Oswald knew the first thing about the horse business. And what a cruel irony that the most skilled horseman around should die in such an absurdly tragic manner.

"Sent for the Sheriff," Maude said, ruefully returning to her story, now that the worst part was behind her. "An inquest was held sometime after midnight. You see, Frank did not have on the high-heeled boots that many riders wear. His foot was apparently caught in the stirrup, and he was dragged to death. The verdict at the inquest was accidental death—misadventure."

"How does it fare with Oswald now, Maude?" I asked tentatively.

"Heartsick, Ezra," she responded quickly. "Blames his own weakness—thinks he killed poor Frank."

When Hannah left the room to get the tea, I attempted to question Maude, but she skittered to other difficulties and became agitated again, her lip quivering, tears forming in her eyes. Since Dan's death, I had wondered whether Maude could manage a large farm by herself as well as care for two young daughters. Some people could not.

On the other hand, Lawrence women had shown great courage in saving their husbands during Quantrill's Raid, one by disguising him in a dress and bonnet, another by dragging her man from their burning home wrapped in a carpet, and still others who poured water on flaming homes even as the murderous marauders continued to set more buildings afire. My Hannah was among that brave cohort: headstrong, bold, and clever, she could best many men, except at tasks where great physical strength is required.

Returning to the office now, Hannah poured tea from our best china teapot and offered brown sugar and milk to our guest. "Forgive my presumptuousness, but do other matters bring you here today?" Hannah inquired. Watching her, I thought of a line from *Hamlet*: "When sorrows come, they come not single spies but in battalions." And so it seemed to be with Maude.

"Vitruvius Bird! *He* also brings me here today!" Her humor suddenly seemed changed, a touch of resentment, perhaps even anger in her voice. "He threatens our farm, you see, and Oswald's advice is of no avail."

"How can Bird do that, Maude?" I asked incredulously. "Your affairs are in order, I believe."

"I must seem a weak and blubbering woman, but I don't know what to do, Ezra." Maude was a large woman—not fat, but big-boned, as we say in Kansas—but since Dan's death, she seemed to have shrunk, been diminished somehow, as old people wither and shrink with extreme age. Even her bearing seemed different. "I must confess to both of you that many a time I have thought of returning to Massachusetts. Depressed in spirits, feeling lonesome and blue."

"So, what has transpired? How has Bird threatened you?"

"Yesterday—the day after Frank's death—Vitruvius Bird, whom I have met once or twice, appeared with two men, both armed, and crossed into our fenced pasture west of the house," Maude replied. "Said to one of my farm hands: 'Widow's been trespassing on land that don't belong to her, and we mean to put a stop to it.' One of the other men said it."

"Ownership of that parcel was never in dispute, was it?" She straightened her black jacket and frowned, shaking her head.

Vitruvius Bird, I knew, although not well. A stocky man with a balding head and gray hair, Bird had a trimmed beard, always wore a suit, usually of a stylish plaid and nicely cut, a silver chain crossing his vest to a fob which undoubtedly concealed a pocket watch—the dress of a businessman, not a farmer. Bird was courteous and well-mannered, even amiable, and had come to town at the end of 1864, shortly after the death of Dan Cornish and the re-election of President Lincoln, when he was known to have purchased several parcels of land near the Cornish farm. I was loath to alarm Maude by telling her that Bird was also thought to be a sharp dealer, so I held my tongue.

Hannah quickly excused herself and left the room as I advised Maude on a course of action: a meeting with Sheriff Ruben Flowers and a civil injunction prohibiting Bird from trespassing on her land. Disputes over land were, in fact, common in the Kansas Territory after the federal government opened the Indian reserves to white settlement, often pitting proslavery Missourians who staked an informal claim to a piece of land against Free-Staters who acquired parcels from land agents—parties opposed in both ideology and politics. Those violent days were now past, I hoped, and civil disputes would be settled in law courts, not by threats and pistols.

When Maude's business in town had been attended to, I instructed young Oswald to ride back if Vitruvius Bird or any of his men set foot on the Cornish land, feeling confident that the dustup at the farm would not lead to violence, and after bidding farewell to the Yankee cousins, I went in search of Eli Foster, who would be closing the Watkins Bank for the day. Like the telegraph office and the newspapers, the two Lawrence banks were springs of information if one knew where to place one's bucket or pitcher. Often, Eli had collected information that assisted me by listening to idle chatter in the bank lobby.

After the bank was locked up, Eli—having pulled the iron grating across the glass-windowed doors—adjusted his jacket and straightened his tie, looking as though he could be a model of deportment in a *Harper's New Monthly Magazine* engraving.

Since his promotion at the bank and his engagement to Prudence Franklin, Eli had, in fact, become a bit of a dandy. "Land disputes and claims—near the Cornish farm, say? Heard of anything?" I greeted him with these questions as he looked at me when I stepped up on the plank sidewalk, knowing that in his fine shoes, he would avoid walking in the road with its mud puddles and horse manure.

"Cornish farm, eh?" Eli mused. "Not a dispute with Bird, by any chance?"

"Yes, with Bird, so says Maude." We had gone into a tavern to get a glass of beer, sitting in a quiet corner where we could talk before Eli left to meet Prudence and walk her back to her boarding house. "I believe Bird wants her farm," I said in a whisper.

"Well, I think Bird's a cheat. Crooked as a dog's hind leg! If you shake hands with him, count your fingers before you leave the room." Eli smiled at his own wit.

"Well, I remember one land dispute before you came to Lawrence. Involved Jim Lane . . . uh, had tragic consequences," I said, taking a drink of my beer. "Occurred only weeks after I arrived, and I remember it well because it involved two Free-Staters, Lane and his neighbor Gaius Jenkins. Well, Jenkins and others from his household began drawing water from a well on disputed land, and he knocked down a gate and came into Lane's yard. Shots were exchanged; Lane was hit in the knee, and Jenkins was riddled with buckshot and died.

"After Jenkins' funeral, Lane was tried and acquitted of murder, but his political career seemed dead and buried—or so most thought. At the time, people joked that though buried six feet under, Lane, cussing and spitting dirt like a diabolical gopher, could claw his way out of any grave, and so in a manner of speaking Lane did just that, since now he is a U.S. Senator, well respected, and a rich man!"

Eli laughed politely. "Think I heard that story before," he said, "but I got a question for you. Why does Bird want that land? You can bet your bottom dollar it's not about farming or running cattle," Eli said and laughed. "It is prime land—probably increased in value since Dan's death. And if the Cornish land were added to Bird's parcels, somebody would have a nice stretch to farm—or sell."

"That's the thing, Eli," I answered. "Maude thinks Bird's trying to intimidate her. *Force* her to sell the farm. And now she may be inclined to do so. Shame if she does."

"There's always talk in town about the value of land among speculators like Bird," Eli said, pensively rubbing his chin. "And talk about railroads too, since the Union Pacific came to Lawrence with the telegraph."

The Pacific Railroad Act of 1862 had allowed the Union Pacific Company, Eastern Division, to build a line westward from Wyandotte, Kansas (adjacent to Kansas City in Missouri). I knew that Senator Lane had used his political skills to have the line rerouted southward to Lawrence, where a depot was constructed on the north bank of the Kansas River directly across from the town; the first train had reached Lawrence after the re-election of President Lincoln, in December of 1864. "Well, Eli," I said, "though I've been critical of Jim Lane, I give him credit for bringing us the railroad."

"Every day we get questions at the bank about railroad bonds, surveys, land sales," Eli averred. He drained his glass. "Lots of money to be made on railroads!" He sank back in his wooden chair, put his hands on the table, and chuckled. Several more drinkers entered, laughing, including Dr. Gafney, physician to our family. Seeing us deep in conversation, he nodded and smiled. "And, of course, Lane's now the President of the Leavenworth, Lawrence, and Ft. Gibson Railroad, so he may be looking for right-of-way to bring another rail line to Lawrence."

"When the war in the West was over, there seemed little to write about except railroads," I opined and finished my beer. "The direct rail link between Kansas City and St. Louis should finally occur by the end of this summer when the Missouri Pacific completes the line from Pleasant Hill to Kansas City. Downing has asked me to write about that and where the broad-gauge Missouri Pacific and the standard-gauge Union Pacific, Eastern Division would join up in a change-of-gauge point. Likely in Kansas City. Could eastern Kansas and Lawrence also be involved somehow?"

"I don't know of any right-of-way which has been acquired or land purchased," Eli said, leaning across the table and lowering his voice.

"Land to be acquired—like the Cornish land, for example?" I whispered. "And could there be other plans afoot for lines to Galveston in Texas or Santa Fe? I wonder if Bird knows anything about any plans."

"You need to find out for Maude's sake."

"'There's no art to find the mind's construction in the face,' Duncan, the Scottish King, says just before the murderous Macbeth makes his entrance in the play. It's a theme Shakespeare loves: does a fair and honest face reveal a loyal heart or does it hide a foul and corrupt one?"

"Yes, that's the question to be asked, Ezra," Eli said, looking me in the eye. "See what he is up to!" He smiled at me, pushed back from the table, and looked at his pocket watch. "Time to go meet Prudence."

As Eli and I walked past the crowded bar, I noticed Big Ears King, and an idea struck me like "the lightning in the collied night," as the Bard says. I would ask Big Ears to find a knowledgeable foreman for Maude from the horsemen who came to his stable, where I had often seen employment notices posted. He was happy to help, he said, even happier when I bought him another beer. Eli said good-bye and hurried off. In the morning, I planned to ride to Maude's horse farm with the answer to one of her difficulties. All might yet end well, I told myself, now enjoying a sense of well-being. As I came out into the street, I could see to the west the huge, treeless bulk of Mount Oread, the sun having just set behind it in a gauzy bank of thin, pink-streaked clouds.

CHAPTER FOUR

LAWYERS CAN NEVER leave well enough alone, some people say, and, as a lawyer, I can perhaps endorse that sentiment, but I do draw the line at being compared to a hog sticking his nose into offal or garbage. I reckon that people could feel the same way about a newspaper correspondent, who often pursues a story even if it means exposing a questionable activity or shameful family secret. On both accounts, as attorney and newsman, I must plead guilty.

Nevertheless, as someone who represented Maude Cornish's interests, it was incumbent upon me to discover what I could about Vitruvius Bird, his commercial affairs and history, so, after riding out to tell Maude of my plan to get her a new foreman, I went to see Dr. Charles Robinson, the state's first governor, with whom I was on friendly terms, unlike some of my fellow townsmen.

The Robinson home was an impressive structure on Massachusetts near the new bridge over the Kansas River. I remembered the times I had entered the elegant front doors, most vividly on Black Friday, the day of Quantrill's bloody raid, when I went there for aid—food, clothing, blankets, boards for coffins—for the devastated survivors. On that day, Robinson himself had gone for an early morning ride up Mount Oread, where from his barn he had watched the entire raid, a sight I felt sure he could not forget.

Today I tied my horse in back near the stable and walked up the brick sidewalk around the house, enjoying the warm morning, dark clouds lowering above me, and mist in the air. Several red-winged blackbirds scrambled through the bushes, chattering, and motionless robins on the lawn, like statues of themselves, listened for worms. Centered in the lawn was a small Judas tree, its bright pink flowers beginning to drop. I wondered if the tree sent a message to Robinson's neighbors.

As agent of the New England Emigrant Aid Society, in 1854, Robinson evicted—some said forcibly ejected—armed Missourians from land purchased for the Lawrence colony. Although a balding man with the mien of a schoolmaster, he had shown great strength of character and perseverance; he was also the rarest of all political beings, a moderate, caught in the struggle between Border Ruffians—proslavery Missourians—and Free-State settlers from northern states like Iowa and Illinois, as well as the east.

Robinson, who also stood for free-soil principles, was not an abolitionist, and the greatest political pressure upon him ironically came from the most militant of the Free-State party: John Brown, Charles Jennison, and James H. Lane.

Some of these were radicals who called themselves—and were called—Jayhawkers. They conducted raids into Missouri to free slaves, but also to "liberate" cattle, horses, and other possessions of the slaveholders. In the 1850s, when the Kansas Territory was still controlled by proslavery officials sent from Washington, Robinson had led the Free-State opposition—part of the time from prison in Lecompton—and after Kansas became a state in January of 1861, he was elected its first governor.

Governor Robinson's tenure in office was, unfortunately, equally turbulent; sworn into office in February of 1861, as Southern states were seceding from the Union, Robinson continued his policy of moderation, attempting to end jayhawking raids into Missouri by the radicals now in power in the state.

Within a year, the governor became the victim of a campaign of lies and vilification after two members of his cabinet were accused and found guilty of misusing funds from state bonds, and Robinson himself was indicted as well. Although he was acquitted by a nearly unanimous vote, his career was ruined, and he resigned rather than face certain defeat in the next election, placing blame on his old enemy, James Lane.

During the war, I called occasionally at the Robinson home to see if the governor was preparing for another campaign for office, although if truth be told, I went because I deplored the callousness with which he had been abandoned. Robinson had become the forgotten man. Although among the wealthiest of Lawrence's citizens, he only wanted gratitude from the state for his steadfast service in a dangerous decade, the captain who had brought his ship safely into harbor through stormy seas.

It was in this house during Territorial Days that I first heard Robinson use his stirring phrase: "Till we have built a New Jerusalem in Kansas!" Now it was the governor himself who responded to the echoing sound of the great brass knocker. "How have you been keeping, Ezra?" he asked, unsmiling, as he opened the door.

"Health and good fortune to you, sir," I said, choosing my words carefully. I noticed that he had used my Christian name, heretofore usually calling me "Mr. Middleton."

"I come on business of sorts," I said, offering my hand, which he shook. "As you may remember, I represent Dan Cornish's widow, Maude." He nodded and gestured toward the parlor. No tea was offered or served, as had been the practice in the past, when he was an avatar of civility and manners, but it was, after all, I who named this a business call. Sitting on the edge of my chair, I quickly laid out Maude's dilemma and asked Robinson what he knew about land titles west of Lawrence. He sat impassively before shaking his head and speaking.

"Well, I do not know Mr. Vitruvius Bird at all, and, in fact, have little intercourse with the citizens of this town or dealings in its commerce now."

"Forgive my presumption, sir, but I wish only to know about land west of Mount Oread—the original titles or deeds—to assist a distressed lady." Robinson moved in his chair, and I believed he was about to rise, but instead he leaned forward, elbow on his knees, pulled open his coat, and spoke.

"Ezra, there are legal documents, of course . . . for the land on which Lawrence stands, land that was surveyed and divided into lots. I also own some grazing land on Mount Oread and elsewhere." He coughed, his voice sounding dry. "But you said original titles."

"Perhaps I'm being naïve," I replied, an edge to my voice that Robinson seemed to notice. "Bills of sale, deeds, land transfers."

Robinson scrutinized me with watery gray eyes. "You should know this: when the Kansas Territory was opened to white settlement . . . not an acre . . . not *one* acre was legally available to buy." Amazement, shock, and confusion overwhelmed me.

"Can this be so?" I implored. "Do you mean that *no* land in Kansas could be legally sold by the Indians or purchased from them?"

"Ezra, the history of our country has been moving the savages into land that *nobody* wanted until *everybody* did. President Jackson moved the Cherokee Nation out of Carolina and the mountains and sent them to the Indian Territory west of Arkansas. Thousands of them died on the harsh trek. And the tribes in the central part of the country were similarly pushed west—again and again—and told, I'm sure, they could stay in the reserves west of the Missouri River, but in fact white people were already trying to claim land in Kansas." He coughed again, his hand in his lap in a gesture of weariness.

"This shocks me," I averred, leaning back in my chair, since my knees were almost touching his. "How did so much land change hands in such a seemingly haphazard way?"

"When I scouted the Territory for a location to place our town," Robinson explained, "the Kansas Indians who lived here had been pushed out by tribes that the government had moved from north of the Ohio River: Delaware, Potawatomi, Shawnee. Their reserves, newly acquired, were then ceded—taken! Remember, the Mexican War had ended in 1848, and California beckoned, and then gold was discovered there. So, land in California was there to take, and here in Kansas as well. Of course, Lawrence now sits on land from the Shawnee Reserve, and on the other side of the Kansas River was Delaware land."

"But the land in Kansas? *How* was it taken from the Indian Nations?" I asked.

"Land brokers with connections in Washington, powerful men like Senator Thomas Hart Benton of Missouri, a proponent of westward expansion, who wanted rail lines to California through Kansas, mixed-blood Indians who betrayed their tribes, corrupt missionaries, inducements or bribes, land speculators . . . shall I go on, Ezra? Gullible savages are easily duped. They were lied to and betrayed. You see, I have fought against Indians on occasion, but I haven't wanted to wipe them out."

"I suppose we were all too concerned about the war, abolitionism sweeping the country. The newspapers . . . the correspondents, I mean," I added, feeling chagrined at my own inattention to the corruption and mistreatment of the Indians. Of course, I had heard about Indian deaths from disease and cold during the bitter winters of '62 and '64, but the country had been absorbed in the war or the emancipation of the Negro.

And I knew how the Indians had been slaughtered, especially the Chivington Massacre at Sand Creek in Colorado, where peaceful Cheyenne and Arapaho, including many women and children, were slaughtered. At that time—late November of 1864—the Kansas Militia had just returned from defeating the Rebel invaders at Westport, and I was calling at the families of those who did not return. So, who was to blame for the betrayal of the Indians? Embarrassed, I felt like the negligent pupil, and Robinson the schoolmaster, lecturing me for inattention.

"And recall how the gold strike of '59 in Colorado sent more migrants across Kansas to the Rockies," he continued, "which posed another threat to the buffalo, already facing destruction throughout the state. Union cavalry posted to newly built forts on the plains, their horses eating the grass where Indian ponies grazed, and troopers cutting down the trees on which Indians relied for firewood to survive the bitter winter. Turbulent times and events conspired against the Indians and often nature as well, you see."

"Yes, I think I understand better now," I replied sheepishly, my voice dropping. "We thought our destiny was to populate the continent. Saw it in our papers every day, heard it in speeches, even in sermons on Sunday. Plenty of blame to go around."

"Not all was lost, thank God. Some mixed-bloods are thriving and others are safely in the Indian Territory—those who weren't killed fighting on one side or the other in *our* war!" I nodded my assent to his sentiments as he watched me. "For Maude, I have no advice. For you, review whatever land deed she may have and be prepared to go to court if you have to." He rose from his chair, saying, "And so I bid you good day, Ezra."

Riding away, I mused on the rivals who had founded and preserved Lawrence, Robinson, and Lane. I had compared them to Brutus and Antony in *Julius Caesar,* the idealist and the demagogue, although Downing had not printed that comparison in the paper, possibly thinking it too literary.

Yet it was apt, Robinson, the aloof man of honor, Lane, hollow-eyed and vulgar, the impassioned orator, known to strip off coat and shirt, moving from harsh whisper to shouts, pointing at his audience like a fire-and-brimstone preacher. And in the end, it was Lane who triumphed and Robinson who was cast aside, bitter and resentful.

The mist had turned to drizzle. On the other side of the river, the train depot and the newly leafed trees, the greenest of greens, were almost hidden by fog. I rode up Massachusetts and turned off at the stables owned by Big Ears King, where I dismounted under cover and untied the India-rubber cape rolled up behind my saddle. "Got a good man for you," Big Ears shouted from the doorway to the barn, stopping to spit tobacco juice. "Name's Agard. Speaks '*Horse,*'" he said, smiling broadly, the prominent freckles on his face moving as his cheeks rose. "Can ride out there today, if you'd like him too. Hard worker too. No malarkey!" He smiled.

Mr. Agard was in his forties, amiable, and seemed to know more about training horses than I did, which, if truth be told, was not much. Since he was eager to work immediately, I tore a page from the commonplace book I always carried and wrote a note to Maude suggesting she hire him for a month on a trial basis and, if he proved satisfactory, consider him for Kittleston's position as foreman, which on a horse farm like Cornish's was a plum job. This arrangement was convenient for me because I had another matter to handle—to talk to Leona Sonnet.

Leona was the widow of Henry Sonnet, the man who had driven me from Westport, Missouri, to Lawrence in May of 1856, as Border Ruffians were sacking the town. When we surveyed the damage, I saw that the Free State Hotel, where I intended to lodge, had been destroyed. Leona asked if I would like to board with them, and there I stayed until I moved to my own house in April 1858, after Hannah and I wed. As my father had taught me the law, so Henry had taught me about the West.

During Quantrill's raid, Henry Sonnet—unarmed—was killed by the Confederate guerrillas who rode into town at sunrise with pistols stuck in their waistbands and burned down his modest home on New Hampshire Street along with much of Lawrence. Leona, deciding to defy fortune, expanded Henry's freight line, built a large storage barn where the house had stood, and named the firm "Henry Sonnet Freight and Wholesale."

Leona also had a family of German stonemasons build her a cottage on Kentucky Street west of the commercial district, and she now traveled from her home to her business property in a buggy driven by a trusted Negro, Isaac Worthy. As a lad, Isaac had been taught to read by Leona and Hannah and had proved a diligent scholar, even learning to read Latin. He was a talented man.

After Quantrill's Raid, Isaac and I had collected bodies, driving our unwilling mules through the smoking town, dug graves together atop Mount Oread, and buried the dead. In every way, Isaac lived up to his name. While it may seem odd for me to say this about a Negro, I admired the young man as I had few others of any age or color.

With Henry and Isaac in my mind, I rode into the Sonnet storage barn, the rain increasing in intensity and the low clouds taking on a faint greenish cast from the newly leafed trees. The barn, smelling of manure and hay, was noisy and busy. Mules brayed, and a wheelwright worked on a wagon wheel. "Get them mules in harness," someone shouted. "That rim ain't gonna last another day," another voice rang out. "Move them mules," the first voice repeated.

"Well, the weather outlook is . . . mud," Isaac jested as I dismounted and wiped water from my saddle and my coat with a gunny sack.

"Well, need the rain, I guess," I opined as he tethered my horse and smiled at my observation. Without question, he was a handsome young man, tan rather than ebony black, dressed in a modest dark suit and neck kerchief. Were he white, he would have looked to be Leona's assistant or someone being prepared for a post in the office.

Of course, in the East, Negroes held such positions, but this was Kansas and the West, and here Black men were just beginning the slow, hard slog toward acceptance. I wondered if Robinson thought Negroes— or Indians for that matter—had a place in his New Jerusalem that was a-building. I thought I would have to give him the benefit of the doubt on that.

Around us, the activity of delivering, unloading, stacking, and unhitching went on, with Isaac supervising but never giving orders; Leona did that from the buggy. "Show the men where to stack the lumber, Isaac," she said. "Have the kegs of nails put along the wall, Isaac, and show them the stalls for the mules."

Because the business prospered and the arrangement seemed to work well, Isaac had a better job than any other Black man in town, and Leona had a superb manager who appeared to be nothing more than a dutiful servant. In the evening, Hannah and I laughed at their hidden drama, and we suspected that Leona and Isaac did as well when the last customer had gone home at the end of the day.

"How are the children, Ezra?" Leona asked, shaking water from her umbrella onto the straw-covered floor of the barn.

"Probably at home, playing in the mud. Yes, very well. Both of them," I answered, recalling how sick they had been less than a year before when I was away with the Kansas Militia at Westport, and Leona helped care for them.

"So, what brings you here today?" Leona asked, and I quickly told her of Vitruvius Bird and the threat he might pose to Maude Cornish.

"Don't know about ownership of land west of town," she said in a low voice, reaching out and taking my hand in her gloved one, "but he seems a bit of a slicker. I assume you can give Maude all the legal advice she needs." Then she laughed. "Of course, I have great sympathy for widows." Then, despite her being nearly fifty, she flashed the same girlish smile she used to give Henry. "You will know what to do, Ezra. And I'll keep my ears open. Lots of folks like to talk, if you know what I mean." Now she gave another merry laugh and patted my hand, then pointed to my horse, which Isaac was already untying.

"Here you be, Mister Ezra," Isaac said, smiling, because I had asked him a hundred times to call me simply 'Ezra,' yet both of us knew he would never so address me. Seeming to be an obsequious Black man, he appeared to enjoy the servile persona he showed the world. Swinging up onto my horse, I winked at him, and he looked at me as though I were a complete stranger.

On this warm, wet evening, I was welcomed home, first by the dogs, Caesar and Brutus, then inside the house by our children, red-haired Samantha, now almost six, and Henley, nearly three, who greeted me by digging in my pockets for the treat I often bought home with me. Both had my green eyes but otherwise favored their mother, especially

Samantha, who had Hannah's golden-red hair. And finally, I was welcomed by Hannah, who left wealth and comfort to be a frontier wife, the woman with whom I fell in love after a ten-minute meeting in St. Louis, who had then followed me west to Kansas and Lawrence.

"Roast and potatoes," she said as I hugged and kissed her. "If that is the question you are about to ask. And then pandowdy for a dessert."

Most men, I believe, have rather formal relationships with their wives, being close only when doing what Shakespeare calls "the act of darkness." Society rightly expects an ordered family, a hierarchy in which everyone knows his or her place and performs the actions and duties commensurate with it. I, on the other hand, have never felt compelled to obey society's dictates unquestioningly but rather followed my heart and found a helpmate. God tells Adam in Genesis that he and Eve shall become one flesh. And one flesh Hannah and I also have been, sharing hopes and disappointments, combining tenderness and desire in our life together.

In bed that night, our children asleep and the house still, I whispered to Hannah as I held her. "What I say now may shock you, sweetheart, but I thought today . . . have been thinking for a long time on and off about Leona and Isaac." I could feel her breath on my neck but could not see her in the darkness. "Forgive me if—if what I say is lewd. It's like I, well, wonder if Leona is like a mother to Isaac . . . but also his paramour." I could feel Hannah move in bed, perhaps to raise herself on her elbow.

"Ezra! You are such a naughty man—a very naughty man indeed." I tried to mumble an apology for my indelicate comment, but Hannah suddenly giggled. "I have had that very thought for some time," she opined.

"It happens, of course. Lots of light-skinned Negroes around."

"A big age difference," she whispered. "What is Isaac? Twenty?" There was excitement in her voice, not shock or censure. "Could it be true?"

"If it were so, and I don't say it is," I replied, "and the town found out, Leona would be ruined and Isaac would be beaten or lynched."

Neither of us spoke for a moment. The house was still as a tomb. Then Hannah broke the silence. "Now I'm frightened for both of them."

"Probably just our fantasies. A conceit, nothing more," I whispered. Hannah moved closer to me, threw her arm across my chest, and was still. Soon she began to breathe more deeply and quickly fell asleep, but I lay awake for some time. I thought of Robinson's last words as I rode away from his house: "Remember, it's *always* about land . . . in California, in Texas, in Kansas." Then lines from Shakespeare, like moths seeking a light, drifted through my mind as they often did when I was sleepless, one now in particular: "Love looks not with the eyes, but with the mind, and therefore is wing'd Cupid painted blind."

CHAPTER FIVE

UP THE MISSOURI from St. Louis, I had come by paddle-wheeler in 1856, arriving at Westport Landing—the original name for Kansas City—a town spreading in wood and red brick buildings across the bluffs above the confluence of that wide brown syrup of mud and the smaller Kansas or Kaw River. A few miles away in Missouri stood the little village of Westport, the gateway to Kansas and the endless rolling prairie.

On several occasions my life bent to events there, like the Big Muddy itself, first as a greenhorn passing through Westport *en route* to Lawrence, where I intended to establish a legal practice and serve as correspondent for the *St. Louis Globe Democrat*.

Although several towns might be considered the gateway to the West—Independence or St. Joseph, for example—Westport deserves the appellation since the well-traveled highways westward, the Santa Fe Road and the California or Oregon Roads, start together there, dividing into two highways at Gardner, some thirty miles away, the aforementioned falling off southwesterly, the other running in a northwesterly direction to Topeka, the Rocky Mountains, and the Pacific.

Without question, I have an affinity with Westport, for it was there that the Kansas Militia deployed to support the undermanned federal army of the Border when General Sterling Price's Confederate army invaded Missouri in October of 1864 in a desperate attempt to salvage an already lost cause. At Westport, and finally at Mine Creek in Kansas two days later, I saw men killed and horses horribly maimed, trying to stay alive myself as well as protect a dozen or so young militiamen from Lawrence and Douglas County, boys half my age, who called me Uncle Ezra.

A year earlier, an event occurred of even greater consequence for me, however, when a rescheduled meeting forced me to stay an additional night in Westport, thus escaping Quantrill's Raid, in which I would almost certainly have perished along with my neighbor Henry Sonnet and two hundred others, both men and boys. Of this I have no doubt! Had Providence spared me when so many others died, and, if so, why? Like Hamlet, I pondered this question and wondered.

Now, each day I considered the newspaper accounts of President Lincoln's funeral train as it moved westward across the country to Springfield, where the man who saved the Republic was buried a week ago on May the first. On the other hand, the story of the flight of John Wilkes Booth and the capture of his co-conspirators held little interest for me. After the assassination, Booth had fled to Maryland and then to Virginia, where on April 26th, he was shot by a Union soldier, Boston Corbett, and died that day.

Many people understandably wanted Lincoln's murderer dispatched like a hog in an abattoir, but that was the fate I wished for another fugitive, the coward and murderer William Quantrill, and so I continued to visit the telegraph office every morning to read the local papers, for there was speculation that Quantrill, who had disappeared at the end of the war, had been seen in Kentucky and might, in fact, have been traveling to Washington to assassinate Lincoln himself. The war was over, but the business of killing was not finished yet.

Then, late in the day on May 10th—a date I would not forget—someone pounded on the front door and our dogs barked wildly.

"Telegram for you, sir!" Young Orville Roden shouted, his voice cracking as he handed me an envelope. "And there's news on the wire now too! Quantrill's been shot in Kentucky! *Quantrill!*" He danced from foot to foot, as though desperately needing to visit the privy, showing his teeth in an apish grin.

"Holy Jesus!" I exclaimed. "Hallelujah! At last, our prayers have been answered!" Young Orville was beaming and snorting in glee to see my excitement, pointing to the telegram unopened in my hand. The paper, as I immediately saw on tearing open the envelope, required no lengthy examination: *quantrill fatally wounded kentucky send story -downing.*

Immediately, I knew what Russell Downing would want: the guts of an account about William Clarke Quantrill, alias Charley Hart, the brutal, sweet-faced Confederate raider whose guerrilla band had burned and murdered in an attempt to destroy Lawrence, the town he hated. Asking Hannah to lock our doors, I hurried into my office, pulled out several sheets of foolscap, dipped my pen in the inkwell, and began to write. Knowing what was wanted, I hastily described the massacre two years before, gave brief accounts of some who had died and some who survived, especially those who had been saved by wives and sweethearts, the brave women of Lawrence.

An hour later, I was in the telegraph office, having pushed and elbowed through a town celebrating the wounding and capture of the despised Quantrill. Like the rejoicing on the snowy January day in '61 when Kansas was admitted to the Union and on the re-election of Lincoln in '64, townspeople, normally staid and industrious, were shouting and holidaying in the streets, although a few who had suffered grievously on Black Friday wept as well.

I was able to jostle my way in until I could hand Orville Roden my sheets of paper with the information for Downing. Behind him stood John Speer of the *Kansas Tribune*, his bald head bowed. I could see tears on his cheeks, holy tears it seemed to me, memorials to his murdered sons, his grief still sharp two years on.

"Get your telegram out soon's I can, Ezra," Roden shouted above the commotion and chuckled, "Pretty busy today." Thanking him, I grabbed Speer by the arm and pulled him close in a hug. Then I shook my head to show I understood his grief, and he nodded as I moved away through the crowd. On the board sidewalk outside, hoping no doubt for news that the hated Quantrill had already died, others gathered, many with copies of the newspapers in hand, and in the street a knot of men, some of whom had been followers of Jim Lane since the days of "Bleeding Kansas"—the ominous name used by newspapers across the country to describe the spring and summer of '56, when violence spread across the nearby Wakarusa Valley.

At that time, I first met Old Osawatomie, John Brown, the militant abolitionist, who, with a small band that included four of his sons, had massacred five proslavery settlers in retribution for the murder of Free-Stater Thomas Barber. As I came to know Brown better over the years,

I realized that he believed that only violence—war—could eradicate slavery and that God had chosen him to be the instrument of His justice, leading to the failed raid at Harpers Ferry and, by my reckoning, the inevitable slide into civil war.

At the center of the group was Big Ears King, the farmer who once worked in a livery stable and dressed in homespun, now a prosperous man of commerce who wore store-bought shirts and a tie but today was coatless in the heat of the afternoon. King, I knew, hated Quantrill as much as I did.

"Wish I could've shot that villain," King announced. "Couldn't abide him. But no one knew what a treacherous coward he was, the bastard." King was red with anger, and spittle came from his mouth with each sentence.

"Nobody did, but maybe we've closed the book on the past, Ears," I opined. "Booth killed, and now Quantrill wounded, fatally they say."

"Ain't so sure, Ezra. Heard Senator Lane say the past don't want to go away."

"How *is* the senator?" I asked. "Haven't heard much about him lately."

"Too ill to be at the Senate some days, I hear," King responded with a look of concern on his face. "We need him there to look out for Kansas interests. But say, I did hear about another old friend of ours." Always the leg-puller or storyteller, he waited for me to question him.

"So, are you going to tell me?" I asked, poking him in the chest in a friendly way. He smiled and spit tobacco juice in the street.

"You can't guess, so I *will* tell you," he said with a hearty laugh. "Hickok! That's who! They call him 'Wild Bill' now," he whispered conspiratorially. "Remember him from Lane's Free-State army?"

"Of course I do," I replied. "Where's he been since the war ended?" I paused, and King eyed me, a bit suspiciously, I thought. "Last I saw him was after the fight at Mine Creek, where we whipped the britches off the Secesh and sent them home bare-ass naked. *Those* that could still run." The men who had now become our audience were asking questions since even those who didn't know Hickok had heard of him, now familiar to many in Kansas and Missouri as "Wild Bill."

"Heard he was a civilian scout for General Sanborn at Westport," someone behind me said. It was Sheriff Flowers who had joined our conversation.

"Heard he was a Union spy at Westport," averred Charlie Vertue, a vulpine little man with dark eyes and heavy sideburns. His face was marred with pockmarks.

"Well, yes, both a scout and a spy at Westport," I declared. As Hickok's friend, I suddenly became the center of attention and object of a barrage of questions, which I tried to answer as modestly as possible. Finally, I got King to answer *my* question about Hickok.

"In Springfield. Just mustered out," he said eagerly. "Saw a fella who talked to Lorenzo."

"His brother," I added for the listeners. "A wagon master in Missouri . . . during the war."

King nodded. "Guess that brought Wild Bill to Springfield," he said. "Seen him shoot at oyster cans thrown in the air. Hit every one." I had, of course, witnessed his shooting prowess too, when he was with Lane's so-called army.

And I had heard stories about him from Will Cody, the Pony Express rider and later member of the Seventh Kansas Volunteer Cavalry (the Jayhawkers), someone who always had a yarn that needed to be told. As though he were reading my mind, Vertue began talking about Cody, remembering him and Hickok from Leavenworth, where the Cody family lived.

"Yes, he and Cody were mates," I said. "Cody was a Pony Express rider back then. When he was thin. Before he filled out."

"Filled out?" Vertue ejaculated. "He was *always* full of it . . . full of shit!" Everyone laughed.

"Well, he did like a yarn," I replied. "Even if he did need to liven them up." Again, the men laughed boisterously, even those who did not know Cody personally.

With supper approaching, I thought it time to return home. Hannah was fond of Hickok and would be pleased to know he had been seen in Missouri. I could return later to the telegraph office to see if Quantrill had died or Downing had wired me.

As I walked home, passing the Sonnet warehouse on New Hampshire, I thought about my friendship with Jim Hickok. I liked him immediately because he was no braggart. Moreover, he talked about assisting escaping slaves in Illinois and his eagerness to go to Kansas to help the Free-State party. After meeting him when he served with Lane, I had seen him in Monticello Township in Kansas, where he had become village constable, and had spent time with him in Leavenworth at the Cody home when he was a freight driver for Russell, Majors, and Waddell.

A giant of a man, a head taller than anyone else I knew, Hickok was slim and graceful, quick as a panther, and handsome as well, with thin lips, narrow nose, and blond mustache. In those days, he wore a frock coat and low-crowned hat and carried his guns butt-forward in the manner of a pistoleer. Union spy, scout, and sharpshooter, Hickok had gained a heroic reputation in the war, marred perhaps only by an incident during the summer when the war started, at Rock Creek in the Nebraska Territory. Hickok was accused of shooting Dave McCanles and two henchmen and was arrested and put on trial for three murders. A jury acquitted him, finding justifiable homicide, a common verdict in the West when both participants had a fair chance to defend themselves. In my experience, gunfights on the frontier were usually provoked by one of three things: cards, whiskey, or a woman—often by all three at once—and of course, Hickok did like gambling and women. (I heard that an attractive woman named Sarah Shull was also involved in the incident and was mysteriously sent away the next day.)

When I heard this story—or rather, several versions of it—Hickok had joined the Union army as a teamster, then later a wagon master. About this time, he also seems to have acquired the name "Wild Bill" after saving a young man accused of horse theft from a murderous mob in Springfield; the mob then suddenly cheered him for his bravery, shouting the name "Wild Bill."

And so, for many, this became his name. He was already becoming a legend on the frontier. When I asked him about the name after the battle of Mine Creek—as we sat by a campfire and watched Sterling Price set his ammunition wagons afire in defeat—Hickok seemed indifferent to the sobriquet, saying only, "Gotta be called something," and laughed. Nevertheless, I continued to call him "Jim," the name which Lorenzo and apparently the whole family used.

"Did you find out more about Quantrill?" Hannah asked when I burst into the kitchen. Since she had seen the slaughter on that hot August morning in 1863 and had been threatened by one of Quantrill's cutthroats, she was delighted at Young Orville's announcement an hour or so earlier. "Justice at last," she proclaimed, "for the many who died on that day."

"Still alive but seems unlikely to recover from his wounds," I replied, "but I *do* know something else of consequence," I said in a teasing voice.

"Oh, Ezra," she said with a touch of lasciviousness in her voice, brushing back a strand of hair, and touching my arm gently. "You must tell me, sweetheart," she whispered.

"And so I shall," I said. "Jim Hickok is in Missouri—Springfield! Out of the army now." Hannah squealed like a girl and laughed. "He promised us a visit when I saw him at Mine Creek when the campaign ended. Maybe he'll head our way again." Hannah nodded, smiling. "I'll write him care of the post office in Springfield."

The voices of Samantha and Henley carried up to us on the warm evening breeze from the sunflowers where they played tag. The plants were several feet high, the black seeds at the center of the yellow blossoms already formed—a tough and hardy flower that thrived in the hot prairie summer. Swifts filled the evening sky, darting about to capture the huge mosquitoes that came up from the river. Only May, but it already felt like summer.

"If Jim comes to visit, perhaps you can get him to talk about his exciting adventures," Hannah mused. "You could write about them."

"Yes, my dear, I have thought about that often and carefully, but I cannot," I answered, almost in a whisper. "Jim's a good man, but he leads a violent life because the West encourages that. He's someone with skills of hand and eyes, not knowledge found in books. Despite having a sharp mind, he's always sought adventure and is bored in society. Except at the gambling table." I laughed, and Hannah nodded and looked up at my face.

"There is already a legend growing around him like a vine with poisonous flowers, a legend of manliness. Riding and fighting, and especially shooting. Who's the best shot, who has the quickest draw, who can act in that split second that determines who lives and who dies? For men like Hickok, reputation's more valuable than money . . . or life itself. Out here, men can build a reputation by horsemanship, shooting, gambling, or taking someone else's woman." I laughed again, and Hannah continued to watch me.

"If I wrote about Jim for a magazine or an eastern paper, they would want shocking, bloody accounts which would only enhance his reputation and encourage foolish boys to challenge him or cause an envious rival to ambush him or shoot him from behind. Someday you'll see cheap novels with woodcuts and sensational magazines with stories of things that never happened. Fights with Indians, bloody shootouts, bandits slain, and readers in St. Louis, Boston, and New York will learn about someone called 'Wild Bill,' not the Civil War hero, just the frontier savage, 'Wild Bill!' I want nothing to do with that!"

"I understand," my wife said, pausing to listen for the children. "Do you think there would be downright lies too?" I nodded. "Ezra, I've been thinking as you spoke, how much Jim is like Othello . . . an 'extravagant and wheeling stranger of here and everywhere,' he is called, a warrior, not a man comfortable in times of peace."

"Yes, I like that line too. But Othello can be savage in the play, and perhaps that is the real similarity with Jim."

I watched Hannah's face change. "Perhaps Jim will be less violent now the war is over," she averred. I felt that she did not understand how dangerous the charming Hickok could be.

After supper, Hannah and I sat on the bench by the lilacs, now completely leafed out, watching our children at play. We loved the long violet evenings in May, listening to the crickets in the grass and watching our children chase the ineffectual fireflies searching for a mate.

"Can we catch some, Papa? And put them in a jar?" Samantha asked. Hannah went into the kitchen and returned with a glass jar and a piece of gunny to cover the top.

"Some people think fairies use the fireflies as lanterns when their soldiers go into battle," I suggested. "When I was a boy in St. Louis, we called them glowworms."

"But they aren't worms, Papa!" Samantha insisted. "Worms don't fly in the sky."

"You are quite correct," I replied, as our daughter ran to me with a firefly cupped in her small hands.

"Be careful you don't hurt him," Hannah cautioned.

Samantha continued to chase the fireflies while Henley ran aimlessly about, flapping his arms as though with enough effort he might begin to rise into the night sky.

"Why so pensive all of a sudden?" Hannah asked after a few minutes of silence.

"Still thinking of Hickok, I reckon," I replied. "And a line from Shakespeare too. Although I can't recall all of it. It's about how closely one's virtues and faults are bound together. A line from *All's Well That Ends Well*. Not a play that everyone knows."

"Not a play I have read, I confess," Hannah admitted with a smile.

"'The web of our life is of a mingled yarn, good and ill together,'" I said. "Part of a longer speech, but I can remember no more of it."

"It's lovely," she whispered, taking my hand and placing it on her breast. "We must read it together, but not tonight. It's bedtime."

CHAPTER SIX

DAY AFTER DAY during May, I began my morning by buying one of the local papers on my way to the telegraph office, expecting to see a headline boldly proclaiming, BLOODY QUANTRILL DEAD! When I stopped at the office to ask one of the operators—either Orville Roden or Skeeter Duncan—what was new on the wire about the dying bush-whacker, both men now met my gaze by shaking their heads—each using the same gesture, as though it were learned and practiced in some operators' school—before averting their eyes. Next, I usually dropped by the Sonnet warehouse to see if Leona was in. She, I knew, would be equally eager to learn if Henry's killer was at last dead. The weekly *Globe Democrat* with my piece on Quantrill had been delivered by mail to Lawrence, and still Quantrill did not die. Downing eschewed sensational headlines, but his more staid one showed the same impatience with a murderer who stubbornly refused to cooperate. Quantrill was now *The Man Who Refused to Die.*

Soon after May had rolled into June, I started my quotidian jour-ney on foot to the telegraph office when I met Edmund Whitman, the staunch abolitionist and friend of martyred John Brown. Ed had been one of eastern Kansas' busiest land agents before the Homestead Act of 1862 had offered government land cheaply. As Ed's profits declined, he began to farm and raise mules on prime land that he had kept for himself.

With him today was his younger son, Jeremiah, who was one of my young militiamen during the Westport campaign. If truth be told, he was my favorite boy, just seventeen at the time, wise-cracking and sarcastic, someone who mocked authority through comic voices—our sergeant, the rich and posh, the lazy, and especially our opponents on the battle-field, "Johnny Reb," also finding in our weevil-filled hardtack and bad meat, a source of endless amusement for our company.

"Come to town to see if Quantrill has died yet," Whitman said, shaking my hand. Whitman, tanned, his hair almost white, looked older than he probably was, too old to have two sons less than twenty. He had replaced his old corncob pipe with a handsome briarwood, which he puffed ostentatiously.

"Not yet, Ed," I answered. "Always was a contrary son of a bitch, Quantrill." Jeremiah had tied up his horse and his father's and now shook my hand and smiled broadly. "That cat fur on your lip is looking mighty fine now, Jeremiah."

"It *was* better, but some bird's been pulling it out at night to line her nest," he replied, his grimace melting into laughter.

"Already getting warm for June," Ed observed. "Need the rain."

"We always seem to need rain in Kansas," I said. "How are your pastures?"

"More worried about my cornfields. Mules eat lots of corn, and I got lots of mules," he replied with a grin.

"Selling lots of mules then?"

"Well, the mule business is good. Jeremiah and Desmond are taking a dozen or so to Missouri to sell." Desmond was the elder son, the quiet one, who, with his brother, was now learning the mule business.

"Missouri?" I queried. "Thought Missouri had plenty of mules of its own."

"Well, they surely do," Jeremiah interjected, "but they're known to be stubborn and ill-tempered. Ours, on the other hand, are gentlemanly mules, you know."

"The boys are taking them to Kansas City in about two weeks. Want to see the big town," their father said with a laugh. "Got a buyer lined up."

"Be good to see the town again. Not that we saw much of it during our campaign," Jeremiah said with what sounded like nostalgia about the military action of a year before.

"You boys watch out for sharpers," I said, smiling. "They're thicker than frogs in Egypt around the grog shops there."

"Just hope them boys come back," Ed laughed. "Hope our revenue accompanies them home as well." Whitman stepped up on the board sidewalk and went into the General Merchandise, and I bid goodbye to Jeremiah, who had exchanged glances with a young woman on the other side of wide Massachusetts Street and quickly lost interest in me.

Several days later, on June 6th, William Clarke Quantrill, the hated man with the strange name, died in a military hospital in Louisville, Kentucky. On that day, I greeted as many of the people as I could who had suffered the terrible losses on Black Friday, the twenty-first of August in 1863, two years earlier, in some ways already seeming long ago but at the same time painfully recent. In Lawrence, we did not celebrate Quantrill's death as we had the news of his capture but marked it with a mixture of revulsion and relief.

Two evenings later, I was able to free Eli Foster from the tender clutches of Prudence Franklin—who, within the month, would be his wife—to reminisce about the day we collected and buried the bodies of the men and boys of Lawrence, since we were about the only able-bodied men left alive. "Can't stay long, you know," Eli apologized. "Got a wedding to help plan." I put the pitcher of beer on the table beside the mugs, which Eli had brought from the bar. "Prudence hasn't a mother or sister to help her, though Hannah has proved a valued friend."

"Haven't been in the Methodist Church since Black Friday," I replied. "I have been thinking about the past, though. There's a phrase from one of Shakespeare's sonnets that seems stuck in my mind: 'I summon up remembrance of things past.'" Indeed, "Sonnet 30" is one of my favorites, this poem of reflection using legal images and financial metaphors—just what would appeal to an attorney like me—causing me to wonder if those who believe Shakespeare had studied the law could be right. But I did not summon up these recollections: they came to me like uninvited guests who intended to stay. Like memories, like the bones of the dead.

"You have a line of poetry for every occasion," Eli laughed, and I smiled and shook my head. "Glad to have finally put Quantrill and the war behind us. People in Kansas have seen too much sorrow." Eli took a cigar from the pocket of his tobacco-brown frock coat and, with his silver pocket-knife, cut off the cigar's end.

"Seems to me the whole country is full of sorrow, my friend," I replied. Eli looked puzzled but nodded. Tonight, he seemed to me to be excessively sanguine, not a doubt on his handsome face. I hoped he would not lose his optimism after his marriage or experience frustrations with his new bride. "My thoughts are dark this evening," I said after we had chatted for a while. "Go back to Prudence. Hannah and I look forward to the wedding. I hope you'll be as happy as I have been in my marriage."

Eli rose, and I emptied my mug as he returned his knife to his coat pocket and shook my hand. "Good times and bad; we have seen them both. You have been a fast friend, Ezra."

I could not stop myself. A quotation from Shakespeare was already on my tongue, "'We have heard the chimes at midnight,'" I said. He looked at me in confusion. Of course, any person who knows the history plays would have recognized the famous line immediately, but Eli's tastes did not run to poetry. As Shakespeare puts it, it was all Greek to him.

Over the next two weeks, as the wedding day approached, I spoke to Hannah about my apprehension at again being in the Methodist Church with its painful memories. On several nights, I lay awake sleepless, and more than once, I awoke in the night tormented by dreams of burned buildings and bleeding bodies lying in the dirt street under the scalding sun. Now that the spring rains had ended, each night we opened the windows to catch the breeze. The cicadas, noisier and more numerous than usual, emitted their dry, high-pitched drone in the trees, and locusts and moths instinctively sought the lights.

After I had spoken to Hannah about my disturbing dreams, she insisted I see Dr. Virgil Gafney, a physician who had come to Lawrence shortly before Quantrill devastated the town. I had watched him care for survivors at the Methodist Church, sweat dripping down his face and soaking his shirt, closing the eyes of the dead and bandaging the wounded well into the night. One of his medical predecessors had been Mortuary Morris, a man whose survival rate was no more noteworthy than his professional diligence. So impressed with Virgil's dedication was I that I asked him to care for our family, which he did, saving the life of our daughter Samantha, who fell dangerously ill with whooping cough while I was away on the Westport campaign.

Virgil said that my experiences were not unusual for someone with my history—the trauma of Quantrill's Raid as well as the Westport action. He explained that such experiences can occasionally manifest themselves some time after an event, as physicians were now noting in treating veterans of the late war.

Then he asked a question that flummoxed me: "Ezra, do you feel guilty that you survived when others that you knew did not?" Naturally, I said that was nonsense, but, as he sat smiling sagely as physicians often do, I allowed as how it might be possible. He then prescribed laudanum, a tincture of morphine, and wrote a note for the chemist. "It's a weak draught, but it should help you sleep and may even give you some pleasant dreams." He chuckled. "Come see me again after Eli's wedding." I was certain that Virgil and I would participate in the chivaree—the noisy and irreverent mock serenade for newly-married couples—banging on pots and singing bawdy bar-room songs that disrupted what was intended to be a romantic night for the newly-weds.

Finally, our first peacetime Fourth of July arrived, although for some of us the holiday was partly overshadowed by the wedding of Eli and Prudence, who were preparing to tie the knot, as country folks put it. The Fourth was a hot day with a slight breeze from the west providing a bit of relief from the afternoon sun. Large white clouds moved slowly across the sky like empty sailing ships riding high in the water, waiting in the harbor to be filled with merchandise, a sight I had seen as a college student in Boston.

The air had the dry smell of cured leather in bales stacked in the sun. Families prepared for a boisterous national holiday with a concert, picnic, speeches, and fireworks. Some of the speakers spoke of our martyred President—eloquently, I suppose—although I wondered if all of those who praised the sacrifice of patriots had themselves ever made any. Although I did not fully understand the cause of my cynicism, I hid it beneath an outward appearance of merriment.

The festivities drew to town those who lived on the surrounding farms, including Maude Cornish, driven in a buggy by her cousin Oswald, and accompanied by her new foreman, Mr. Agard; Ed Whitman; several of the boys from the militia company; and even Vitruvius Bird, sweating in a high collar, suit, and waistcoat with a small group of his farm workers. The townspeople whom I knew best were also in attendance: Prudence and Eli, about to be united in matrimony, the Saltmarsh brothers, Hovey

Lowman and his competitor, John Speers, Big Ears King, Larby Jones in his wagon, Skeeter Duncan, and Sheriff Flowers.

Lemonade in cups cooled by ice was passed around, and later the men would share kegs of lager or whiskey from stoneware jugs while they smoked pipes or chewed tobacco. Many of the women carried parasols to protect their tender skin from the harsh Kansas sun, and those who did not wore a bonnet. While the revelers ate—a process that continued from dinner time almost through supper—the men pitched horseshoes, and the boys played ball. To stay cool, I wore a soft collar and had rolled up my sleeves, as had many of the other men. The women, in long dresses, looked hot and uncomfortable, even in the shade. After the last speech, an old Negro played the fiddle, his mournful melody reminding me poignantly of the military campfires and the soldiers—thousands of them, from both sides—who did not return from the battlefield.

For me, there was a sadness that even the fireworks could not dispel. After struggling to stay awake, little Henley—who usually ran around like a barnyard rooster—had fallen asleep before the fireworks began. He slept in my arms; even the aerial bombs could not awaken him.

At last, the wedding day arrived; on another hot Kansas morning with the kind of haze that seems to rise up from the land when the air is still. Although the ceremony was intended to be a simple country wedding, the preparations busied much of the town. I was greatly pleased that six-year-old Samantha was to participate in the ceremony, and, of course, Hannah and I stood up for our friends. Nevertheless, I could not entirely banish memories of that terrible day in August two years before, when the Church was filled with the injured and dying. Those memories will stay with me until my dying day.

Two weeks after the wedding, I came across Whitman's two boys, returned from their mule-selling adventure, riding down Massachusetts in a two-wheeled buggy. "How was the Show Me state, boys? Get back with any of your money?" I shouted.

"Well, I declare, Uncle Ezra, we did. What was left after we visited the fancy houses in Kansas City," Jeremiah said with a laugh as he poked his brother with his elbow. Both boys were in their shirtsleeves, the day already hot. "Wait till you hear all our stories," he exulted.

Desmond smiled at the younger man, who stroked his sketchy mustache and goatee. "Why don't you just show Ezra what you got for him?"

Desmond had pulled the buggy into the shade of a building. I followed him, jumped down from my horse, and tied the reins to the buggy's wheel.

"Ezra's a writer, Des, and needs to know the . . . what's the word? Context?"

"Yes, *context* would work fine," Desmond said, continuing before his brother could snatch the narrative away.

"Wants to steal my chickens, you see," Jeremiah responded in mock outrage, not chastened by his brother's words.

"Anyhow," Desmond interjected. "Got to Kansas City with our mules, met a fella there, and learned we could get more for them in Harrisonville, where we met another fella—from Sedalia!"

"Not Sedalia! Springfield!" Jeremiah shouted. I laughed, and people on the board sidewalk watched in amusement. Jeremiah took off his straw hat and wiped his forehead with his kerchief. I thought he might be ready to take a bow.

"You finish it then," Desmond said to his brother, who quickly picked up the story.

"Remember after we kicked the Secesh all to smash at Westport, and they went off dragging their bollocks behind them, our militia trying to bivouac . . . in the middle of the Federal Seventh Cavalry, who had came at them from the east . . . and you saw the fella, the trooper you knew whose mouth ran a mile a minute. Remember him?"

"Yes, of course. A private in the Seventh, name of Cody," I said, remembering my surprise at seeing someone from my past so unexpectedly. "He told me about a scout in Sanborn's Brigade named Hickok, an old friend from Lane's Free-State army."

"You were trying to find him in the confusion," Jeremiah replied, excitement in his voice. "Militiamen and troopers . . . and their horses. The wounded too, and commissary wagons and ambulances. Broken-down horses. Never seen such chaos."

"Cavalry wanted to get after Price and the Secesh 'fore he could escape south. Ha!"

"Forget about Price, Uncle Ezra. I'm talking about Hickok—Wild Bill, they call him now! Killed a man in Springfield a few days ago." Desmond had opened the carpet bag on the floor of the buggy and was searching for something inside. Although surprised to hear about

Hickok, I was not shocked to learn of a violent death, for death seemed to follow him around like a familiar dog, friendly but lethal.

"How'd it happen?"

"Des has got the paper," Jeremiah said. "Newspaper we got in Harrisonville from the Springfield fella." He cast a look at his brother, who nodded, extracted the paper from the bag, and handed it to me.

"GUNFIGHT ON SQUARE!" The headline said. I quickly read the story. *Davis or Dave Tutt was shot in the public square at six o'clock, p.m. by James B. Hickok, better known as "Wild Bill," aged twenty-six, residing in Springfield,* the article began. My eyes ran down the page. *The two had played cards together regularly. Tutt claimed Hickok owed him $35 and took his Waltham repeater watch, defying Hickok, who warned Tutt not to wear the watch on the square. According to witnesses, the next day, Tutt crossed the square, pulling out his pistol, and Hickok drew his, both fired—the shots sounding as one—and Tutt fell.*

Without waiting to see if he had hit his opponent, Hickok spun on his heels and pointed his pistol at Tutt's friends, saying: "Are you satisfied, gentlemen?" Hickok is also reported to have said, "I'd rather not have killed him, but there's been hard feelings between us a long while and he tried to degrade me and I couldn't stand for that." The article continued: *The next day, a bench warrant was issued by the military authorities for Hickok's arrest, and bail was granted. Hickok now faces trial in August.* The folded newspaper in my hands was the *Springfield, Missouri Weekly Patriot.*

"Thanks, Des," I said. "May I keep the paper?" He nodded. "My friend's a dangerous man. Just goes to show you should choose your friends wisely," I remarked, making my statement into a jest and laughing. Both of them seemed puzzled, but I did not wish to explain Hickok to them at the moment.

Bidding them farewell, I swung up onto my horse and trotted over to Sonnet Freight and Wholesale, where I was to meet Leona and deliver the legal documents that my copyist had prepared. Back East, she might have been called a scrivener. Here she was just called a copyist, but no one I knew had as beautiful a hand as that of Molly Garnett, widowed by Quantrill's renegades, who now supported herself copying out my legal work, much of it for Leona. Tying up my horse, I went to Leona's office.

"You're going to own half of Lawrence soon," I teased Leona. "Everybody thought you'd lose business when the railroad came to town, but you've got more than ever." I looked at Isaac, who smiled faintly and brushed dust off his white shirt. "How is that, Isaac?" I looked at them as I handed Leona the completed documents from Molly.

"Miss Leona knows there's money to be made bringing merchandise up from the station," Isaac replied politely. "And taking it to places where the rail lines don't go. Mules don't need rails." I laughed, but all I got in return was a quick nod from the taciturn Negro.

Since Henry Sonnet's death in 1863, his widow had expanded his freight business, built a new and bigger storage barn in New Hampshire where their burned-out house had stood, and became a wholesaler as well. Early in '65, she built a second barn in North Lawrence next to the new depot for the Union Pacific Railway, Eastern Division.

As Leona bought and sold property, people began to say, "That Leona's got a real nose for commerce!" And of course they were right. Witness her purchase of a barn beside the Kansas River, where ice was sawn into blocks in the winter and stored in sawdust to await use in the summer. With a fleet of mule-drawn wagons, she quickly cornered the ice business in town.

"Think that's the last of that batch of papers," I said. "Molly's the best copyist I've ever seen, even in St. Louis. Not all the Quantrill widows have done as well."

"How'd you find her, Ezra? Remind me of that," she asked.

"Oh, Hannah did," I responded. "Went around to visit some of the widows after the massacre. Hannah saw that she wrote a beautiful hand and asked if I could use her to make fair copies for me. Between us, you and I can probably give her lots of work."

"Tell Hannah I'll come by to see her tomorrow. Didn't get to talk to her much at the wedding."

"You look busy this morning," I said. Indeed, the barn always looked busy as wagons came and went, and merchandise was unloaded under Isaac's watchful eyes. "Noontime's approaching, and I need to get home for my dinner." Leona gave me a hug as she always did.

Arriving at home, only minutes away, walking or riding, I put my horse in the stable, making sure he was fed and watered, and walked briskly to the house, glad to get out of the hot sun and eager to tell Hannah my news of Jim Hickok, which would likely please and worry her in equal measure.

There was more to the Hickok story, however, than the editor of
the Springfield paper knew. After Price's retreating Confederate army
suffered a second, more devastating defeat, at Mine Creek, I had found
Hickok, now a civilian scout with General Sanborn's Brigade, and we
discussed the Westport campaign at a campfire on a night when our
rations did not arrive and the Union Seventh Cavalry and the Kansas
militia had nothing to eat but air.

He told me that he and his "mate," presumably another Union spy
or scout, had been betrayed by Dave Tutt and that, surrounded by the
Secesh, he had to flee to save his own life. I remember his words, spoken
calmly and deliberatively in the light of the fire: "Guess I'll see Tutt again
down the way."

Why Hickok and Tutt were both in Springfield playing cards together
for some days is unknown to me. Did Hickok remain in Springfield to
take vengeance on a man who had betrayed him? Did he see the gunfight
as just retribution for the death of a Union comrade? What I do know
and remember well are Hickok's words about Tutt, and I believe that
the gunfight in Springfield was about something other than a Waltham
watch or a thirty-five-dollar gambling debt.

CHAPTER SEVEN

"**I KNOW DEATH** hath ten thousand several doors for men to take their exits," so speaks the Duchess of Malfi, awaiting her execution in John Webster's eponymous tragedy. Jim Hickok's shooting of Dave Tutt had the feeling of a denouement, and, at first, I foolishly thought the killing on the Border might be coming to an end. Although I was pleased to learn that Hickok was quickly exonerated, reflection during the late summer and early autumn months convinced me that the Missouri bushwhackers were still a present threat to the peace.

In Kansas, Southern sympathizers had long been swept away by the flood of patriotism after statehood, but in Missouri, division still smoldered between Union loyalists and the guerrilla bands that were left behind with all their anger and resentment when Sterling Price's Rebel army fled the state, abandoning what was left of their lost cause.

As the war was ending on the Border, some bushwhacker chieftains were picked off like ripe fruit: two of Quantrill's lieutenants, George Todd, killed at the Little Blue River two days before the Battle of Westport, and Bloody Bill Anderson, who scalped and mutilated the bodies of his opponents, shot by Union soldiers in Orrick, Missouri, also in October. The list I had made of the Quantrill raiders had ticks after many of the names now, but over the two years since the terrible event, I had learned more names, and so the list grew, most of the raiders still in Missouri.

The year 1865 was finally coming to an end, a year so momentous that we believed we would never see another like it. Lawrence was now peaceful and thriving. Maples and oaks had been planted since Quantrill's

Raid, and now we were treed in red and gold in the shimmering autumn light, while along the country roads the parchment-tan of cornstalks set off the scarlet of sumac and the orange berries of the bittersweet. Finally, Indian summer slid away beneath the gray skies of November, and in one night, as the wind shifted from westerly to northerly, the last leaves were stripped from the trees.

As Thanksgiving approached, Hannah and I decided that—despite a few guerrilla attacks on stagecoaches and travelers—Missouri was now safe enough for us to take the Union Pacific train to Kansas City and from there the Pacific Railroad of Missouri to St. Louis, its last stretch, delayed during the war, finally completed. Now we could travel in greater comfort and safety with Samantha and Henley than on the slow Missouri River steamboats.

My parents were dead, but, according to the report, Hannah's mother was thriving, and her father, George Waterhouse, although suffering the problems of decrepitude, was in good spirits, and my two brothers and their families were all doing well. Of course, I also wanted to see Russell Downing to discuss my future with the *Globe Democrat* now that the telegraph was changing the newspaper across America.

It had been five years since either of our families had seen us—Henley not even born on our last trip to St. Louis. Hannah's mother was still the most gracious and charming of women, her father beginning to slip into what Shakespeare calls "the last scene of all, second childishness and mere oblivion," retaining only a trace of his boisterous good humor, his boom-ing voice now gone. The St. Louis cousins questioned our children about Indians and buffalo and were disappointed to learn we didn't live in a sod house or tepee or have a Texas Longhorn steer in our barn. I could tell by looking at Hannah that she believed this Thanksgiving dinner might be the last such meal she would share with her father.

In the morning, the barber who came to shave George Waterhouse also shaved me in anticipation of my meeting with Russell Downing. I had been clean shaven my entire life except for the Westport campaign, when, of necessity, I grew a beard; on my return home, Hannah touched my chin as though it were a porcupine, citing Beatrice in *Much Ado,* who announced that she could never endure a bearded husband, saying she "had rather lie in the woolen."

We were to dine at Downing's club in busy, bustling St. Louis—no mud streets, pigs running loose, dog packs, farm wagons, or beeves driven toward the railway station. I wore my best suit with a waistcoat and thought I could pass muster. All morning, I had been apprehensive, fearing Downing would tell me he no longer needed my occasional piece for the *Globe Democrat*, eastern Kansas now quiet and peaceful, far removed from the Indian wars which continued in western Kansas and parts of the Nebraska Territory. Although I did not need the emoluments from my writing, I knew I would miss the excitement of the telegraph office and the pleasure of occasionally seeing my words in print.

Downing seemed much older, of course. I figured he must be seventy, his hair, what little he had left, whiter, and his eyes puffy and moist, but he was as cheery and full of life as he had been that April evening in 1856 when he proposed that I work for the *Globe Democrat* in Kansas. "I can see your father in you, Ezra," he said. "He would have been pleased to know that you are a successful attorney and news correspondent—two careers, and in a strange and violent land."

I swallowed hard and felt tears form in my eyes, mumbling thanks as he shook my hand and directed me to a table. "I may have a bit of excitement for you today," he exclaimed, his eyes fastened on mine. "After we have dined and had a cigar, as we all used to do at your father's." He took off his glasses to wipe the lenses with his napkin, and I realized that I did not remember whether he wore glasses when we were last together. I inquired about his health, and he asked about my family before we ordered our dinner, served by crisply attired Negroes.

Our excellent dinner completed, Downing led the way to the library, where a fire burned in the cold, overcast afternoon, its flames reflected by the silver and brass of the elegantly furnished room. "I know you wish to know about all the lawlessness in Missouri, Ezra," he said after we had settled into our chairs, near enough to the fireplace to feel the warmth, "but I held the subject in abeyance until my other guest arrives." He took his watch from his pocket, glanced at it, and gestured to the waiter standing near the door, who nodded. Then, Downing laughed and said, "My guest is so prompt one can set a watch by him—like the conductor on the railroad." Within moments, the waiter returned with a decanter of whiskey, three glasses, and a box of cigars.

Through the door behind the waiter appeared a tall and sinewy man, ramrod straight, with high forehead, shoulder-length hair, and trimmed beard set off by lustrous pearl-gray eyes. Despite his gray-blond hair, he seemed not much older than me. I knew immediately that he had been in the military, the Union army, I supposed. He strode across the room, nodded imperceptibly to me, and offered his hand. I had a strange feeling—perhaps a fear—that this man could change my life, but whether for good or ill, I could not know.

"Ezra, let me introduce you to Colonel Frederick Benjamin Maypole of the Missouri Militia," Downing spoke quietly but distinctly, as though every word and sentiment were significant but not to be heard by anyone else, even the waiter, who had, in any case, now disappeared.

"An honor to meet you," the new arrival, sober of face, said, taking my hand. "Call me Maypole or Colonel," he said, "but, for God's sake, not Fred. Can't abide the name 'Fred.'" There was amusement in his voice, although his face remained solemn. He squeezed my hand, and I gripped his firmly, as I did not wish to be outdone by the Colonel.

"A pleasure to make your acquaintance, Colonel," I responded. Downing had pulled up a chair for the newcomer so that we formed a crescent before the fire. He poured whiskey into Maypole's glass, which the Colonel raised to us and took a swallow.

"Let me explain why I brought the two of you together," Downing said softly. "I have wanted to do so for some time. Your trip to St. Louis, Ezra," he said, looking at me, "gave me the opportunity. Missouri's in chaos today—in some ways worse than during Price's invasion of the state a year ago, the Confederacy's last breath in the West, as it were. The truth is, many of the Rebels from the war years remain here, and the state still seems almost equally divided between Loyalists and Confederate sympathizers, who either refuse to believe the South has surrendered or have no other way to survive except to pass counterfeit bills, steal, and kill, as they did during the war. When that fool Price invaded Missouri, his army was comprised of veteran Confederate cavalry who had battled the Union army along the Arkansas border."

Downing paused but continued to look at me, glancing occasionally at the Colonel. "Many bushwhackers—hating the federal government and the Union army—had flocked to Price's columns in '64 as the

Rebel army rode westward along the Missouri River, and—as you know, Ezra—he needed all the bushwhackers he could get because there were two Union armies opposing him, one following him and another—the Army of the Border—at the Kansas line. Desertions there were, of course, but the toughest stayed with Price or tried to divert the Union forces."

Colonel Maypole looked at him, but his eyes kept returning to *my* face as though he were assessing me, sizing me up as we say in Kansas, in much the same way Old John Brown studied people with the gold-speckled eyes of a snake (as many said), although I believed they resembled the eyes of a hawk, patiently watching his prey.

"You see, the bushwhackers had gotten more brutal in the last months of the war . . . reached a new level of turpitude!" Maypole said, looking me in the face. "After the Centralia Massacre." He paused. "You know of Centralia, Mr. Middleton?" Of course I did, just as I knew about the Rebels' massacre of captured Negro troops at Poison Springs in Arkansas, showing them no quarter when they tried to surrender.

"Poison Springs was bad too," I replied. "That was April of '64. Kansas Colored Infantry lost 300 men, most killed as they tried to surrender, and many bodies mutilated and scalped Indian style. I knew some of them, several from Lawrence." I stopped for a moment to collect my thoughts. "Still, nothing was as bad as what happened in Lawrence, sir. Unarmed civilians, some of them boys. Just boys."

"Without doubt," the Colonel averred. "Only meant to suggest that when their hopes were dashed, the bushwhackers became more savage. Their discipline was utterly gone, and they began routinely to scalp, mutilate bodies, and even rape. Only *Black* servant women, of course, since they thought of themselves as Southern gentlemen, eh?" In the quiet of the library, Maypole's voice, brittle with anger, rang out.

"Twenty-four unarmed soldiers executed at the train station in Centralia, and then about a hundred others killed in an ambush when they rode into town to help." Maypole held his cigar, unlighted, in his hand, with his other hand poking at me for emphasis while Downing sat back in his chair with his cigar and whiskey, content for the moment to be a listener, perhaps a bit embarrassed by the other's outburst.

"Let me interrupt, sir, to say that I knew about many of the bushwhackers at Centralia since they had also been with Quantrill in

Lawrence." I reached into my coat pocket and withdrew a little book, what many call a commonplace book. "Here I have recorded the names of the leaders of the Lawrence Massacre as I learned of them. Many were also at Centralia. George Todd, for one."

The Colonel's eyebrows went up, and a slight smile crossed his face. "He died on the Little Blue River near Independence in October," I said, "killed just before the Battle of Westport. As they get killed, I tick them off my list. And Dave Poole. Also, at both Lawrence and Centralia. And the greatest savage of them all—Bloody Bill Anderson." I looked at Downing and continued, "He decorated his horse's bridle with scalps. He was a madman!" His eyes wide, Downing seemed shocked at the depravity, although, of course, he knew of Anderson from his own paper.

"Indeed, you are quite right, sir," the Colonel said. "A right villain that one was, with the black beard of a pirate, carried a lanyard with fifty-three knots—one for each man he had killed. William T—Bloody Bill—Anderson, shot by Union troops on October 26th in Orrick, Missouri, a few days after Todd died. I know the lanyard story to be true. A militiaman I know saw his dead body. Heard that fifteen of those knots were for men or boys he murdered in Lawrence."

I sat back in my chair, having leaned forward while Maypole was speaking. "I had hoped to see him dead on the battlefield at Westport," I said, after clearing my throat. "A vain hope, of course. He was already dead." I reached for my whiskey and laughed at my own folly. The Colonel got up and stepped to the fire, turning his back to it as though to warm himself. Seeing again how tall and thin he was, I speculated whether anyone had ever called him "Colonel Beanpole," but immediately knew nobody would dare to do so, his presence being so intimidating. Nevertheless, an amusing thought.

"Continue, if you will," the Colonel said, rolling the unlit cigar on his fingertips. It was almost as if he had been reading my mind. His voice had now dropped to a whisper.

"Frank James," I replied, "was also at Centralia, I believe." Downing nodded to me.

"Certainly was," Colonel Maypole said. "With his younger brother, Jesse, just seventeen." He now placed the cigar in his mouth but still did not light it.

"To my knowledge, Jesse wasn't with Quantrill in Lawrence. Too young, I expect. But Archie Clement was." I had my whiskey glass in one hand and my little book in the other.

"Yes, Little Arch," the Colonel responded. "The size of a boy. Called Anderson's 'Scalping Lieutenant' in the newspapers. Worse than one of the red-skinned savages. Good God, a white man doing such a thing!" The Colonel shook his head at the depravity of the bushwhackers, holding his still-unlit cigar. "Of course, these villains saw themselves as Confederate rangers, but they never wore the gray uniform, dressing themselves in Union blue coats taken from murdered soldiers to hide their identities, a disgrace to any army." He spit out these words, but I could see that his rage was completely under control, only a slight twitch of his moustache showing his suppressed passion. He stood looking into the fire for a moment, turned on his heel, and quickly returned to his armchair.

"Now you can see why I wanted to bring you two together," Downing explained, breaking the mood as the Colonel and I watched him. "Many of the most dangerous bushwhackers are dead, Ezra, but not all. Frank and Jesse James are in hiding—in Clay County, I suppose—ignored or tolerated by the authorities. Archie Clement is alive, as are the Younger brothers." Downing ran his hand through his thinning hair, straightened his waistcoat, and leaned toward me. "Our new governor, Thomas Fletcher, a Republican and ardent abolitionist, was inaugurated last January."

Because I knew about Fletcher, I grunted agreement as Downing spoke. "Many of the bluecoats who kept the peace in Missouri have been mustered out, leaving the local authorities to deal with the bushwhackers. Of course, local sheriffs will never arrest them, and our militia can only do so much. The bushwhackers have ingratiated themselves with the townspeople, who believe they are like old Robin Hood of England, who stole from the rich and gave to the poor."

"Most likely, they stole from the rich and kept it for themselves," said Colonel Maypole with a grin and a snort.

Impatient at Downing's explanation, as was I, the Colonel now began to chew on his cigar. Of course, I had continued to follow Missouri politics, even after the war ended. "And so, Ezra, I have been advising the governor on certain matters. I need not tell you this is confidential in every sense. Colonel Maypole has been put in charge of surveillance of the bushwhackers, much like the federal agency, which was formed in 1861, the Secret Service Force, set up by Allan Pinkerton, to gather information on the battlefield and elsewhere."

I had heard about the Secret Service and Allan Pinkerton and learned that he ran a detective agency in Chicago before enlisting for service with President Lincoln to set up what was called a "spy network." I had read accounts of his techniques and accomplishments, including a story that he foiled an assassination attempt on Lincoln before the inauguration, although I knew of no corroborative evidence for that. There was, however, much speculation about Pinkerton during the war, and it was said that his secret information made possible some Union successes on the battlefield.

Colonel Maypole watched me with what card players call a poker face. He nodded, acknowledging Downing's account. "Our friend told me you know more about the Jayhawkers and the bushwhackers than anyone he knows. Indeed, five minutes with you has convinced me too. Well, I need someone to help me gather information in western Missouri—including that area on the north bank of the Missouri River near Kansas City, some call 'Little Dixie.'"

For the first time, Frederick Maypole broke into a smile. He was, in fact, an attractive man when his somber features softened, but I began to realize how dangerous the task he had in mind was, and my spine began to tingle, the sensation running into the back of my thighs. "Of course, you will want to consider my offer, and we will also need to discuss compensation. You can write what you want for Russell. In fact, you should do so because your safety in Missouri may depend on how convincing you are as a *mere* newspaper correspondent." His voice was deep and convincing, probably too convincing.

"Spies frequently end up dead, and these may be the most dangerous men in the country," I said as my mind began working. Hannah and my children had to be my first consideration. I had served in the war with the Kansas militia. Did I now have to serve again? Would Hannah willingly have me go?

"We shall not have to meet often. Send your news accounts to Russell as you have done in the past, but add information about subjects and events in which I have an interest. I will review your telegrams or letters for what I need, and Russell can use what fits *his* use for the *Globe Democrat*. No secret codes, no meetings, no documents that could compromise you. What could be simpler? And you will get paid twice!" He laughed and waved his chewed cigar like an officer's baton. Colonel Maypole was assuming I would accept his offer. I wondered if he was married, but supposed not. Whatever his expectations, I needed to explain to him that my family would come first, and so we agreed to meet again on the morrow, after I had discussed this with Hannah. A sensible man would have immediately turned down the proposal, but I had to admit to myself that becoming a government spy was intriguing.

We shook hands at the door, Colonel Maypole and Downing leaving together, and I walking in the opposite direction to catch the horse car back to the Waterhouse residence. I pulled up the collar of my overcoat in the gray afternoon, feeling the damp creep in like fog from the Mississippi River. Then, just before me, I saw a surprising sight: Vitruvius Bird in a large fur hat, accompanied by two well-dressed, derby-wearing men in black, going down a side street to my left. Bird had not noticed me, engrossed as he was in conversation. What, I wondered, could he be doing in St. Louis?

CHAPTER EIGHT

AS **WE PULLED** into the depot in Lawrence, sleet, driven from an empty gray sky, hit the train windows like broadcast wheat seed or grains of sand. As I expected, Leona's man, Isaac, was waiting with an open, mule-drawn buckboard and an umbrella for Hannah and the children, although the latter—Samantha and Henley—sat with their faces to the wind, catching the sleet in open mouths, giggling, and talking of snowmen. I knew the winter air was too dry for snow to form; in fact, snowfall on Christmas Day was rare enough in Kansas, heavy snow seldom occurring before the New Year, often not until mid-winter.

Since the railroad had come to town only the year before, the whistle marking the train's approach was still exciting for the children, who tooted and shrieked in reply, while their elders also stopped to listen, nodding their heads as if to say "high time we got the rails in Lawrence," or "nothing can stop us now—hooray!"

The war had been a lid on a pot which now boiled over, the lid being removed. The country was again on the move westward as it had been when prospectors and adventurers had rushed to California in '49 and to Colorado in '58, but those of us who lived west of the Missouri River knew our future well-being depended not on gold fields to be discovered in the mountains but on railroads which would carry in settlers and, over time, could carry out the produce of this rich, new land. When a higher cause and self-interest move in tandem, things seem to happen, even if the gain be the kind of brazen greed which the Bastard in Shakespeare's *King John* calls "commodity." In Lawrence, we had recovered from Quantrill's

Raid and Price's invasion of Missouri, but Kansas was still behind many of the western states and territories.

Now everyone talked of railroads. North of the Missouri River, the railroads like the Hannibal and St. Joseph were standard gauge; south of the river, the railroads like the Pacific Railroad of Missouri were broad gauge. Lawrence had hoped to become a change of gauge point, but Kansas City, with a larger population and better location, had been chosen. Moreover, the hope that the Union Pacific, Eastern Division, would become the main transcontinental route and go through Kansas, lost out to the Union Pacific line from Omaha, Nebraska Territory, where construction had begun in 1863.

If Lawrence did not get any of these plums, there were plans for other lines, including one from Leavenworth, which only weeks before had been renamed the Leavenworth, Lawrence, and Galveston, and could carry freight to the Gulf of Mexico.

Before leaving St. Louis, I had met again with Colonel Maypole to discuss our special relationship. Hannah had given a frosty assent to my playing the spy in Missouri after I assured her there was little danger in my doing so. It was apparent that she often knew my state of mind better than I did, and if truth be told, I *was* becoming bored with my law books, wills, contracts, sales and purchases of land, charters, and bonds, and needed a bit of adventure. She knew it too.

Now, as the Christmas season approached, I prepared for the change in my life by seeking out Big Ears King. A name like "Big Ears" might seem insulting to most people, but he took it as a sign of friendship, as much a part of him as his hardy laugh, freckled face, and the wad of tobacco in his jaw. I explained to him that I would now devote less time to the law and more to the newspaper.

Since King had long been an associate of Senator Jim Lane, and through his livery business knew people far and wide, I was counting on him to announce to the town my return to the *Globe Democrat* by telling him it was confidential, thus ensuring that the news would get out as fast as greased lightning. I had new *cartes de visite* with "*St. Louis Globe Democrat*" printed on them, replacing the phrase, "Attorney at Law." Through a recent innovation, these cards had a photographic image of my face printed on paper and gummed to the back of the card.

Hannah also played her part in spreading the news by mentioning around town that I would again be pursuing railroad stories for the *Globe Democrat*, which, in fact, was exactly what I intended to do. I knew Hannah to be everyone's friend. Leona had said it was because "she don't ever put on airs or exhibit ostentation in manners or dress." Since Kansans are so plain spoken, "not putting on airs" was a high compliment.

Hannah had two abiding causes in her life, and one was securing the vote for women. I had told her jokingly that the franchise for women would not come until the Conversion of the Jews, although that did not deter her from continuing to discuss suffrage with her female friends, as well as with me. Hannah said she might not get the vote herself, but believed that Samantha almost certainly would. In this, I hoped that she was prescient.

Hannah had been outraged when she discovered that the Fifteenth Amendment to the Constitution would not guarantee women the franchise that had already been granted to Black men. She spoke to her women friends and wrote to friends and family in other states about what she called "the great inequity," but only a few claimed to see her side of the argument, and fewer still offered either hope or support.

Her other cause was the plight of the Negro. Her tutelage of Isaac Worthy had made her eager to take on another young person. Despite our state's abolitionist history, colored people found themselves ignored and often mistreated in Lawrence. It was one of the many ironies of the war that after helping to free the slaves, white Kansans seemed not to know what to do with them. In fact, attitudes toward Negroes seemed to have hardened since the war ended.

Many Black men who had served valiantly for the Union returned to seek work but found only jobs shoveling horse shit from the streets. Lawrence seemed to have forgotten the old Underground Railroad stations in town and the bravery of the conductors, Black and white. The state, which seemed like the Promised Land now for the Negro had begun to be the land of lost promise.

So it seemed almost providential when our friend Virgil Gafney told us of a Negro girl who could help Hannah to keep house. She was Phoebe, fourteen years of age and recently orphaned. I was both surprised and pleased to learn her surname: "Brown." John Brown had kidnapped—freed—Black families from Missouri in the years before and during the war, and in gratitude, some of those families took the old abolitionist's name.

The skinny little girl whom Dr. Gafney brought us seemed frightened and confused, but it was six-year-old Samantha, not Hannah or I, who was first able to gain her trust. "Will we be sisters?" our daughter innocently asked. Phoebe began to smile when our daughter took her hand and led her to the bedroom, which they would share. It would take time, I knew, but we trusted in the spirit of Christmas, St. Nicholas, and the holiday traditions the German immigrants had introduced to Lawrence. With the new child in the house, I felt more at ease in leaving my family, and Leona and Isaac would also be nearby. Besides, Hannah had our old shotgun and knew how to use it.

After the war, Russell Downing's *Globe Democrat* had become a source for railroad information in the Missouri River Valley: new and projected lines, railway bonds, land ownership, and subsidies, in fact, everything pertaining to the railroad, a source superior to the local newspapers with their hearsay and speculation.

I was familiar with the Hannibal and St. Joseph Railroad, which made the 190-mile journey across northern Missouri; this line carried the mail from the east to that small city in northwest Missouri where, during its brief existence in 1860 and '61, slim young men like my friend, Bill Cody, rode for the Pony Express. In St. Joe, the mail was put into a mochila (a saddle bag with mail pouches on which the rider sat) before horse and rider took a ferry across the river into Kansas Territory at Elwood—where in December of '59 I had heard then-candidate Lincoln speak—and from there west to Marysville in Kansas, into the Nebraska Territory, and so on toward California.

I also knew Leavenworth, where the Cody family lived, and Atchison, farther up the Missouri River on the Kansas side, but it was to Clay County in Missouri, where the great muddy river makes a sharp turn east before it snakes its way toward St. Louis, that I would travel after the New Year.

Downing knew a new railroad line to Chicago was being contemplated to transport beeves from the Kansas grasslands or even from the Indian Territory, Texas, or Abilene at the end of the Chisholm

Trail, perhaps passing through Clay County on the north bank of the Missouri River. And it was no coincidence that I should be sent there since Colonel Maypole thought it to be a nest of dangerous, unregenerate bushwhackers.

When I left in mid-January on my journey into that part of Missouri some called "Little Dixie" for its Southern sympathies, the holidays were still on my mind. Phoebe had quickly become part of our family and, when asked by the curious about our plans for her, we simply called her "our little girl" and smiled. It was bright and cold, good weather to travel since the muddy roads froze at night and often didn't thaw until mid-day, although I had not ridden from Lawrence but instead had taken the train to Wyandotte, just across the state line from Kansas City, and from there had hailed a steam ferry to the hilly land across the river, my horse so spooked by the clanking, hissing steam engine of the ferry that it took both the pilot and me to get him aboard.

Before we landed in Fishing River Township in Clay County, the river pilot, Barney Appleyard, a blond young man of about twenty years, proved to be as skilled in weaving tales as he was accomplished with boats and horses.

"Railroads putting the watermen out of business, sir," he complained, drawing on his clay pipe. "Guess I was borned at the wrong time. Not my fault, of course, when you was borned, is it? Didn't *ask* to be borned!" he laughed. The Missouri was a dangerous river with submerged logs and sandbars, floating branches and other detritus, so he kept close watch on both sides of the boat as he grinned and sucked on his pipe. "River traffic way down since the rail connection to St. Louie opened. Traffic mostly local trade now. Goods to the little towns and, of course, passengers crossing the Muddy, sir, such as yourself."

I had explained on embarking that I was a newspaperman and handed him my card. If President Andrew Johnson had himself been invited on board, he could not have been welcomed with more deference and respect than I was.

"Talk 'bout a railroad bridge near Kansas City—iron, I reckon—but that won't come 'til a railroad puts a line through from Chicago." He glanced at me, but his eyes quickly returned to the treacherous waters. "Ole Muddy floods at times. Reason Kansas City's built so high up from the river, since the bottom land floods some spring times . . . most springs, in fact," Barney said laughing. One of the other passengers, a young man with a satchel, now came up to us. "When the bridge is finished and the train comes directly from Chicago," the young pilot pronounced the adverb with a strong stress on the first syllable, "well, maybe I have to leave the river for good!" He laughed again, not bitterly but as though his own bleak future might prove a slight source of amusement for his passengers.

The boat moved steadily downstream, the engine clanging and hissing like an ancient grist mill afloat in the dirty water. A farm couple in muddy attire who said they hailed from Crab Orchard in Ray County, sitting on a bench near us, viewed the pilot's words with the equanimity of seasoned river travelers and smiled at me.

"Take milk, for instance," Appleyard pronounced, waving his arms like a preacher on Sunday morning, his pipe clenched in his teeth. "If we had a bridge and rail, milk would get to Kansas City within an hour of milking. Now our milk is rancid 'fore it gets to market or maybe churned to butter by the roads."

"But don't you profit from taking it across the river?" I asked in a low voice.

"You're a sharp one, sir," he replied, laughing. "Saw the flaw in my argument. Well, my sacrifice for the greater good, I guess. So, then Clay County farmers would clear more land, buy more cows, have more pasture." He removed the pipe from his mouth and snorted. "Stead of sitting round whittling." He scrutinized the shore ahead.

"Well, that's the quay over yonder," Barney announced. "Said it was a short trip. Only stop there long enough to pick up wood and get the horses unloaded." The derelict quay looked as though it had been fashioned with debris pulled from the river, and the old woman who waited at the woodpile—stacked wood covered with a canvas—could have been one of *Macbeth*'s three witches, the Weird Sisters (so they are called), who greet Macbeth and Banquo in the Scottish play. She seemed as old as the mighty river itself, gray hair escaping a dirty wool cap, missing some teeth in front, but spry enough to spring to life and throw pieces of wood into the bin near the glowing firebox as the pilot helped the two horses step onto the quay and then solid ground.

As Barney Appleyard pulled his steam ferry back into the current, my fellow passenger and I exchanged greetings, and I handed him my *carte de visite*. Since he had no card to give me, he apologized before saying he was Sidney Mulligan, traveling to the town of Liberty, which I knew to be less than ten miles north of the river. Sidney awkwardly mounted his horse, and I thought he might be a wounded veteran of the war like Leona's driver, Larby Jones, who lost part of his leg at Westport, but began to realize he was lame, a clubfoot I suspected, rather than a war injury.

We left the cluster of houses that constituted the heart of Fishing River Township behind us, riding together up the hill into the silent, leafless woods. In eastern Kansas, the prairie is often edged by woods, but here the woods commanded the landscape, with empty fields and orchards surrounding frame houses and barns, crops seeming almost an afterthought. My companion was a dyspeptic fellow, but his clothes were clean, if a bit shabby. Rather than the broad-brimmed hat of the West, he had on a round-topped hat like a loaf of bread, which had failed to rise.

"Folks seem to pinch pennies nowadays," he mumbled, whether to himself or me I could not tell.

"Maybe your luck will change in Liberty," I replied, hoping to cheer him up. "You been here before?" When he did not answer, I tried again. "First time I've been to Liberty, though I travel around Missouri and Kansas for my paper, although I've never been out on the high plains of Kansas. With the buffalo," I added, laughing at myself.

"Me neither," he said after some consideration. "Mostly stay close to Kansas City." After a moment, he turned in the saddle to look at me. "After Liberty, reckon I'll go on to Excelsior Springs, then up to St. Joe before I come back down river." He clenched his teeth in what I took for a stiff smile. "I practice the dental arts, sir." He patted affectionately the satchel which rested awkwardly across his thighs. "Tools of the trade. Have to take special care of my chloroform. Some folks need it for a stubborn or broken tooth that must be drawn." I had expected him to say "pulled," but practitioners of the "dental arts" should be entitled to their special language, as we attorneys have our Latin phrases.

With the sun well above the trees now, the air had warmed and the birds chattered or sang in the thick woods, blackbirds, tits, cardinals, sparrows—the summer birds like the robins having gone south to Texas.

With each gust of wind, the bare limbs rattled like unearthed bones, making a grim music. Squirrels scrambled into the branches, always staying behind the trunk until popping out to look at us with curious eyes before disappearing again and scampering away through the fallen leaves.

When we reached Liberty, Mulligan, the dentist, began looking for a rooming house. I, on the other hand, needed to be seen and known in town, both to observe and be observed, and so I took a room in the hotel, near the livery stable and across from the bank—the Clay County Savings Association—where I meant to introduce myself to the business community as a correspondent for the *St. Louis Globe Democrat*.

Liberty was a quiet town, smaller than Lawrence, which nestled below a beetling escarpment once called Hogback Ridge, now referred to as Mount Oread; there the new university would admit its first students in September to a lone brick building on the northeast slope, overlooking the town and far from the cemetery where were located the graves into which Eli Foster and I had lowered the bodies of those who had died in Quantrill's Massacre. I strolled around like any visitor to Liberty, stopping at the tavern across from the livery stable where my horse was lodged and ordering a plate of stew and a whiskey since I was still chilled from the cold.

I gave the tavern keeper my *carte de visite* to introduce myself as a newspaper correspondent, but did not reveal I was a Kansan since feelings might still be touchy here after years of conflict between the Missouri Bushwhackers who raided Kansas and the Jayhawkers who ravaged western Missouri before and during the war. Since the tavern keeper was an affable man, I began to ask about railroads because I assumed everyone favored railroads in this rural corner of the state, cut off by the river from the thriving metropolis of Kansas City across the water.

"Who decides where the lines go anyway?" he asked. "Rail barons in Chicago? Bankers in Philadelphia or St. Louis?"

I shook my head. "I don't know where decisions to put in new lines are made, so I try to report on where land is purchased to lay the rails."

"What I'm thinking is *that* very thing," he said emphatically, as though he had just discovered how to extract whale oil from river catfish. "See where land is being bought up!" He pulled at his vest and walked down the bar to retrieve two empty glasses.

"You have something there," I averred as he returned to where I stood. "Friend of mine likes to say, 'It's always about land.' We think as you do." I leaned toward him conspiratorially. "That's what I aim to report to my paper. Anyone bought land in these parts that could be used for railroad right of way?"

"Let me tell you. Someone's going to make money, and it ain't me."

"Me either, brother," I replied, and he grinned.

"You be around here long?"

"Not long, but I should be back to inquire about land sales for my paper. Appreciate whatever you could tell me." And I bought another whiskey even though I didn't fancy one.

I walked across the hard-packed dirt street to the bank—the Clay County Savings Association—the air still chilly despite the sun. The bank manager was Oscar Pevensey, a bespectacled, balding man who seemed as pleased to accept my card as if I had handed him a large silver certificate to deposit. I asked him about land purchases and other matters related to railroads. On several subjects, he politely and respectfully demurred, saying, "That would be a confidential matter, sir," and smiled obsequiously, so after a handshake, I departed, walking into the slanting rays of the afternoon sun.

During the day, I had inquired about the best places for supper and was told that the rooming house where the dentist, Mulligan, was staying had good food, so there I went as the sun set, not wanting to be on the streets after dark, and there I saw Mulligan engaged in conversation with several men whom I thought coarse-looking. After my meal, I walked to the door and touched my hat brim to him, and he nodded, exhibiting a rueful countenance. During the day, I had learned some things about commerce north of the river, which I could put in my story for Downing, but I had no information on the persons of interest to Maypole.

Of course, I knew where the James brothers lived—in Kearney, about three miles from Liberty—but inquiring about them could well prove suicidal. Any ne'er-do-well or farmer might be in their employ, and Archie Clement or the Younger brothers could also be nearby. This scheme of the Colonel's now seemed to me the most quixotic of missions, and I told myself that he should be the one to attempt to smoke out Frank and Jesse James since he was the one who needed to find them. Tomorrow I would ask more questions about land and railroads. but I had already arranged to meet Barney Appleyard at sundown to be carried back across the river to Kansas City.

In the morning, I roved around town, stopping at the office of the newspaper to find it closed, and then went into the land office to ask about recent purchases of land, only to learn few pieces had changed hands in the last year. I wrote down the names of the biggest landowners in the township and made other notes. Since it was cold and damp, I had another whiskey and left earlier than I intended, riding through woods under tree branches that chattered like skeletal fingers. Sundown was approaching, the light failing, and owls were already hooting before beginning their night's hunt.

My watch told me I had come early for my appointment with young Appleyard, but soon I heard the arrival of the ferry, or rather my horse did, for his ears became erect and he pawed the ground, sensing its approach. The pilot swung into the quay and tied up the boat. As my frightened horse was being loaded on the ferry by the pilot and me, I heard hoof beats on the road down which I had recently ridden and the haloes of a horseman—none other than the dentist, riding as though the whole Sioux Nation, spears and knives in hand. were close behind him. Into my mind came the image of Ichabod Crane fleeing the headless horseman, and I laughed at Mulligan's unintentionally comic arrival. Without doubt, he was holding on to his saddle for dear life.

After the pilot had led Mulligan's exhausted mount on board, he untied the ferry and pushed off, while the dentist cowered against the pilot's cabin, holding his satchel to his chest, ashen-faced and gulping for air.

"Not going to Excelsior Springs, Sidney?" I asked. "Why were you riding so fast?"

"Savages!" Mulligan declared with a sputter and a cough. "Thought they would kill me." He was still breathing heavily. "Let me tell you . . . Mister Middleton. Had a terrifying experience." The sun had now dropped in the January sky, and night was beginning to close in. The oil lantern, which hung above us, illuminated little of Mulligan's face, which was shadowed by his hat.

"You was in some hurry, sir," young Appleyard said, steering the ferry a bit upstream so the sluggish current would bring us precisely into the quay on the Kansas City side of the river.

"Some men said a friend needed my skills. Tough-looking they were," Mulligan explained, calmer now that he had escaped the pursuers he imagined were behind him. "Went to a cabin out of town to meet my patient . . . a little man, no bigger than a boy . . . but mean." He swallowed and went on with his story as Appleyard intently watched his shadowed face. I wasn't sure whether to laugh at Mulligan's tale or pity him.

"Bad tooth he wanted pulled. Could see he was in pain . . . but when I tried to examine him, he swore at me something fierce and grabbed me by the collar. Waved his knife and swore again. Terrible language! 'You don't do this right, him or me will cut your bollocks off and stuff them down your throat.' The pain of threatening me enraged him more, and one of his . . . devilish companions had his knife out too." He lapsed into exhausted silence. "Never seen such a big knife," he said weakly.

"Did you get the tooth out?" I asked, then again asked, "You did get paid, didn't you?"

"Got paid before I went out to the cabin," he said. "Gave the little fella whiskey . . . Lots of whiskey. Luckily, the tooth came right out . . . or they would have killed me . . . or worse."

"Must've been shitting your pants," the pilot said, laughing as we came to the quay. Mulligan didn't answer, stepping off the ferry as Appleyard held the horse for him to mount. I paid my fare and that of the dentist, who was already riding wildly toward Kansas City, clutching his bag of dental instruments.

"Thanks for paying his fare, sir," the river pilot said as he handed me my reins and laughed boisterously at the dentist.

"Think I know who the patient was," I said as I led my skittish horse away from the hissing steam ferry. "Never saw him but heard enough about him."

"Spect you do," he responded as I continued to watch his face, concealed by the night. "Little Archie Clement, I think it was. Took over Bloody Bill's gang, I hear. Known in Clay County and down the river as far as Lexington." He shook out the rope to tie up the ferry. "But nobody talks about him much. People just stay out of his way, and you should too if you go back to Fishing River, sir." He turned from me and, saying farewell, I mounted and rode toward the telegraph office in Kansas City.

Leaving my horse at the nearby livery stable, I marveled at the difference between the busy streets of Kansas City, bright under its lights, and Clay County, as I walked to the Pacific House, the finest hotel in the city. It was there on a hot August night in 1863 that I met with General Thomas Ewing, Jr., recently appointed to command the District of the Border and end the Missouri bushwhacker guerrilla raids into Kansas. For a decade, raids by partisans brought destruction to both sides of the Border, and when the actual war started with Southern Succession, in Missouri—which stayed in the Union—a war within a war began between Confederate sympathizers and Union loyalists in that state. Who was it said to me then—Ed Whitman, I think it was—"History don't ever come to an end. It just goes on and on like a river." The truth of that struck me again as I entered the fine hotel, but I would add this addendum—about the irony of events.

If I had kept to my schedule and had not stayed that night in Kansas City, I would have been home in Lawrence when Quantrill's raiders invaded the sleeping town, murdered my friend, Henry Sonnet, and two hundred men and boys, and torched the commercial district. What Colonel Maypole called the War of the Rebellion was not over yet; to be sure, it was a fire that would not go out, extinguished, but then would reignite, as I had seen in Clay County.

In the telegraph office, I felt I did not have time to imbed in my story for Downing the information for "our friend," as I was to call Maypole. I simply wired Downing that I could place in Liberty "the dwarf," our name for Archie Clement. I counted on Downing to get that news to Maypole without delay. And perhaps the Colonel could get the Missouri militia there and surprise the deadly little man before he could disappear again into the safety of the dark Missouri woods.

CHAPTER NINE

HAPPY TO BE home after two days as a rover in Missouri, I spent the morning with my family, which now included Phoebe, whose loving nature was more evident each day. As yet, the full fury of winter had not stampeded across the prairie, the weather remaining relatively mild, with clear skies and cold, sunny days. As I sorted through my papers and looked at notes I would use in my story for Downing, during the dinner hour, Eli knocked at the door.

Although I had complete trust in my friend, I had told him only that I was going to Missouri for the newspaper, nothing about spying for Colonel Benjamin Frederick Maypole; even the most trustworthy person can accidentally let slip a secret. Today, Eli, however, had no interest in my peregrinations in Clay County, because something important had occurred in my absence: word had come that Maude Cornish's father had died in Massachusetts. It had been brought to the Watkins Bank by Little Joe Oscar, the half-breed ranch hand who, shortly before Christmas, had replaced Agard as foreman.

"When did she hear, Eli?" I asked.

"Yesterday," he responded. "We haven't told anyone in town yet. Been waiting for you." I went into our kitchen, where Hannah sat with Phoebe at a table near the stove, working on the young lady's studies.

"Poor Maude," Hannah exclaimed when I told her the news. "First, the Captain killed at Westport, then Frank Kittleston dead in the accident, and now the loss of a parent." My wife wore a dove gray dress, her red hair pulled back in the fashion that pleased me most. There was a look of uncertainty on her face, and I immediately knew what she was thinking: what would Maude do? Eli had a similar look, and I had questions of my own: with legal matters pertaining to the death, could I represent Maude effectively and still sniff around the dangerous pie cupboard that was Clay County? I told myself I could, and so would immediately ride out to see Maude. Hannah could later visit her to offer the kind of consolation that only a woman can give.

"She will need your help. Her cousin is worthless," Eli cried out. "Worthless! Couldn't teach a dog to bark!" A smile crossed Hannah's solemn face as she giggled at Eli's remark, and I swallowed a laugh.

When I arrived at the Cornish horse farm, I asked for Maude, who, in winter, was known to suffer from the blues, as women called them. Oswald said Dr. Gafney had called the day before and had left medicines. Maude, again clad in black, came from her bedchamber when she heard my arrival. Her appearance shocked me: red, sunken eyes, chalky face, and tears that had marked her cheeks. Sitting beside her on the love seat, I offered her my hand, which she gripped hard and would not let go. Finally, she could command herself enough to speak.

"Ezra, you must help me leave this cursed land. This land of death!" As a man who lives by words, I must admit I could find none to comfort her, although I tried.

For some time, I sat beside this woman, about ten years older than me, now overcome with loss and fear of the future. Oswald had seated himself across the room; he seemed afraid of her, as though she had a disease and he wished to avoid contagion. It was the look I had seen after battle—from men reluctant to touch a bleeding or dead body. I smiled at him, and he timidly returned my smile. As I watched Maude in her black satin blouse with puffed sleeves, skirt to her shoes, words from *Hamlet* came into my mind: "like Niobe, all tears."

Certainly, it was illogical to blame Kansas or the raw prairie for her father's death in Massachusetts, but her reaction was not altogether surprising. Strong women—and men too—were driven to distraction by the bitter winds of a Kansas winter, drought that destroyed crops, babies and children who died from diseases no longer seen in the East. It seemed a wonder her spirit had not been broken earlier. For some time, I discussed with her the consequences of her ridding herself of the farm and returning to the East—liquidating her assets, as we attorneys say.

Realizing that I had no recourse, I told her that if she insisted on leaving, I would help her sell the horse farm that Dan had made into one of the finest in the state. Maude would never be happy in Kansas, I knew, and the best thing I could do for her and for my dead friend, Dan, was to help her sell the farm and the horses, perhaps separately. Before I did anything, I would ask for advice from my friend Charles Robinson, the biggest landowner in Douglas County, and Ed Whitman, formerly a land agent.

For some time I had suspected that Vitruvius Bird wanted the Cornish farm, not for farming or raising horses but for a possible railroad right of way, for there were rumors that a direct line from Chicago to Kansas City might continue through Lawrence to Topeka and on to Dodge City at the head of the Western Trail up from Texas, or to Abilene on the Chisholm Trail. Whoever owned land the railroad wanted would be in the catbird's seat. Bird had attempted before to force Maude to sell by threats, and he might attempt to intimidate other bidders now.

I needed to plan carefully if he were the only potential buyer, so I made Maude promise me she would not sell unless I approved the bid. Since the sale of the farm seemed inevitable, I was determined to outwit Bird and make the widow a rich woman when she left town.

That afternoon, I discussed my plan with Maude, who had tears in her eyes when she took my hands in gratitude. No one must know what we had in mind, especially not Oswald, whom I thought a weak and feckless young man. I remembered a line from *Hamlet* as the Prince contemplates revenge against his devious and murderous uncle, Claudius: "O, 'tis most sweet when in one line two crafts directly meet." Here, Shakespeare describes two intricate and deadly plots on a collision course from opposite directions, striking together. I was determined that in any contest with Bird, our craft should prevail.

Spending time with Maude always brought back memories of her husband. When the Border Ruffians with their black flags and decorated cannons invaded Kansas in September of 1856, five months after the sack of Lawrence and my arrival in town, Dan, older than I by about ten years, was a fully-grown man, while I felt myself still a boy. As the Missouri invaders approached Lawrence, I was given an old shotgun, and Dan, an excellent shot, a Sharps rifle, and we waited all day crouched in a cornfield before Governor Geary brokered a truce, and terrible blood-shed was averted.

During the war, after Quantrill's Raid, I enlisted in Dan's regiment of the Kansas Militia and was nearby when he was shot from his bay horse at the Battle of Westport on that cold October morning in 1864. These memories were quick and fresh in my mind as I sat in his widow's parlor, explaining my design to extricate her from her onerous attachment to the horse farm. As I talked, Maude's eyes seemed to brighten, her face to gain color, and her bosom and shoulders to rise. I thought myself the *deus ex machina* who arrived to end her drama with a happy resolution.

With the stage set, we let the death of Maude's father circulate through town along with the rumor that she was considering the sale of the horse farm. As her attorney, I began to get inquiries and responded with what I hoped was skilled equivocation. We would not be rushed, I told Maude, and we did not want Bird or any other potential buyer to fetch us in.

I continued to discuss the value of the farm with Leona Sonnet and Ed Whitman, who still had a gimlet eye for land. Soon, the only topic of conversation in town was the sale of the Cornish farm and its valuable horses. Colonel Maypole was eager for me to go back to Clay County, but I had much to accomplish here before I could return to Missouri—then things changed.

On the morning of St. Valentine's Day, as I lit our kitchen fire and placed my card on the breakfast table so Hannah would see it when she came into the room, there was a sudden knocking on our back door. It was Eli, a scarf wrapped around his neck and frozen breath escaping his mouth.

"Terrible cold last night," he mumbled, lips numbed by the cold, as he pushed past me and rushed to the stove. "On my way to the bank . . . saw the *Journal* . . . paper just off the press. Bank robbery in Missouri. Wasn't that where you were? Liberty?" For a moment, he stood over the stove, rubbing his hands together while I examined the newspaper he handed me. "Gotta get to the bank. Give Hannah a kiss for me. Thought you should know." He stalked to the door and pulled it open, and as he ran out, the cold air rushed in.

As I tried to comprehend his news, Hannah came into the kitchen, pulling a robe over her nightdress, and walked toward the stove as she saw my valentine. "Lovely," she whispered, her voice thick with sleep, as she started toward me. "Wasn't that Eli?" We had laughed that Eli's visits at the breakfast hour had greatly diminished after he acquired his nubile young wife, but here he was today.

"Sorry to ruin this day for you . . . it's shocking news," I declared. "Robbery yesterday in Liberty, where I was two weeks or so ago." She looked at me, confusion on her face. "Daytime apparently . . . a *bank*! Not a railroad train. Never happened before." I paused as the reason for my distress seemed to become apparent to her. "I never thought this could happen."

"Where will you go now?" She inquired, beginning to cut a slice of bread for me.

"To the papers and then the telegraph office to ask Orville what's new on the wire."

"Off you go then," she responded, giving me my coat, scarf, and a slice of bread. Her smile lit up the morning, as it always did. "Happy Valentine's Day, dear," she said. "I'll see to the slops." Both of us laughed as I kissed her and ran out the door into the cold.

The papers had nearly identical stories—the account from the wire, to which each editor had given his particular flourish. I hurried to the telegraph office to see if more had come in overnight.

"You just there, Ezra?" Orville Roden asked, and then exclaimed, "Liberty?" Turning in his chair, he added, "Holy Jesus. A regular bank! Guess they got into the vault. Heard they got sixty thousand dollars— sixty thousand!" Holding the two local papers in a hand stiff from the cold, I swatted at my leg in frustration. I was as astonished as Roden and as outraged. No one thought robbers could attack a bank and invade its impregnable vault. This was peacetime. And now we knew that a boy had been killed when gunfire was exchanged in the street. Had Sheriff Ashton tried to stop the robbers? Which of the many Missouri outlaws had done it?

Roden pointed to the table where several envelopes were arrayed. "Telegram for you there some place, Ezra," he said, returning to the chattering machine. "Haven't got the boy to deliver them yet. Name's on the envelope." Picking up mine from the four or five on the table, I tore it open and discovered it was from Downing and made reference to "our friend." Maypole wanted to meet me in Kansas City as soon as possible, and since no firm offer on Maude's property had been made, I could accommodate him.

Ed Whitman, a cautious man of unimpeachable integrity and knowledgeable in land values, whom I had enlisted to assist me, could handle any offer tendered in my absence, and, in any case, he could reach me by telegraph. It was perhaps not surprising that Vitruvius Bird had not communicated with us; was he still interested in the land since his trip to St. Louis? In any event, we were ready if he were playing a waiting game. The bank robbery in Liberty had replaced the sale of the farm as the subject of speculation for the small groups of people who gathered in the cold on Massachusetts Street.

The next morning, I asked Hannah to drive me to the railroad station so that I could slip away with little fanfare, and, though reluctant to leave home again so soon, I felt a tingle of excitement about spying for Maypole. When I arrived at the station, snow was falling, the wind out of the north, and I was happy to board the car, where an iron stove warmed the three of us on board, riding the rail in comfort to Wyandotte How easy it was, I thought, to become accustomed to this modern mode of travel, speeding down the tracks at almost twenty miles an hour.

Since it was early in the day when we arrived, I went, not to the hotel but to the quay on the Missouri River, where I hoped to find the ferry boat captain Barney Appleyard, who had probably crossed the river at least once since the robbery. Barney soaked up information like a sponge, as people say, and he, I believed, might know more about the robbers.

My journey to the quay was in vain, however, since Appleyard was nowhere to be found, and I learned he was unlikely to return until late in the day. A number of passengers waited in the little hut out of the falling snow, but since the intercourse of the group was the cold weather blowing in from the north and not the robbery in Liberty, I went to the livery stable to hire a buggy to take me to the hotel, a short ride up the hill to the center of town. So strong was the tang of horse urine, I could have found my way to the stable in pitch darkness.

Waiting for me in the lobby of the Pacific House was Colonel Maypole, pretending to read a book while carefully noting the persons who unwrapped after coming into the lobby or others, carrying bags, who were exiting the hotel.

"Happy to see you again, Colonel," I declared as he slid himself to full height, his legs and torso like the sections of a small hand telescope. His grim face suggested our meeting to be a weighty one, and he showed me to a corner of the lobby where we were not likely to be overheard.

"The villains have raised the stakes, Mr. Middleton," the Colonel said fiercely. "I don't like to be caught out like this." The vehemence of his words surprised me and, coupled with his contemptuous sneer, reminded me of the monomania of General William Blunt, who commanded the Union Cavalry at Westport, a real Ahab, as one literate officer described him, a volatile bully.

"Do we know with certainty who the robbers were? I assume it was the Archie Clement gang."

"Those outlaw bands coalesce and separate like blobs of mercury. Difficult to tell who's in which gang," Colonel Maypole replied. "I've heard there were six or eight robbers in the bank. Maybe more in the streets—as lookouts. One of my men talked to the Sheriff, name of Ashton. Do you know him?" I knew of Ashton, of course. I had observed him when I was in Liberty: a short man with a big gut and folds of fat in his neck, who waddled up the street. "Yes, I have seen him. Slow and fat. I assume the outlaws pay him to wink at what they do."

"Crooked as a dog's hind leg, I'm sure," he said. "You think there's anyone in Liberty we can trust?"

"Several we might get information from." I paused before I continued. "But trust? No sir. Too many outlaws. The James brothers and the Youngers may be in Clay County too. Dave Poole and his gang are back in the deep woods somewhere. Probably more villains than honest folk." I smiled, realizing I had used the Colonel's term for the bushwhackers, just as I had picked up his name for the war—the War of the Rebellion.

"We need to draw them out, Ezra," he said emphatically and rose from the chair into which he had lowered his body only minutes before. Maypole seemed never to sit still for long, nervous energy running through him like a line charged with electricity. "If we know their thoughts before they think them, we can wrong-foot them in a moment of weakness and stamp on their necks." He shot me a sinister smile. "I've arranged for a private dining room where we can speak our minds without fear of being overheard. Lord, things have gone to smash in Clay County!"

When we had removed ourselves to the small room, we ordered our supper and, as we were beginning to eat, the Colonel spoke. "You know, I learned about spycraft during the war under Allan Pinkerton—or Major Allan, as we referred to him." I nodded, and the Colonel continued. "Pinkerton's method was to write down everything we knew about a person, or place, or event, and share that information. Everybody contributed information." I watched him in the candlelight, his face becoming a grotesque mask as the flame flickered.

"Yes, I can see how the method worked," I replied to him. "One person might add a single datum that completed a portrait or provided one fact that a general, say, needed to know."

"Indeed! Like the method of inquiry in natural philosophy." He paused and folded his arms. "Many times it afforded us an advantage on the battlefield," he said, a look of satisfaction on his face. "So every word you write to me may have value to someone."

We talked into the night, and the Colonel made notes as I told him what I knew about Little Archie Clement and the town of Liberty, including the layout of the two-story brick bank, the number of windows, the side streets, and the alley behind the bank. He had an interest in the smallest detail. By one o'clock, I was exhausted, and since I intended to be at the quay before sunrise to see Appleyard, I suggested we call it a day, and so we did.

As I walked to the quay in the bone-piercing cold of the morning, the eastern sky began to grow light, the dusting of snow still unbroken by footprints. In the hut near the river, an ancient Negro crouched in the corner, having started a fire in a stove that looked almost as old as he was. He would tend the fire all day as passengers came and went. I reckoned he had spent most of his life as a slave, for years of toil and sadness were etched into his face. A younger man, perhaps his son, arrived carrying in wood.

"Come in, sir," the old man said, slowly standing and shuffling toward me. "You look stiffer 'an a frozen snake. I know 'cause I feel like a frozen snake when I get away from the fire." His clothes were worn and carefully patched, and a scarf—a cast-off from the Union army, I thought—was wrapped around his head to cover his ears, tied at the top of his head. When I asked for Appleyard, the ferry pilot, the old man nodded. "Clever pup, he is," he chortled. "Going 'cross the river today. You going there, sir?" I shook my head.

"Not crossing today. Just wanted to talk to Appleyard," I answered, moving closer to the stove.

"You picked a sharp one, sir," he averred. "He's good at talking. Seems sometimes his tongue moves so fast you'd think it's not attached to his mouth at all." He laughed and tottered to the door. "Got to keep the fire in the boiler going."

Through the window, I could see Barney Appleyard near his boat, talking to the passengers who had just arrived. He remembered me. "Didn't bring your friend, the dentist, along today, did you?" He cackled and shook my hand as I mumbled my reply.

"Want to talk to you about the bank robbery," I said in a low voice. "Look, I'm not trying to stick my nose in where it doesn't belong, but a bank robbery in peacetime is news. Here's what I think: Archie Clement and his gang robbed that bank. If I don't write a story, other correspondents will come digging around here."

"Maybe that's a good thing for the ferry business," he laughed. "But, no, I'll tell you what I know . . . which ain't much." He moved closer to me. "Talked to a man who saw it all—including the young fella who got killed in the crossfire. Clement was inside the bank with five others. Might have been the James brothers . . . he wasn't sure. Dave Poole was in the street, a lookout, I guess."

"Where was the sheriff?" I asked.

"Got there after the gunfight started. Everybody was shooting when the gang took to horse."

"Blow the vault open, did they?" I asked.

"Oh, no, just threatened the teller with a cocked revolver. Nothing simpler."

"Sounds too easy," I said with a sigh. "Little Arch will just do it again. Maybe kill a few inside the bank next time. Nobody's going to try to bluff *him*! But who got the story to the wire?" I asked.

"Oh, Rupert Marsh—*Kansas City Daily Journal of Commerce*. Over in Liberty to talk about pigs and pork," Appleyard said, drawing even closer to me. "Goes on and on," he said, "the violence." He pulled his pipe from his pocket but did not put it in his mouth. "Been thinking, the past's got a grip on us like a Missouri River snapping turtle that just won't let go." I nodded to him to show my agreement. "And if you resist, that snapping turtle can take your finger clean off. "

There was a pensive look on his face as he turned his back, made a flourish with his hand, jumped on the ferry, and, without looking back, pushed off from the quay. The two Negroes stood at the door of the now-empty hut. As I passed, I handed the older one a shiny dime, and, satchel in hand, looked for a buggy to take me across the state line into Wyandotte and my train to Lawrence.

CHAPTER TEN

"**KNEW YOU WOULD** be on this one, Uncle Ezra," Jeremiah Whitman shouted, using the name which the boys in the militia company called me, as I came from the railroad car, bag in hand. "Only one coming up from Wyandotte this afternoon," he said with a laugh. I was always delighted to see Edmund Whitman's wisecracking youngest son and clapped him on the shoulder. "Got the buggy here." The winter evening was already closing in, and lamps were lit in the station. It had been a bleak, stone-gray day, cold as a tomb, and snow looked to be coming.

"Papa sent me to your house, and Hannah sent me here," he said in mock complaint as we climbed into the buggy. It was pulled by one of his father's mules, and Jeremiah evidently enjoyed the humorous incongruity of the big mule pulling a small two-wheeled trap buggy. "Papa got this offer from Mr. Bird. Says you won't like it." He laughed as he handed me the folded note, and I glanced at it and then back at Jeremiah, who waited for my comment.

"Well, I don't," I replied.

"With respect, I say this. Got his head so far up his ass he farts out his ear!" We laughed together, the young man continuing to chuckle. The offer was below—about $20,000 below—the price we could accept and didn't include the valuable horses.

"Been smoking the locoweed, I guess," I said. "So, we just wait him out and hope for other offers."

"Hope it works, Uncle Ezra," he said, getting into the buggy and untying the reins.

"Yeah, me too," I replied as Jeremiah called to the mule, whose name was Helen, or so the boy said. We crossed the new stone bridge into Lawrence, bouncing past the mansion of Charles Robinson near the bridge's foot. A suffocating blanket of gray cloud hung across the sky, and damp air seemed to penetrate our garments. Riding with Jeremiah was always an adventure: he managed to maneuver the buggy to strike every bump and rut in broad, dirt-packed Massachusetts Street before sharply turning onto Rhode Island and our home.

"How's that for a ride," he chortled, and, I swear, the big mule laughed too. I jumped down from the buggy with my bag, and Jeremiah swatted the mule with the reins, and off they went.

"Tell your father I thank him," I yelled as the buggy jumped forward, and Jeremiah lifted his hat to me without looking back. Hannah stood at the open door as Caesar and Brutus behind the fence barked an excited welcome. The children ran out to meet me; I was especially delighted that Phoebe no longer stood back but embraced me.

In fact, Phoebe was quickly adapting to our family life. Hannah and I bought her the kind of clothes that well-bred young ladies wore. On our first visit to church, Hannah and I observed that all eyes were on us as we walked down the aisle. Phoebe was, of course, the only Black face in the congregation, but we had prepared her, explaining that expectations might be different, the service perhaps less boisterous and more solemn than what she had previously experienced. Eli and Prudence—the latter visibly with child—were the first to greet Phoebe, and some others followed.

My time in Cambridge and Boston had accustomed me to Negroes in elegant dress with refined manners, but in Kansas, they did not yet appear in polite society or attend church with whites. Our success with Phoebe belonged to Hannah, whose political views—on suffrage and education for Blacks and women—were well known, if not entirely appreciated by many in town. When Hannah went on horseback, it was in a riding costume since she abhorred riding sidesaddle. She was—to use a word that had come up from Texas—a "maverick," or unbranded calf. She laughed when I first associated the word with her, knowing it also meant difficult to handle. We did not, however, try to force our opinions on others, hoping only that our new daughter could have a happy life in an often-remorseless land.

I was pleased to be home. Hannah handed me a letter as I stepped to the glowing fireplace to remove my heavy coat and warm my backside. I immediately noted it was addressed to Hannah and, recognizing the handwriting, I gave a laugh. It was from our friend Jim Hickok, who had, in jest, said he would always send any letter to Hannah so she could "mend" his spelling before she gave the missive to me. In truth, Jim's spelling often did not follow proper conventions, although his handwriting was beautiful, the letters well-formed and regular. With joy in her voice, Hannah spoke as I perused the letter: "Jim will arrive in Lawrence tomorrow and stay at the Eldridge."

"And a good thing too. We have so little space for guests since Phoebe came to us," I replied. "Good to see him again and hear about his new adventures. You will be pleased too." I had teased her about Hickok when she saw him several years earlier. Of course, I had last seen him at Mine Creek, where the Seventh Cavalry and the Kansas Militia caught Price's fleeing cavalry in late October of '64 to end the Rebels' invasion of Missouri. Now I wondered what was bringing him back to Lawrence—probably not just to see the Middleton family.

Chicken soup simmered on the stove, and the two girls were setting the table while Henley played on the floor with a wooden pistol. Even before I heard the knocking at the door, I knew we had visitors because the dogs were barking, but at least we were not yet at the table. Big Ears King was our caller, his broad smile seeming to announce good news. Phoebe was fascinated by his ears—like barn doors thrown wide open, people said—but knew not to stare or ask about the freckles thick across his face like paint spattered by a careless painter.

"Hickok's on his way here," Big Ears trumpeted. "Be here tomorrow!"

"Just got a letter to that effect," I said. Big Ears looked crestfallen, and I immediately felt sorry for him. "Good to have you confirm it though," I added lamely. "I've been to Kansas City on a newspaper errand."

Big Ears looked around the kitchen to see the girls finishing the setting of the table. "Sorry to come at supper time, but I've got more good news. Man named Weekly is interested in the widow's horses. Don't want the farm—just the horses!" King seemed pleased with himself. "From out near Topeka. Earl B. Weekly." And Big Ears spelled the surname for me, although I was not in doubt about the spelling. Then, in a flurry of thanks from me, he departed, and my family assembled at the table.

The next day, I wrote two letters, one to Vitruvius Bird, rejecting his offer for the Cornish farm, and another to Maude, informing her that I had not accepted an offer from Bird, ending my letter with, "Trust me as Dan did. All will be well."

Hickok did not arrive Saturday, as expected, and our family went to church on a cold and bleak Sunday morning, wondering if he would appear at all. Several persons expressed interest in the Cornish farm, and I smiled and equivocated. "Well, we shall see," I said with a sage look on my face when asked if a sale were imminent, hoping that in my wisdom I was not playing the fool.

By Sunday morning, Big Ears King, having foretold the arrival of Hickok on Saturday, rushed around town in a state of chagrin mixed with panic. When the train from Wyandotte arrived late in the day, a number of people were waiting at the station in North Lawrence to see if this hero of the war was on it. Everyone had heard or read of "Wild Bill," and a few might remember him from the days of James Lane's militia.

Although eager to see my friend, I did not gather with the crowd at the station but instead went to our barn, where I hitched two horses to the buggy and listened for the locomotive whistle to sound as the train pulled into the station. By leaving with the shrill blast of the whistle and racing through the empty streets, I was able to reach the station as Jim stepped down from the car.

When the crowd saw Hickok, there were shouts and ejaculations, as in the beginning of *Julius Caesar*, when the Roman citizens welcome the triumphant Caesar into the city. Some who knew Hickok rushed to shake his hand, and others stood further back to point out for their wives or children the famous man, although they need not have done so since Hickok was a head taller than anyone else and instantly recognizable. In all the shouts, he was "Wild Bill," a name never used within his family, nor by me for that matter. He laughed and jested, even with those he did not seem to know, before slowly moving toward me when he saw me standing at my buggy.

"Take me to see your gal, Hannah, Ezra?" he asked with a grin.

"We thought you might never come back to Lawrence," I said with a laugh. "Sure glad you did. Even if you are a day late."

"Couldn't be helped. Big card game last night in Kansas City. Had to stay and win some money to pay my hotel bill!" Hickok waved again to the dispersing crowd. As we drove away, I glanced back to see Big Ears still surrounded by a few people. Like a stone wall that stores the sun's heat to give off its warmth later, he basked in the glory of Hickok, and now his face emanated both affability and satisfaction.

Later at our front door, Jim, dressed in a Prince Albert frock coat, over which he wore a cloak that kept his guns exposed, was warmly welcomed by Hannah and our three children. He seemed unsurprised by Phoebe and charmed her when he bowed to her, telling her, as he took off his cloak, the story of Sir Walter Raleigh, Queen Elizabeth, and the puddle.

Henley was fascinated by the big Navy revolvers, which Hickok wore butts forward. Samantha did not take her eyes off him, fascinated by his size, I supposed. Later, when we sat at the supper table, all of us had questions. Hannah's first one was the reason for his trip to Lawrence, and it elicited a long account of his travels since the war ended, although he did not mention the shooting of Tutt in Springfield. Interrupting him, she teasingly asked his destination.

"Well, I only spend one night here at the Eldridge and then take a train tomorrow for Fort Riley—well, Junction City, which is not far away, as I recall. I've been appointed a deputy U.S. Marshall by my friend Captain R.B. Owen," he said, leaning back in his chair between bites of food.

"And what will you be doing there, Jim?" I asked.

"Nothing too exciting or dangerous," he replied. "Guess it'll be recovering stolen mules—Uncle Sam's long-eared soldiers." He smiled as we all laughed politely, except for Henley, who guffawed. "Maybe transporting federal prisoners." Four-year-old Henley seemed disappointed.

"Will you kill anybody?" Henley asked. Hickok grunted and shook his head, and I tried to shift the conversation.

"No, it's a good question, Ezra," Hickok said. "The answer is, I try *not* to kill anybody, but sometimes I have to shoot at someone." Henley frowned, clearly wanting more details. "Might have to arrest deserters from time to time, but I don't want to shoot them. They're in *our* army, but they have to go to jail to teach them a lesson."

"Many men still here from your days with Jim Lane?" I asked.

"No, not many," Hickok replied. "Say, who's the fella with flaps for ears who seemed to know me?" He smiled and winked at Henley.

"Big Ears King," I answered.

"Who gave him that name?"

"His mother most likely." Everyone chuckled at my comment, but Henley continued to laugh loudly until Hannah gave him the eye.

"I may see you more often with the new job." He thought for a minute before he continued. "Fact is, I been in some bad scrapes since the war ended . . . but I got a respectable job now with the government." He chuckled.

"You need to find yourself a wife . . . and settle down," Hannah quickly retorted, a smile on her face. It was a game she played with him, eliciting excuses for staying single.

"I keep my eyes out for a gal like you." She shook her head in comic frustration, and, with Phoebe's assistance, took the young children to bed, while I poured two glasses of whiskey and led Jim to chairs before the fireplace.

"Ever hear from Cody?" I asked. Hickok shook his head and sipped his whiskey. The conversation lagged, as happens when the interlocutors are strangers or friends who have been long separated, the tie that binds having frayed. "I remember his tales."

"Good tales," Hickok responded. "Some of them—on occasion—true." I laughed and thought of Falstaff, Shakespeare's comic liar, but did not mention the name, which would have been meaningless to Jim, not a reader of poems and plays.

Hannah returned, and we three chatted, but I felt we had to search for topics to discuss. Soon Jim Hickok stood up. I offered to hitch up the horses to the buggy again, but he objected. "Only a short walk from here. Same place as the old Eldridge?" he asked.

"Built on the foundation of the old hotel," I explained. "Up to Massachusetts and then one block south. Beautiful building—biggest in town."

We said our good-byes and promised to meet again, but I wondered whether we would. After he finished with the army, he would likely continue west or perhaps go north to Wyoming or the Dakotas. Eastern Kansas had become too civilized for him.

As I looked out the window in the morning, I could see the snow falling heavily, but it wasn't until I walked to the barn that I realized that the sun in the east glowed like a lantern behind the clouds from which large flakes dropped. Although the Kansas sky is ordinarily broad and bright, today the clouds were like gauze on a wound, a bandage soaking up blood. After breakfast, I dressed warmly to ride to King's livery stable to see if Earl Weekly might be on the morning train from Topeka, enjoying, as I rode, the prints my horse made in the fresh snow.

"Got news here you'll like," Big Ears called out as I approached the livery stable, his rough voice almost melodious. "Telegram from Weekly an hour ago. Brother's coming with him too." Not surprising, I thought, that both brothers were coming to see the horses, since Cornish's animals were highly prized and sold well at auctions, and I was pleased that we now had serious bidders, leaving me free to winnow prospects for the farm itself since Bird had evinced no further interest.

"I should ride out to let the widow know you will be coming," I said, leaning down from the saddle to shake the hand offered me. "Maude and I are in your debt and always will be."

"And I in yours, Ezra," Big Ears replied, smiling so broadly that I could scarcely see his eyes, his freckles riding up his cheeks. "You could have called me out about Hickok. Actually, I didn't know him much at all, but you never challenged me on that." I shook my head.

"Better head out to the horse farm to make sure they're ready," I said, touching my horse's sides with my heels. "You bringing them out in a buggy?" I called back to him and turned to see him nodding.

After discussions with Ed Whitman, who knew horses almost as well as he knew mules, and several other knowledgeable persons, I had settled on a price for the horses to be sold, forty or so animals. Maude's new foreman, Little Joe Oscar, a half-blood Delaware who exhibited his Indian heritage in high cheekbones and a hook nose, had the farm spruced up in anticipation of horse buyers.

As I sat on my horse in the snowy lane, I looked at the two-story brick house that soon would be empty, and barns and outbuildings soon to be vacant. In the big corral, many of the handsomest horses enjoyed the cold weather and freedom from the stalls, nipping at one another and kicking their heels. Maude was relieved that our plans seemed finally to be moving forward. I suggested she pay the hands for an extra month if the sale price was favorable, and she agreed to do so. I felt sure knowledgeable horse breeders would show an interest in such superior stock. Nevertheless, I could not banish my sadness when I thought of Dan.

The snow lay heavy across the meadows and in the nearby woods, on bare branches and fence posts, a farm wagon near the barn, and the roofs of buildings. In the pastures, the snow was unbroken, except for a few animal tracks, but the road was clear. Sitting in the parlor before the fireplace, Maude reflected on her years before Dan went to war with the Kansas Militia. "You know, Ezra, I could have lived here most happily with Daniel, despite the prairie winds . . . but when he was taken away . . . I found it difficult to go on alone." I noticed she did not say "die," and I hoped she would not break down when the Weekly brothers came to inspect the horses.

By and by, barking dogs in the barnyard announced the arrival of the brothers and, rather than a buggy, King drove a buckboard to accommodate four men, who were—as I learned—Arlo, the foreman of their Topeka ranch, and Mr. Weaver, identified as a "horse doc" in addition to the brothers. The Weeklys were younger than I, which is to say, about thirty or so, with heavy jaws. Earl, looking the elder, had streaks of white in his black beard; David, his shorter beard unsullied by signs of age. Both were well dressed in tweeds and wore boots, the others more simply dressed in denim and overcoats. I introduced Maude Cornish, who stood on the steps out of the snow, with Little Joe Oscar. I gave the older brother my card—the one identifying me as an attorney, not the one for the *Globe Democrat*. Although it seemed stuffy, I said, "I represent Mrs. Cornish and handle her business affairs."

For two hours, we looked at horses. I stayed back so the brothers could confer. Little Joe Oscar brought horses from the stalls to walk and run in the corral, and he took the brothers and the "horse doc" through the stalls so they could examine and re-examine the stock. The brothers expressed satisfaction with everything they saw and complimented Joe Oscar on the farm itself. I watched the brothers glance at each other and whisper. "How many horses do you plan to sell?" Earl Weekly finally asked.

"As many as you want to buy, sir," I said with a chuckle. "Except for several older ones, they are all in peak condition. Mr. King will buy those." I waited a few moments in the wintery silence before I spoke. "Let's say forty. I can give you a price for that number."

"I know of the reputation of these horses," Earl said, looking at his brother. "But I am getting married in the spring, so our business will be changing some. We couldn't keep forty more horses on our farm right now." My heart sank a little hearing his words, and I did not like his "but."

"You see, Earl and I have done most things together since our parents died," David said, quickly glancing at his brother. "If we can agree on a price, we might buy some of your horses, but my brother and I must confer about this. May we meet again in the morning, Mr. Middleton?" I agreed and we headed back to Lawrence, I on horseback and the others in King's buckboard. I did not know whether we might sell all of the horses, or some, or none at all.

The next morning, the sun shone on yesterday's snow, and every patch on the ground and the branches sparkled in the cold air. I wanted to sell the horses together, if possible, because I thought them more valuable that way; if we sold them one by one, we would spend much time in pointless dickering.

When I picked up the Weekly brothers at Mrs. Chester's boarding house, I was told Arlo and Weaver were already at the station waiting to take the Union Pacific west to Topeka. On the way to the Cornish farm in my buggy, the three of us did not speak of the horses at all. Instead, Earl talked of Price's invasion of Missouri in '64, the fighting at Westport and later at Mine Creek in Kansas.

"Our younger brother died at the Hockabee farm with the Kansas Militia at Westport," he said. "Only a boy . . . but proud to serve under the Stars and Stripes. He was a bugler."

"Captain Cornish died at Westport two days later, sir. A Sunday morning," I added. "Commanded the Douglas County Regiment."

"Earl and I were with the Union army, mostly in Tennessee," David said, speaking now for the first time. Earl seemed to do most of the talking. "You ever hear of Captain Potter of the Shawnee County Regiment?" the younger brother asked. "The one that took heavy casualties along the Big Blue?"

"Yes, yes, of course!" I interjected excitedly. "He was put in charge of our regiment after Cornish was killed. A good man: bought wagons with his own money to take our wounded home when we ran out of ambulances."

"Knew him from Topeka," David cried. "Friend of our dad's, eh, Earl." He swatted his brother in good humor, and they smiled at each other.

"David and I were at Chickamauga with Rosecrans. Reckon we got to know Tennessee better than we wanted to." He chuckled.

"So, you knew Captain Potter?" I asked incredulously. "Well, he marched us down to Mine Creek, where we beat the Rebs again, and then marched us home!" I said with some passion. "Over two years now. Good old Captain Potter," I said as I turned the buggy into the barnyard and waved to Joe Oscar, standing by the barn.

"You got a price on the horses? On forty, say, if we could take them all?" It was Earl who suddenly spoke, and I felt my heart jump in my chest. Would they, then, buy *all* the horses? Since we were still in the buggy, I jumped down, holding the reins so the brothers could climb down.

"Well, yes. We do have a price for the herd . . . not including the three old ones." But I was afraid to name the price Ed Whitman and I had set. I swallowed and did name my price, and watched the brothers' faces break into smiles.

"Holy Jesus!" Earl snorted with joy, and I gripped the reins tightly, afraid he would spook the horses. "That's only two hundred dollars more than the price *we* would have offered."

"Well, I can accept the lower price," I said, laughing. "Gladly!" And we shook hands all around. "Let's go in and talk to Maude Cornish, and then we can go to town and get the sale written up."

We rode back to Lawrence in the gayest of moods, and as I was dropping them off at Mrs. Chester's boarding house, David coughed and spoke. "Has Mrs. Cornish set a price on the farm yet?" It was as though I had fallen from the buggy and had the breath knocked out of me.

"Let me leave you here," I said, taking a deep breath. "I shall pick up all my papers on the property, drop off the draft for the sale of the horses at my copyist, and meet you back at Mrs. Chester's. Back in an hour from now!" Swatting the rears of the horses lightly, off I went.

At home, I quickly tied up the buggy and ran into the house. "Guess what!" I shouted to Hannah as I hurried into my study. Always neat as a boy and as a student, I carried those habits into adulthood, and so my papers on the Cornish property were in a large envelope in a desk drawer.

"What are you so excited about?" Hannah asked as she entered. The draft for the horse sale sat on my desk, only the dollar figure needing to be added. Dipping my pen in the inkwell, I stood behind my desk and wrote in the figure.

"Hannah, my love," I announced. "We may have sold the *whole* damn farm!"

She watched for a second. "Oh, Ezra," she squealed with delight. "Have you done it in truth?"

"I'm going back to give them a price now." I hugged her tightly and ran for the door. Driving to Molly's house, I told myself again and again that the brothers would not be able to meet our asking price for the farm. I had spoken too heedlessly to Hannah, raising false expectations and playing the fool in my enthusiasm.

Molly said she could draw up a bill of sale immediately since it was a simple document. We would attach a description of the forty horses later, if either party wished. I watched Molly draw up a bill of sale for the horses while I cursed myself. Thanking Molly, I put the finished bill of sale into the envelope and quickly left.

When I reached the boarding house, Mrs. Chester had just finished serving dinner, and the brothers were about to rise from the table. She was a white-haired old lady with dark brows, looking like a ravenous crow eyeing a June bug.

"Afternoon, Mrs. Chester," I greeted her. "The two gentlemen from Topeka and I would like a private room for a bit of business." She glared at me but smiled at them and nodded.

"Don't you have an office, Mr. Middleton?" she growled under her breath. "Well, never mind then, but don't be too long about it."

Shown into a small parlor, the three of us smiled. I opened the envelope and took out the sheaf of papers, and we sat down. Two identical copies of the bill of sale were quickly signed, and we agreed that I would send them a description of the forty horses sold—all but the three old horses, which I would sell to King for a small sum.

"I must say, sirs, that I was surprised to learn of your interest in possibly purchasing the Cornish farm," I began.

"When we came here, we had no such interest," Earl said, stroking his beard. "None at all."

"But when we saw how fine this land is, inspected the house and other buildings . . . well, we began to whisper and wondered about buying the farm," David said. "You may have noticed. I loved this farm the moment I first saw it."

"Depending on the price you have set," Earl interrupted, ever the practical one. "As you know, I am marrying in the spring and will stay in our house with my new bride, so we would have to build another house for my brother. We could only build on our best pasture, however, and we are now *adding* horses." He shrugged and held out his hands, palms up in a gesture of futility. I was nodding during these comments, wondering where he was going with his explanation. "So, we ask you, sir, what does Mrs. Cornish want for the farm?"

I opened the large envelope on my lap and took out the remaining sheaf of papers. "This price has been set by Mrs. Cornish." I coughed to clear my throat—or perhaps it was a theatrical flourish such as one might use in a courtroom to command attention—and placed the paper before my observers. "I have given you two figures on this paper," I said. "The first is for the land and all the buildings, and the second one includes the furnishings in the house as well." The brothers carefully examined the figures I had set before them.

"Well now," Earl said, looking at his brother and then at me. "You see, Mr. Middleton, our father worked for the railroad in Chicago before he retired and came west. He made provision for David in his will." I waited for a further statement, but Earl Weekly continued to examine my face. "May we confer in private once again?"

I left the room and, through the door, could hear muffled voices. Since the sales price was a large sum, I did not expect a quick response unless it was a flat refusal. Shortly, the door opened, and I believed the deal had fallen through. Earl's face was somber, although I discerned the hint of a smile on David's. Perhaps they had disagreed.

"Mr. Middleton, we are of like minds here," Earl said. "We can accept the first price if you will throw in all the furnishings at no additional cost."

"You, sir, have a deal then—sirs, both of you I mean. Fine furniture like hers should never be sold at auction. The widow will be happy to have the furniture stay with the farm."

"I shall live here," David said. "Half the horses will go to Topeka with Earl, and the remainder will stay here with me on my new farm."

"What I can say is this: all's well that ends well, as the poet says." To me, it almost sounded like a benison.

CHAPTER ELEVEN

IT FELT LIKE an ending, the sale of the Cornish farm to the Weekly brothers of Topeka. For several reasons, I was happy to include, at no cost
to the buyers, the furniture. Selling at auction the fine furniture that the
Cornishes had loved and used was something I had been dreading; only
Governor Robinson's house had more elegant furnishings. For many of
us, an auction would have been painful, especially if the resulting income
were meager, and the experience of seeing family treasures knocked down
at auction in the barnyard would have broken Maude's heart.

Upon further consideration, I thought it fitting for Maude to give
the older horses to Big Ears King for acting as an agent, and she was
pleased to do so. Moreover, she was delighted that Vitruvius Bird, who
had coveted her farm since her husband's death, did not end up acquiring
it, thwarted in his avarice.

Three days after the sale of the farm, her personal possessions packed
in cases, a rich woman, she began her journey with her two young daughters and cousin Oswald, across the continent to Massachusetts by rail,
so, in addition to my fee, I received the satisfaction of believing I had, in
some measure, repaid Captain Cornish for our friendship. It pleased me
as well that David Weekly kept Little Joe Oscar on as foreman of his new
horse farm. It was, in other words, like the ending of a Shakespearean
comedy where happiness reigns and goodness is rewarded in an overt
display of poetic justice.

But, of course, this was neither Illyria nor the Forest of Arden but
the raw and remorseless plains of Kansas and the lawlessness of western

Missouri. As I had been befriended by Henry and Leona Sonnet a decade earlier when I came to Lawrence, so I presented David Weekly— or Davey, as he preferred to be called—to persons congenial or useful in his new life; I should have been remiss in common courtesy had I done otherwise. Much like my friend Eli, he was an affable young man, although perhaps less outgoing, and I realized that in helping Maude sell the Cornish farm to someone other than the ostracized Vitruvius Bird, I had increased my own standing in the community. Davey, moreover, asked if I would represent him in commercial matters.

"Untoot!" my father had said to me as a boy, meaning I should not toot my own horn, as the saying goes. In truth, I have always been of a reserved nature and disliked the accolades now accorded me. So, I resolved to "untoot" in my dealings with others, although doing so might be difficult since I was a friend of the military hero and gunman Jim Hickok, who was now rounding up deserters at Fort Riley, north of Junction City, and about twenty miles from Abilene and the famous cattle trail.

To the west, about twenty miles, was Salina, regarded as the edge of civilization. Beyond were five scattered army forts, restless and angry Indians, and a rapidly diminishing population of buffalo. Perhaps there on the treeless plains, Hickok's dangerous pursuit of what Shakespeare calls "the bubble reputation" would be subsumed in the discipline of federal service.

In Kansas, March is a fickle month with a rare balmy day followed by a week of bitter cold and snow. A mild winter could usher in a blizzard late in the month or even early April, with the wind howling as though it were coming from the ends of the earth. On one such windy morning in early March, I began my day as I usually did by arising early, breaking the ice on the trough, and pumping enough water for Hannah to begin the day's chores.

After eating breakfast, gathering eggs with Phoebe and Samantha, and feeding our animals, I stopped by the telegraph office to see whether I had received a missive from either Russell Downing or Colonel Frederick Maypole, but I had nothing to show for my early start except a cold nose and stiff fingers. As usual, my next stop was at the Post Office. Standing at the cage was Jeremiah Whitman, looking unusually dapper.

"Good day, Uncle Ezra," he said, his nose and cheeks red from the wind, seeming to lower his head in deference to me. "Cold as all get out today!"

"Why are you out so early on a cold day?" I asked, knowing it to be a long ride in from the Whitman mule farm west of town. "Folks all right?"

"Due some heavy snow before March is finished with us—or so my father says." His merry laugh filled the room, and Hal, the postal clerk, a young man about Jeremiah's age, laughed along with him.

"Got a girl," the clerk said from his barred cage. "Why, he comes to town so often, Mr. Middleton." Hal left and quickly returned and handed me a letter, the paper folded over carefully to produce a secure envelope. I noticed immediately the small, neat hand of Colonel Maypole, and I stuck the letter in my pocket to read at home, where I could devote full attention to its sentiments.

Outside the building, the young Negro who assisted the Postmaster poured ashes from the stove over icy patches of the board sidewalk where water from the roof had refrozen overnight. On the mud of Massachusetts Street, dray horses pulling loaded wagons snorted frozen breath. In early March, people said, "Spring can't be far away," but this month was wetter and colder than usual, and the crocuses, tulips, and daffodils were slow to break through the earth, except on the south side of buildings where sunlight warmed the soil.

Since the day had gotten no warmer, heavy clouds stifling the sun, Hannah had lighted a fire in our hearth to warm the house, and there before the flaming hearth I stationed myself to read Maypole's letter. It was written in a hand so crabbed it seemed he might have squeezed his pen in frustration or anguish as he wrote, and I wondered if his handwriting showed a troubled state of mind. He began with information which caught my attention. Missouri Governor Thomas C. Fletcher had urged the legislature to take action against the lawlessness that affected the state when federal troops began withdrawing, and it became apparent local authorities had neither the will nor resources to end the violence in areas like Little Dixie.

One new law required that all adult males register for the state militia, not that there was any expectation that the bushwhackers would ever put on a uniform. The Colonel explained that the new laws might serve to flush some bushwhackers, "villains," he dubbed them, out of their sanctuaries in the woods. The Colonel's new assignment was to find a bushwhacker or two who might be induced to assist in this process. My trips to Clay County, he further informed me, would be discontinued since one of his operatives—a term of Allan Pinkerton's from the war—had been killed, presumably by the James gang, literal cutthroats, who guarded the area around Kearney. He promised me additional assignments, although I had decided not to return to Liberty and Clay County.

The Ides of March came and went, and I told my children about Julius Caesar—the most famous man from ancient times, after Jesus of Nazareth, of course—and I explained that in school they might read about his military campaigns. Only Henley showed any curiosity about Caesar, but he quickly lost interest when I explained that the Roman didn't carry revolvers like Jim Hickok.

Within a week, the days seemed to lengthen, the lowering clouds were replaced by intervals of showers and sunlight, and the broad land began to awaken. Buds, feeling the warmth of the sun, swelled on apple and cherry trees, and the woods were clothed in the garments of spring. The rich smell of newly turned soil drifted from the farms of the Kaw and Wakarusa Valleys, along with the smell of new grass. Birds of every size and color chattered, sang, and called from the woods and farmlands: nightingales, cardinals, finches, jays, blackbirds, robins, and sparrows, but no larks or swallows, the birds of high summer, which swooped and scooped insects from the sky.

The trees planted in town by the first settlers—redbuds and crab apples with their flowers of rose or cerise—mixed their color with the linen white of pear blossoms and the borrowed fragrance from the sweetest of all, the pale lilacs blooming in our dooryard. On the first warm day, my senses responded to the sights and smells of the spring, so even the smells of the barnyard had an odor not unpleasant to me. It was as though the earth had split open and the rich flora from Proserpina's bower had burst forth into the welcoming sunlight.

In due course, spring began to give way to early summer. Tassels and purple silk appeared on the corn, the first fruit—peaches, cherries, and pears—began to form, vegetables were dug or picked, and piglets and lambs born. I put up a scarecrow in our garden to frighten away the blackbirds, and our children threw clods of dirt to drive them away, but to no avail. This year, the rains had come at a propitious time as storms swept in on winds that tore at our trees.

I liked best the storms that left behind ragged banks of clouds, which at sunset streaked orange or golden across the sky, and on occasion, the fiery vermillion of a furnace, before the curtained night was drawn across the flames. Still, as the sunflowers grew taller than a man and the seed-heavy heads bent toward the ground, I received no assignment from the Colonel or message from Russell Downing. Then in July, everything changed.

On the first day of July, the Lawrence papers carried the news that James Henry Lane, United States Senator from Kansas, had shot himself and was dying. Shortly afterwards came a telegram from Downing requesting a story about a man I knew well.

When I arrived in Lawrence in 1856, as the town was threatened with invasion by Missouri Border Ruffians, Charles Robinson, along with Lane—who had commanded Indiana volunteers in the Mexican War—organized the defenses of the small settlement. Lane, the Grim Chieftain as the newspapers christened him, raised a military force called the Free-State army, which raided Missouri and freed slaves, although many people thought its real objective was to steal livestock and furniture from houses before they were burned down.

During the Civil War, Lane recruited and trained the Kansas Brigade, which fought Confederates on the Border, and he raised the Kansas Colored Volunteers, who were, I believe, the first Negro troops to engage in conflict with the enemy, at Island Mound in Bates County, Missouri in October of 1862, a year earlier than when the Black troops of the Fifty-Fourth Massachusetts saw combat. Without doubt, he was an energetic leader and mesmerizing orator, but he was unscrupulous, devious, and, according to his numerous enemies, utterly corrupt.

Although sometimes called an abolitionist, Senator Lane was, in actuality, a Free Soil Republican like Abraham Lincoln. Some in Lawrence never forgave him for leading his Jayhawkers against the town of Osceola, Missouri, burning, killing, and thus increasing anti-Unionist sentiment in Missouri; one newspaper even contended that Quantrill's raid on Lawrence in 1863 had been undertaken in part to avenge Lane's raid on Osceola. Perhaps this is so.

In my story for Downing, I credited the senator with helping to bring the railroad to Lawrence, supporting Kansas rail interests in Washington, and later serving as President of the Lawrence, Leavenworth, and Fort Gibson Railroad, as well as other economic schemes for the state.

Looking back, I found it difficult to separate the good from the bad in Lane, and this I tried to explain in my story too. I often sided with Charles Robinson since I thought him more dispassionate and equitable than his rival, who was often moored only by self-interest. At the end of his career, Lane was finally betrayed by his own devious nature when he abandoned his fellow Radical Republicans and backed Andrew Johnson's reconstruction policies, voting to uphold the new President's veto of the Civil Rights Bill, and losing support both in Congress and back home in Kansas.

Sick and despondent, facing charges of financial malfeasance, Senator Lane shot himself in the head on leaving his brother-in-law's carriage in Leavenworth and died ten days later. He was buried with great ceremony in the new Oak Hill Cemetery in Lawrence. At the burial, amidst bouquets of flowers, I remembered Antony's eulogy on the Roman dictator in *Julius Caesar*: *The evil that men do lives after them: The good is oft interred with their bones.* Sometimes, however, good and evil are so thoroughly mixed in a particular man that perhaps they cannot be separated, one quality forever bound to its opposite. Was this the case with James Lane?

When I finished my account of the late senator, to test my judgments, I walked around town to speak with some of the citizens of Lawrence, and I first talked to one of his strongest admirers, Big Ears King. For many years, King had watched over Lane's business interests and had risen with him, climbing from hanger-on and toady to respectable livery stable owner, while his dress changed from homespun to suits of store-bought plaid, his chewing tobacco replaced by fat cigars that looked like sausages.

Since Big Ears was grieving, I suggested we get out of the July heat to drink a beer in the saloon as we reminisced. Both of us remembered the Lane of Territorial Days and the times his speeches set a fire under an audience gathered in the streets: his wild and tangled locks of black hair tossed as his head jerked, his voice rising from sinister whisper to ejaculations of "Great God!" as he tore off his neck cloth, shirt, and collar while his body heated up with his rhetoric and his eyes burned into those of listeners hypnotized by his voice.

Tears began to form in King's eyes, and I was amazed that what I found to be Lane's reckless clowning, my interlocutor saw as moving and noble discourse. Feeling ashamed, I was holding up to ridicule conduct that King admired. I quickly ended our conversation, throwing down the rest of my beer, slapping him gently on the shoulder, and making an excuse for leaving. "May he rest in peace," I mumbled and believed I almost meant it.

Without question, in Missouri, most people still hated Lane, while in Kansas, people found things to admire about him, even if they believed that as a politician, he had outlived his usefulness. If, to me, the sale of the Cornish property had seemed the last act of a drama, then Jim Lane's death was a sad, unsought encore.

Three men had been the Giants of early Kansas: John Brown, Charles Robinson, and James Lane. Men not drawn together by religious belief or political party but by the accidents of geography and a belief in freedom, although they would never have been able to agree on what freedom meant. They were not friendly rivals but bitter opponents who hated one another and would have scorned any suggestion that they work together for the common good. Now two of them were dead: Captain Brown, hanged for treason after the abortive raid at Harpers Ferry, Virginia, and Senator Lane, by his own hand. The bones of Lane, the rabble-rouser, now lay in the soil of Kansas. Only Robinson remained.

CHAPTER TWELVE

ONE WEEK BEFORE James Henry Lane died, the Fourth of July celebration for our nation had attracted Lawrencians to South Park—to the very place where, in another July, Quantrill's raiders, four hundred strong, had assembled in a stifling dawn before sweeping with orchestrated cruelty through town—waiting now for orators to speak of the two famous men of the prairie, Abe Lincoln of Illinois and Lane of Kansas, the one dead, the other at that very moment waiting for death, the speakers drawing for their audience what I thought were spurious parallels between the two lives. Still, the occasion reminded me that history is no simple thread of events but an abstruse strand of persons, places, and events which must be carefully picked apart and closely examined before being woven together again.

For me, past and present time are so knotted together that I can walk from one into the other as effortlessly as from room to room in my house. Three years had come and gone since the Massacre, and Lawrence, Phoenix-like, had risen from the ashes, a flourishing town of stone and brick buildings, and the deep-rutted California Road from Westport by which the raiders entered town, could still be seen working its way up the gentle back slope of Hogback Ridge past the cemetery where victims of the raid had been buried, some in a mass grave, before the bodies could putrefy in the heat.

Above us as we listened that evening to the speeches and the prayers for Senator Lane, rose the beetling face of the hill where, carpeted by pink-seeded tall prairie grass, now stood the three-story brick building of the University of Kansas, on the escarpment that had, of course, now been renamed Mount Oread, although only in Kansas could a bald, tree-less hill be called Mount *Anything*.

In the first year of statehood, Topeka had been selected the state capital by a vote of the people, and competition for state institutions was fierce: Leavenworth had received the prison, Manhattan the agricultural college, Emporia the normal school, and Lawrence the state university—all these in a state where resources were meager and there were scarcely enough properly-prepared young persons for *one* institution of higher learning.

Nevertheless, Lawrence desperately wanted one—and did receive one—although I regretted that decisions in the young state were often made through bribes and horse-trading. Moreover, because I had attended college in the East, where some schools had been established a hundred or more years earlier, I had many questions about faculty and curriculum and, indeed, whether so many institutions could survive in a state impoverished by war and assaulted by such inimical forces of nature as the occasional flood and the periodic drought. And so, we sat there in the descending darkness, waiting for Lane to die.

After the fireworks had ended and the smell of powder and smoke had drifted away, supper's crumbs swept up, the last drops from the last whiskey jug poured into the last cup, my family trudged wearily home-ward, Phoebe carrying Henley and Samantha walking beside Hannah, all of us guided by a sliver of moon in the eastern sky. While he lived, Senator Lane had staked out a claim in my mind, and when, a week later, he finally succumbed to his self-inflicted wound, I immediately missed him.

Now I waited for word from Russell Downing, and when his letter came, I was surprised to learn of an incident in Independence, Missouri, no mention of which had been made in either of the Lawrence papers or the *Globe Democrat*, in the latter case an omission I attributed to Downing's advancing age or inattention. Exactly a month before, in Jackson County on the outskirts of Kansas City, several armed men thought to be members of the James gang had broken into a gaol, killed a guard, and freed two bushwhackers associated with Quantrill's Raid during the war years. Now bushwhackers—whether led by Little Archie

Clement, Dave Poole, or the James brothers—seemed both emboldened and able to strike anywhere in western Missouri, and I began to wonder whether the Colonel's plan to draw out and imprison the leaders had any chance of success.

"To be once in doubt, is once to be resolved," Othello says about himself, and I felt Shakespeare's words applied to Maypole, another soldier who could not tolerate uncertainty or ambiguity. Despite some reservations, I conceded that some bloodletting might be necessary to restore the health of the body politic in Missouri, and I waited to see whether the legislature's plan to register adult males for the state militia would come to fruition.

Across the Missouri River Valley, summers are hot and dry as the days creep slowly toward autumn—"dog days," they are called. Here in Kansas, I watched with interest as September's scholars matriculated at the new university, not one of them—so I was told—prepared for college. Heat hung in the air, the grainy tufts of milo were ready for cutting, and dried cornstalks waited for a fall rain that refused to come. In the trees, cicadas, which had escaped the parched earth, droned like tuneless violins, protesting the heat. Day after day, I looked at my calendar and waited for Russell Downing to send an assignment. The waiting, Hannah told me, was making me peevish and ill-tempered.

My humor changed with the arrival of the first fall rains, for, to be sure, October has long been my favorite month of the year, cooler days following the baking summer. Pale sunlight now drew color from the trees along the Kansas River, and now clumps of sumac in the bushy ravine which bisects West Lawrence turned bright crimson, reminding me of the sumac at the Battle of Westport two years earlier, when the Kansas militia wore sprigs of the bush in our hats.

Within a fortnight, mornings brought a slight chill, although afternoons were still pleasant enough for our dogs to sleep in the sun. The falling leaves meant that farm animals were ready for slaughter, the piglets of spring disappearing one morning when the men from the abattoir arrived to carry our fat hogs away. Our children were not encouraged to treat the farm animals as part of the family, giving them names, although occasionally a runt did receive a name and perhaps a longer life.

And so, the year began to slide slowly toward winter as the sun sank earlier and earlier in the western sky, its light as pallid as that of the moon. I waited impatiently for the Colonel's trap for the bushwhackers to be sprung, not that I had any part to play except perhaps to record it for the *Globe Democrat* and to receive satisfaction for the capture or death of one or more of Quantrill's raiders.

Then, during October's last week, Young Orville, the son of Orville Roden, knocked at our door several hours after sunrise to deliver the telegram from Downing, which I had expected for several months, but instead of instructions to haste to Lexington, Downing's terse message to me was, "sit tight."

I hurried to the telegraph office to see what might be on the wire and discovered that the Alexander Mitchell and Company bank in Lexington had been robbed that morning, apparently by Clement's gang of ruffians, little more than two weeks before the fall election was to take place. Every day, like the Ghost in *Hamlet,* I haunted the offices of the *Kansas Tribune* and the *Kansas Journal* in search of information about the robbery; little money had been taken—only two thousand dollars—and no one had been apprehended.

Election Day in Lawrence was cold, gray, and quiet, but in Lexington, Missouri, violence had occurred early in the day, as I learned at the *Tribune;* an attack by what were said to be one hundred bushwhackers had disrupted the election there. Governor Fletcher had announced he was sending the state militia to Lexington and Lafayette County to apprehend the bushwhackers and restore order. What had happened, I wondered, to the Colonel's plan to draw Clement from the woods and, beyond that, perhaps mount an action against the James gang in Clay County.

Now the word came from Downing: I was to meet the Colonel in Lexington, forty miles downriver from Kansas City, where he was ready to spring his trap and attempt to arrest Little Archie Clement, who seemed to present the biggest obstacle to peace and normalcy in western Missouri. From the beginning, I had reservations about the governor's stratagem to enroll the bushwhackers in the state militia, not that the tactic of enlisting or sending into combat deserters or captured enemy was new or untried, having been employed routinely since Roman times, perhaps earlier.

In Missouri, however, the political climate was dangerously unstable, as the rampage at the polls had demonstrated. Perhaps the enrollment scheme would work if the Union army were to be involved, but I was not certain that the Missouri militia could be counted on, despite the Colonel's confidence in them. Many things could go wrong.

Nevertheless, a week later, Thanksgiving Day behind us, I boarded a train which whisked me to Wyandotte, where a trap buggy carried me across the state line to the Kansas City quay, the great muddy river still the quickest and most direct route to Lexington, on the southern bank. Twice Lexington had been fought over—in September of 1861 and again during the Westport campaign in October of '64—but this time, if our scheme went as planned, we hoped for a peaceful and blood-less denouement.

When I reached the quay, I found that the pilot of the waiting steam ferry was not Barney Appleyard but a muscular, blond, and bearded Missourian called Jericho, his teeth stained by chewing tobacco. "Where's Barney?" I asked, getting on board.

"Ain't sure, exactly," he replied. "Gone to work on the railroad, I hear." I would miss the witty Barney, but since Jericho seemed deter-mined to get us to Lexington in time for supper, the new pilot satisfied me. Lexington was a much bigger town than Liberty with more com-mercial establishments and industry, and when we pulled into the quay later in the day, the streets seemed quiet and orderly.

That evening, I met the Colonel for supper in a private room at the City Hotel. Since his enigmatic countenance seldom betrayed his pas-sions, his expression could have suggested retribution for the election fiasco. After supper, he ordered whiskey for us, brought out a small case, offered me a cigar, and selected one for himself. Calmly, he cut off the tips and proposed a toast to our missing friend, Downing.

"Despite several setbacks—including the disturbance at the polls last month—our scheme is to be put into effect tomorrow. Dave Poole is, as you know, a downright—" Nodding, I interrupted with a grunt. "Yes, I know he rode with Quantrill and probably killed men in Lawrence, but here's the point, Ezra. He wants a pardon, and he is willing to get Little Archie into town and his men enrolled in the militia. That's the law now."

"And you will have to give them safe conduct too," I added.

"I should like to shoot all of them, but we can use Poole to get Little Archie, that pernicious devil." With that phase, Maypole's eyes narrowed slightly, and a bitter grin twisted his face. And he was, of course, correct about Clement; the little man had discovered he loved killing and loved scalping, loved it even more than Bloody Bill Anderson, who brought Indian-style scalping to Border warfare.

There was no polite name for someone like Clement, but Shakespeare had a phrase that fit such men; they possessed "some vicious mole of nature," a carbuncle, a pervading evil that corrupted the whole body. Although there had been an arrest warrant for him after the Liberty robbery, Little Arch would be guaranteed safe conduct to and from town on the morrow, and the platoon of militia under Major Bacon Montgomery was there only to supervise the enrollment, not to arrest anyone.

Since the Colonel rarely talked of himself, during dinner that evening, I asked about his service during the war. Initially, he demurred, but after cleaning his supper plate, he leaned back, poured himself another glass of whiskey, and began to talk. "Well, Ezra," he commenced, "when the Southern states began to leave the Union and Missouri teetered on the edge—would we stay or would we join the Confederacy? I opined that if Missouri left, the Union would lose the war that everyone knew was coming. So just before Lincoln's inauguration, my father got me a commission . . . Eighth Missouri State Militia."

In his stylish tweed suit and waistcoat, he cut a handsome figure with his silver-blond hair and trimmed beard. His eyes did not leave my face. "Later, I joined the Union army and ended up in Washington, which was full of Confederate spies. That's where I met Allan Pinkerton. He was crude and a bully in some ways, but he was brilliant, and he taught us what he called spy craft—helped us win the war, and one time saved Lincoln's life."

He paused and a faint smile crossed his face. I wanted to question him, but he would allow no interruption, beginning quickly again. "So, being mustered out when the South surrendered, I returned to Missouri and rejoined the militia, knowing the turmoil here and the need to restore order. I am tied to the state of Missouri." He reached across the table to offer me more whiskey, but I declined his offer with a wave of my hand.

"Any chance Clement's outlaws will ravage the town as they did in November?" I asked.

"Not likely," the Colonel said with a chuckle as he blew cigar smoke into the air above my head. "*That* was an election day. Tonight, we got a platoon of unpleasant gentlemen . . . with carbines, camped outside town on the old battlefield."

"In the Eighth Missouri Militia, were you, sir?" I asked.

"Action along the Arkansas border mostly," Colonel Maypole said, nodding. "Cavalry raids, but men died. Wilson's Creek, where the Rebels won in '61. And Pea Ridge the next March, and *we* won this one." His expression did not change, but his eyes brightened as though he could see his comrades through the tangle of years. "Named for the wild peas that perfumed the air there, I heard. Of course, not in March, when we fought." He shook his head and seemed to smile again. "Then I was off to Washington, the Union army, and the secret service force of Allan Pinkerton."

"Pal of mine was at Pea Ridge with the Eighth Missouri," I interrupted. "Was a sharpshooter there, I believe." Colonel Maypole's eyes narrowed again as he nodded. "Name of Hickok. Crack shot . . . with Lane's old Free-State army in Kansas, where I met him."

"Had several sharpshooters at Pea Ridge," my companion said.

"Jim Hickok," I added, "though people now call him Wild Bill."

"Lot of men had such names, but I do remember one tall fella. Think maybe he shot some ruffian on the square in Sedalia after the war?" the Colonel asked. "Might have been your friend." We rose at the same time and nodded to each other. "I believe I am needed elsewhere, Ezra," he added. He walked out the front door of the hotel into the cold night, and I went to my room to await the morrow.

The next morning—the thirteenth day of December—was clear and, despite the chill, people filled the main street, scurrying like ants from a disturbed hill to get the best vantage point to observe Clement's gang enroll under the watching eyes of the Missouri militia. Dan Poole, who had been promised a full pardon, rode into town, his horse snorting in the frigid air, followed by Little Archie Clement, a tiny man, but heavily armed and wary as a wild turkey.

He had brought about twenty-five men with him, all armed and smiling arrogantly at the troopers as they watched while the bushwhackers tied up their horses. In faded blue Union jackets and flat-crowned hats, the militia sat their horses still and stoically, carbines resting across their saddles. I could understand why Poole had agreed to be an intermediary, but what had impelled Clement's bushwhackers to come to town to enroll: a taunt or dangerous joke after disrupting the election a month before, or simple hubris?

The cold wind carried the smell of the river up to the hotel's porch where I stood with the Colonel, who watched, a sidearm at his waist, as a flag snapped above us, saddles groaned and brass jingled, and from time to time a horse pissed in the street. Major Bacon Montgomery ushered the bushwhackers into the meeting hall where the ceremony would take place, and we waited, my feet and nose beginning to feel uncomfortable.

Then I could hear the Major make a short speech, and some of the bushwhackers gave a cheer before they wandered out of the building, mounted their horses, turning from side to side to smile and joke with bystanders, like merry guests leaving a wedding feast, before they slowly rode together up the street toward the edge of town.

"Guess that about concludes it," I said to the Colonel, who now seemed to watch his own men more closely than the Bushwhackers. The spectators in the street had begun to drift away, perhaps disappointed that not even a fistfight had broken out, and some of the militia began to wander up the street to look in shop windows while others meandered into the bar of the City Hotel. I went to look for the Major to hear what had transpired in the hall, but he had disappeared into the throng that now filled the lobby of the hotel and spilled into the bar behind us. The mood was convivial: a tense ceremony had concluded without dispute, and I took solace in the outcome.

Suddenly, shouts and gunfire sounded from the bar, and men pushed into the lobby, jostling and elbowing, impeding entry into the bar. Running to the front of the hotel to look through the window, I could see Clement, who had returned to town. He was shooting at someone behind him in the alley. Then from the windows of the hotel I could see him, now on horseback, turning to shoot back into the alley, then suddenly jerking in the saddle and pitching from his horse into the dirt street, cursing as he attempted to crawl, when he was hit again, now fumbling with his revolver and trying to cock it with his teeth, his body soaked in blood.

In front of the hotel, Major Montgomery was in the street where a crowd was gathering—shopkeepers, a woman, several troopers. The

Colonel had appeared and was trying to move the crowd back, and someone had grabbed the bridle of Clement's horse. Why had Clement returned to town after leaving under safe conduct? Who had started the brawl in the bar? Had anyone else been shot . . . who had shot Clement?

People forming a circle around his body now spoke in lowered voices and inched forward. Little Arch was propped up to be photographed, gouts of blood on his face, his coat wet with gore. He was, in fact, no bigger than a boy, a boy the size of Squirrel Searcy, the smallest militiaman in our Westport Company, often mistaken for a drummer boy.

What exactly *had* happened? Would I write for Downing that it had been a fiasco, a flawed plan? Or that the return and death of Clement was simple chance or caprice? Major Montgomery had a look of triumph on his face, but the Colonel had a countenance which I found difficult to describe. It was the expression I imagined on the face of a stage Othello who has just strangled Desdemona, the wife he mistakenly believed had betrayed him. I struggled for words to describe that face: it was a look of horror.

CHAPTER THIRTEEN

AS I WAS writing my story for the *Globe Democrat*, Little Archie's face refused to leave my mind, a pentimento beneath the accumulating impressions on the day's canvas, not easily erased or rubbed from my memory. It was not that I was squeamish about the blood, for I had seen battle's ghastly wounds as well as the barnyard butchery of animals, in which I had assisted. The little man who had viciously killed in Lawrence, Centralia, and elsewhere across Kansas and Missouri—desecrating bodies as no white man ought ever to do, even in times of war—deserved no pity, and I felt none for him.

Major Montgomery had exulted in Clement's death, and his troops laughed and celebrated wildly, causing me to wonder whether the Missouri militia had perhaps set him up in the hotel's bar. If it *were* fortuitous, why did everything seem too pat, so opportune, so exactly right.

Several of the troopers were eager to talk to me, each one insisting that, in the bar, Clement had resisted arrest, a handy excuse to justify the killing of a troublemaker. As I expected, they were unanimous in the opinion that Little Archie had drawn and shot first. After listening to the many voices, all I can say for certain is that Clement had returned to Lexington after his safe conduct had ended and that the Major had an arrest warrant for the February robbery of the bank in Liberty. Of the dozen or so robbers, Clement was the only one who had been positively identified at the bank, although Dave Poole and the James brothers were also thought to have been involved—and so Little Archie had gotten *all* the blame.

One of the troopers opined that another man might have accompanied Clement on his return to town, but no such friend or confederate could be found and identified. Strangely, in such tight quarters, no one else had been shot or wounded, save one of the town's butchers who had suffered a superficial wound to the arm.

Colonel Maypole talked to the Major and many of the militiamen before coming over to me in the hotel's lobby. I wanted to ask him about the look of horror on his face as he knelt over the little man's body: what did it signify? Could it be that the Colonel had come to have a kind of affection for the man he knew he must destroy?

That notion I quickly dismissed as the fiction of a lady novel-writer who might celebrate the myth of a romantic and chivalric South inhabited by ladies with snowy bosoms, curled blonde hair, pastel crinoline ball gowns, surrounded by cheerful "darkies" who lived conveniently away from the white masters except when they were needed and who sang—melodiously—on cue. That world had no more foundation than the fable that the James and Younger gangs lived like Old Robin Hood of England, stole only from the rich, and gave everything to the poor.

I have heard it said that the *winners* of wars get to write the history of the times and erect for posterity what Shakespeare calls the gilded monuments of princes; rather it is sometimes the *losers* who create a mythic narrative of an event, and so in Missouri and across much of the South the defeated had begun to tell of a heroic struggle to preserve the "traditional Southern way of life," and so protect those values from "Yankees" who invaded from the North. Unlike Kansas, where the repeated blows of conflict had forged a solidity of purpose, Missouri and the other Border states were still riven by disagreements between Unionists and Confederate sympathizers, segregationists, Democrats, and Whigs.

Because Missouri—one of the loyal Border states—did not secede from the Union, Lincoln's Emancipation Proclamation of 1863 did not free Missouri's slaves, but, anticipating ratification of the Thirteenth Amendment to the Constitution, Missouri's Republican Governor, Thomas Clement Fletcher, emancipated the state's Negroes in January of 1865 shortly after taking office, forever abolishing that evil practice in the state.

Russell Downing and Lincoln had been lockstep on policy, but I believed Downing thought Andrew Johnson's policies to be ineffective and, even worse, dangerous. For one thing, Lincoln had been inching toward Black suffrage before the assassination, supported protection for the rights of the freedmen, and had, in his speeches, recognized Blacks to be part of the nation.

Although called "Reconstruction," Johnson's version was simply to leave the old Southern political system in place and restore the former powers of the rebellious states as they prepared to re-enter the Union, leaving the details up to those states, with, in many cases, the old Confederate officials again in charge. These men had never been punished; President Jefferson Davis did not spend one day in prison for his acts of rebellion, nor did his generals.

Already, secret societies were forming in the South, and biased laws ("Black Codes"), indentures, peonage, and sharecropping, in effect, continued many of the practices of slavery. Reports of lynching in the South seemed to be increasing. The publisher of the *Globe Democrat* also thought that land reform should have been undertaken, giving some of the freedmen their own land to farm, a goal of Radical Reconstruction as well, but that was now impossible with Johnson. A revolution was taking place in America, and I could only observe it from afar.

The Republicans in Congress continued to push *their* Reconstruction agenda, passing the Fourteenth Amendment and sending it to President Johnson, who promptly vetoed it, an action which Congress then overrode, giving Johnson a stinging defeat when the amendment was submitted to the states for ratification. What might have escaped notice by some people at first was that Negro *male* suffrage was guaranteed, but not *female* right to vote. After decades of patience, Hannah and other progressive women were outraged, as was I.

As the sternwheeler carried me up the Missouri from Lexington, I stood on the empty deck, watching the cold wind tear the smoke from the top of the chimneys and seeing the droplets of water dripping from the huge paddle wheel and seeming to freeze in the air. Wrapped in a heavy rug and hugging myself closely, I felt the wind scour the memory of the previous day from my mind until involuntary shivers coursed through my body, and I sought relief in the warmth of the cabin. Going inside, I glanced toward the wheelhouse to see a familiar face, that of the ferryman Barney Appleyard. I waved and touched the brim of my hat, and he mouthed the words, "see you at the quay."

"You get aboard in Lexington, Mr. Middleton?" Barney asked after pumping my hand in greeting. "Big doings there a day ago, I hear." He held his clay pipe in his left hand and wore a river pilot's cap and a heavy wool jacket against the damp and cold.

"Yeah, I saw Little Archie get himself killed."

"Didn't do it all by hisself, I'm thinking," Barney said with a laugh. "Got some assistance from the militia." He looked me in the eye. "What will you say in your story, sir?"

"Have already written it . . . but I still don't know what happened," I said, smiling, eager to change the subject. "Thought you got a job with the railroad, but here you are still on the river."

"Thought about it, but as you can see, I got advancement to the sternwheeler." He laughed again when I congratulated him. "Still poor as Job's turkey though," he said, smiling at my puzzlement. "My father used to say it. Never sure exactly *what* it meant." Barney pulled his jacket up to his chin. "Not enough work in western Missouri and too many mules pulling in different directions," he opined, looking closely at me again. Perhaps I had frowned because I knew I had to get across the state line to Wyandotte to catch the train west, the last one of the day.

By the time I did cross into Kansas for the train to Topeka, the wind had abated as, carrying my valise, I joined the cluster of passengers, my thoughts on my wife and family. Finding my seat, I made a pillow of my overcoat and, asking the conductor to wake me when we got to Lawrence, I immediately fell asleep. As the only passenger leaving the train, I jumped from the carriage and entered the depot.

A single lamp was still lit and, as I hurried toward the street, a familiar voice called my name; it was Larby Jones, the friend who had lost his leg at Westport two years before. I shall never forget the names or faces of those who fought with me, those who survived and those who did not return. The temperature continued its steady drop. Larby's mule snorted clouds of frozen breath and shook his head.

"Going to the warehouse, Ezra! Drop you off at home," he shouted as he lifted a wooden box into his freight wagon and limped to his mule.

"Much obliged," I replied, climbing onto the bench. The stationmaster was closing and locking the gate in the dusk and had already banked the coals in the depot's Franklin stove. "Maybe Hannah will have an extra plate of supper for you."

"Always like to join you lovebirds," he laughed, "but I got an invite from a widow lady tonight." There were, of course, still some widows from Quantrill's Raid, but their number was shrinking. Larby tapped his nose, which meant, I believe, that the identity of his hostess would remain secret.

Our dogs began barking as the Sonnet freight wagon came down our street, now in full darkness. Bidding Larby farewell, I hurried through the barnyard toward the back door, which opened to reveal, not Hannah, as I expected, but Phoebe, holding a kerosene lamp. I hugged my three children, taking time to kiss each of them in turn before embracing my wife.

I knew what she would say before she said it because, when sending me a note, she always addressed me with one phrase: *my much loved husband!* To me, it sounded devotional or literary, but at the same time deeply personal. Because it would freeze overnight, Hannah had pots of water ready on the stove in case the pump was frozen tomorrow. Frost had already etched patterns on the window in the kitchen, and because of the cold, the dogs would need to sleep in the kitchen overnight. In my home again, my heart overflowed with joy at returning to my wife—*my much loved wife.*

The kitchen was warm, and a fire burned in the parlor; supper, prepared by Phoebe, was merry, with rich smells and laughter at the table. Phoebe seemed to have grown several inches in the several days I had been gone. Now almost sixteen, she was nearly as tall as I, graceful and beautiful. I was as proud of her as the children of my own body. She was already a woman, and men—Black and white—were beginning to take notice of her. One who did was Leona's assistant, Isaac Worthy, who had become like a brother to me on those days when we buried the dead after Quantrill's attack on our sleeping town.

Isaac was one of the most proper young men I had ever known, meticulous in dress, bearing, and speech. As a Black man and a white man, we could never become proper friends in society—like Eli and me, for example—but beneath his façade of deference, Isaac, I am certain, felt a brotherly love for me too. Lighter-skinned than Phoebe, Isaac seldom spoke to her, but I noticed recently his quick, furtive glances in her direction. She seemed determined never to catch his eye, and that, in itself, might mean something, but, in any event, Hannah and I believed Phoebe was much too young to consider marriage.

Our three children were excited about the upcoming holiday, especially after Hannah's mother sent an Advent calendar from St. Louis. While in our church we never celebrate Advent—the four Sundays before Christmas—our children nevertheless demanded we use the calendar with its little paper door for every day, a religious picture behind each one. Phoebe was especially enamored with the Annunciation, when the angel Gabriel announced to Mary that she would bear the baby Jesus, for her own life also seemed to provide evidence of miracles.

John Brown, whom I believed to be the person who snatched her from bondage, must have seemed as powerful as Gabriel to Phoebe, and angels had become as real to her as the mules and horses in our barn. Indeed, I supposed that to Phoebe, Gabriel must have looked exactly like Brown, with a long white beard. Our daughter asked me again and again to tell her stories about Captain Brown, and I was happy to comply, grateful that the old man still lived in the memory of our daughter, as he lived in mine. And just as Mary, heavy with child, walked with Joseph to Bethlehem, so Prudence, also with child, walked the streets of Lawrence on sunny days in December, where Phoebe could descry her.

Eli and Prudence believed their child would be a girl and decided on the name Christine to acknowledge the Nativity. Phoebe loved Prudence and asked to touch her swelling belly whenever we saw the couple. The Fosters, in fact, were protective of Phoebe when many in Lawrence ignored her or crossed the street to avoid speaking to us, treatment which caused Hannah to rage in private, while suppressing her anger in public. Acknowledging that some of our neighbors were insulting and callous, I continued to believe that the New Jerusalem we were building here in the West would have streets where white and Black could walk together in peace and harmony.

"And women too?" Hannah asked sharply.

"Yes," I averred, "and Indians too, I guess, but it may take time, my dear."

"And how long must we *wait* then?" Hannah asked. I knew it was a question about race, but it was also one about female suffrage too, both legitimate questions, for neither of them did I have a ready answer.

So as excitement increased in our household and the December nights lengthened with the approach of St. Lucy's Day—the shortest day of the year—it seemed our children, like inflated balloons, could hold no more excitement, even before Hannah hung the stockings by the mantle in the parlor. In a land of cottonwoods, ash, oaks, and hackberry, we had no pines or spruce to cut down and carry into the house for Yule trees, but the children, ignoring the continuing bitter cold and praying for a snowfall, decorated a small holly in our garden with chains of colored paper.

Every morning Eli sent word that Prudence believed the baby was about to come, and the midwife, Mrs. Seligmann, waited to be summoned. Eli, stolid and calm in combat at Westport, was now as jittery as a colt. He told me in confidence that he had ordered a German doll in Kansas City for the baby. "Has a painted face made of bisque—a kind of porcelain. Just waiting to be sure it *is* a girl." Everything was ready, and Prudence, a portrait of health, impatiently awaited her baby's appearance. Our children, with the shortsightedness of youthful optimism, had convinced themselves that the baby and a heavy snow would arrive, as if by miracle, on Christmas morning along with gifts delivered by St. Nicholas.

On Christmas Eve, our family attended a service of music, and the children's excitement—impossibly!—grew yet again. Because Eli insisted that Prudence remain at home to guard against the frigid wind blowing in from the north, Phoebe now was certain that the baby would soon arrive, as did the Christ Child almost two thousand years ago in far-off Bethlehem, surrounded by farm animals, shepherds, and angels singing in praise of God. At Phoebe's insistence, I promised to go before breakfast to Eli's house as soon as we had opened our gifts, including those left by St. Nicholas himself.

The morning was chilly but not as cold as the previous day, and the clouds hung in the sky like a whorl of gray wool sheared from a great ram. Our children were already opening their small packages, squealing with delight at every gift. Hannah and I, still in our bedclothes, stood at the back door looking at last year's dead plants in our garden while Phoebe watched to see if I was about to get dressed for the short trip to Eli's house. The day was still, and no one was on the street when snow-flakes floated down, spinning on their descent to earth. The sun behind the clouds dyed them a milky pink on their tumbled edges. "A baby born on Christmas," Hannah said. "It will be a blessing to them." I was about to tell the children to look outside at the snow they had awaited when our dogs began to bark.

Lolly, the girl Eli had hired to cook and clean, came around the barn, running awkwardly. "Here's Lolly with news," I said, noticing larger snowflakes beginning to fall from the sky. "A perfect Christmas now," I whispered to Hannah, who had stepped outside and lifted her face as the snow began to stick in her copper hair.

"Children!" Hannah shouted. "See the snow come down!"

Lolly, a chubby girl, could not get her breath and wheezed my name as she handed me the single piece of paper, which I unfolded. It read: *Ezra. Come.* I pulled on my pants and boots and grabbed my heavy coat. Hannah pushed the children away from the door. The baby had come at last, they assumed, and now they argued about who should hold her first, for they all agreed it was a girl.

"Will send word," I shouted to Hannah as I ran after Lolly, who had spun around and, like a frightened heifer separated from the herd, stumbled and slipped ahead, finally falling to her knees, exhausted. I trotted, careful to keep my feet in the snow. The inhabitants of Lawrence were outside now, welcoming the snowstorm, and many hailed me as I ran down the street, careful to keep my balance, and ran across the dried grass toward the front door. I beat on it, and Eli appeared—in a wrinkled shirt, shoeless, who looked grimly at me with tears in his eyes.

"What is it? Prudence? How are they?" I asked.

He choked out the words. "Ezra, the baby is dead."

CHAPTER FOURTEEN

IN TIMES OF trouble, pious people often rely on religion for consolation; I, on the other hand, more frequently turn to poetry to ease my suffering. Although Shakespeare provides many passages about profound grief—Lear's raw cry of anguish over Cordelia's body, for example, "thou'lt come no more"—but the line, however, that I saw in my mind, as though written in the elegant cursive of Molly Garnett was one by Shakespeare's rival playwright Ben Jonson on the death of his first son, beautiful in its simplicity: "Rest in soft peace, and, asked, say: here doth lie Ben Jonson, his best piece of poetry." As I remembered Eli's dead child, I was cognizant of the fragile lives of my own children and the words spoken by other grieving parents.

On my return from Eli's on Christmas day, Hannah had thrown a shawl over her shoulders and, leaving the children in my care, hurried through the snow, which now covered the ground to a depth of several inches. What should have been a joyous Christmas morning was instead a tenebrous time, a day of deepest sorrow. The children were calmly told there would be no baby—that Christine had died.

The two younger ones seemed almost indifferent to the announcement; since, I supposed, because they had not seen the baby, she had no more actuality than persons in the stories I read to them at bedtime, but Phoebe's response was different—after wrenching sobs, like a small child, she ran to the comfort of my arms.

Now wearing the black armband of mourning, I assisted Eli in such things that accompany a death: visiting the funeral parlor, discussing the

burial ceremony with Reverend Cordley, and inspecting the snowy Oak
Hills Cemetery, where the baby Christine was to be interred the next
day. The temperature had moderated, the board sidewalks in town had
been swept, and all traces of snow had been obliterated by the traffic on
the streets, leaving in corners small, dirty piles of snow, like chaff in the
bottom of a feed box.

Since Prudence and Eli were blond, I had assumed the baby would
be blonde as well, perhaps with the coloring of the German doll which
Eli intended to purchase for her, but I did not ever see the baby because
Eli had wrapped her in a blanket, as if to protect her from a chill, and
even on our trip to the funeral parlor, carried her tenderly as if she were
alive. Prudence did not leave her bedroom until the day of the interment,
when she emerged wan and red-eyed into an overcast gray day.

Since the ground was still frozen down several inches, on the pre-
ceding day, men with pickaxes and shovels had to dig a hole for the
tiny coffin. We huddled together as the Reverend Cordley read from
Ecclesiastes: "To everything there is a season, and a time to every purpose
under heaven." The coffin was placed in the grave, we sang "The Shining
Shore," and the service ended.

As we left the cemetery, Davey Weekly nodded, indicating that he
wished to speak to me, and I fell behind Ed Whitman and his boys to
attend to Davey. Hannah and our children walked ahead with Eli and
Prudence, who continued to dab at her eyes with her handkerchief.

"How are things out near Blanton's Bridge, Davey?" I asked him.

"A rueful day, Ezra. We are still cold about the heart." He leaned
closer to me as though he might speak and then seemed about to turn
away. "I hesitate to tell you this, but fear I must," he whispered. "Being
said by a person or two." He paused. "Hateful things. . . ." Davey is not
one to gossip, so his warning was especially alarming.

"What things?" I whispered, making certain we were not overheard.

"Think it was . . . said to me . . . so it would get back to you."

"Tell me, Davey," I replied, taking his arm and pulling him further
aside into the snow.

"Promise to do nothing rash," he whispered to me. I have never been
known as an impulsive man or one easily given to choler. Nor am I burly
or likely to pick a fight. "Here's what was said: 'Consorting with such

people.' Uh, he did say: 'They are not clean.' Can't remember much else. Most of it gabble."

The choler rose within me, the back of my thighs tightened, and my face burned despite the cold. I could, however, guess who the interlocutor might be. And, of course, I knew instantly who was being spoken about—Phoebe. "Tell me who said it!" I demanded of Davey, drawing him close to me. "He needs to be taught a lesson."

"Don't be a fool, Ezra," Weekly said in a harsh whisper. "You have a position in town. You can't go around punching people." He looked in my eyes. "Said all I'm going to. Don't do *anything*!" And of course Davey was right. His interlocutor, I guessed, probably was Charlie Vertue, the vulpine, caustic-tongued agent for Vitruvius Bird. Vertue had never liked me, and Bird surely blamed me, for the Cornish horse farm had gone to the Weeklys.

Bird's own farm lay fallow—or at least most of it was unused—but I assumed he thought the Cornish farm could have been used in one of his schemes, perhaps sold with some of his own land for railroad right of way. Well, the two of them were best left alone where they could stew in their own bile. As I became calmer, I hurried to catch up with Eli and swatted him gently on the shoulder and he smiled.

This would be remembered, I thought, as a bitter Christmas, a holy day when we felt we had fallen through a hole or tear in the fabric of time, dropping from joy to despair in an instant. Death on the prairie in winter, however, although rare, is not unknown; many families in Lawrence had lost a newborn or infant during a cold winter, occasionally a mother in childbirth—yet life goes on, as people say. That was not, of course, a sentiment I intended to share with Prudence and Eli. This year, the New Year's celebrations were restrained, but week by week, the collective pain seemed to lessen. Although the weather was cold with unkennelled winds howling from the north, the snowfall was meager and icy, but on milder days, people gathered on the street to buzz about the hope for spring rains.

Before the rains came, however, the first signs of spring appeared on the west side of our house where the winter sun warmed the ground, even on chilly days: a few brave crocuses in purple or violet popped up in a place where bulbs had been planted. When those fragile flowers began to fade, lily of the valley blossomed, tiny white bells on slender stalks.

Since my father had told me they were my mother's favorite flower, in memory of her, I brought fragrant stalks every morning in season to Hannah in a small glass vase, as my father might have done for my mother. Now, cattails appeared along the Kansas River in sheltered pools where the water was sluggish, and a pellicle of ice covered the brown water.

There is an order to events in nature which can be observed. The Judas tree or redbud covers its branches with pink blossoms before any leaves appear, the bloom of the crab apple perhaps comes next, with the apple and pear close behind, and finally across field and forest the shimmering green leaves of the deciduous trees. These signs of the spring reminded me of the unromantic task of hauling manure from the midden behind the barn to the flower beds and the vegetable garden, where it would be dug in.

Although I was kept busy with legal work during the winter, my life had become as dull as unseasoned porridge, and the warming weather caused me to want the adventure of the road. And so I began to think of Colonel Maypole, from whom I had heard nothing since the killing of Little Archie in December, nor had I heard from Russell Downing. Early in March, however, I received a copy of *Harper's New Monthly Magazine* in the mail, dated February 1867, with an account of the life and adventures of Jim Hickok, called "Wild Bill" throughout by the author, Colonel George Ward Nichols. Pinned to the magazine was a note from Russell: *Isn't this your friend?*

Did he want my comment? Of course he did, and after reading Nichols' article, I was happy to oblige. I wired in reply: *Woodcut of Hickok excellent. Known Hickok for ten years, so regarding claim he killed hundreds—utter nonsense.* In the past, I had refused to think about writing of Jim's exploits because I believed that doing so would make him more of a target for hotheads who might want to try to outdraw him or, worse, shoot him from behind at cards, or in a dark alley. Now Colonel Nichols had done just what I feared—made him a target.

In Kansas City, Leavenworth, and Lawrence, Jim was a Civil War hero; now, as "Wild Bill," he would be known across the country as a bloodthirsty killer. However, to wax paradoxical, Jim was back in the "safety" of the US Army, serving as a scout for the Seventh Cavalry, according to Big Ears King, who ran down news and gossip like a shepherd's collie with a skittish flock. The Seventh was attempting to put down the latest Indian trouble in western Kansas.

With the vast herds of buffalo beginning to disappear from the state, railroads moving inexorably across the prairie, and the rich virgin land plowed up for crops, the Indian tribes were threatened—perhaps more than during the war when Indian troops were used by both sides as combatants.

General Winfield Scott Hancock, a hero at Gettysburg, had been sent to Kansas to end the unrest on the plains, but "Hancock's Indian War," as it was derisively called, had been inconclusive, and the Cheyenne, led by Chief Black Kettle, were more desperate than ever. Big Ears had information that Hickok was now a scout for George Armstrong Custer, the handsome and charismatic commander of the Seventh Cavalry.

I had never seen Custer, who had achieved the brevet rank of major general in the Civil War, but he was said to be brave and daring as well as handsome, and I thought of Shakespeare's Henry IV, who says of himself: "I could not stir but like a comet I was wondered at." It seemed a line written for Custer. Like Grant, who already had a boundless political future waiting for him, Custer would also have great prospects if he could finally end the Indian problem in the West. And how would Hickok, the plainsman, compare with the elegantly uniformed "boy general" as he was called in the papers, a comet crossing the Kansas skies?

It was, on the other hand, Hickok, not Custer, who was in my thoughts—as well as Hannah's—since we had received no letter from him since he last visited us in Lawrence. Big Ears beamed and chuckled since he believed he possessed information about which we knew little, but since Jim was thought to have been seen recently in Leavenworth and Kansas City, it was likely he would pop up in Lawrence like a prairie dog from his underground city.

It was not, however, the Plains Indians who dominated conversation on the streets of Lawrence in the two years since the war ended, but railroads and cattle. Kansas, of course, had not been selected as the route of the Union Pacific transcontinental railway, which instead had gone through the Nebraska Territory, running from Omaha to Cheyenne in Wyoming Territory and so on to California.

The Union Pacific, Eastern Division, bisecting Kansas, was still a plum for the state, running to Denver, where the Denver Pacific followed the foothills of the Rocky Mountains until it joined the transcontinental railway at Cheyenne. Along this east–west axis in Kansas were nine principal forts, some dating back to the days of the old Santa Fe Road and the Conestoga wagons which carried the pioneers in their westward travels to prospect for gold. Kansas also had a north–south railroad, the Leavenworth, Lawrence, and Galveston, formerly headed by Senator James Lane, now dead by his own hand.

Along the spine of rails and the "wood and water" stations that supplied the trains, towns developed, often around a nearby fort. In the early days, antelope, deer, and wild turkey were abundant, as were buffalo—then in huge herds which shook the earth when they passed—and the work crews that laid the rails were fed with freshly-killed buffalo meat, often from beasts shot from train windows. Settlement followed the Union Pacific westward across the seemingly endless, open plains. When the war ended, only the eastern third of the state was inhabited by white men, and Abilene or Salina (twenty miles to the west of Abilene) seemed to mark the edge of civilization, although buffalo hunters, trappers, and the federal cavalry might dispute that. The Union Pacific, Eastern Division had reached the Colorado state line in January of 1866, although there were few regular passenger trains running in the sparsely-settled state, and the cavalry was hard-pressed to protect those trains from periodic Indian attacks.

Cattle had been trailed up from Texas and the Indian Territory since the war ended, and there was an inordinate demand for beef in Chicago. I knew a thing or two about beeves, but with new ploughs and harrows, wheat drills and barbed wire, and especially the new seed wheat—Turkey Red seed—that the Mennonites had brought from Russia, I thought farming the rich soil would better comport with the economic needs of Kansas than trailing cattle from the southwest.

Central Kansas, however, changed suddenly when Joseph G. McCoy realized that Abilene, a rude village on the old Spanish Chisholm Trail that ran north from San Antonio, was an ideal location for a shipping yard from which Texas cattle could be loaded and sent directly to Chicago by rail.

Located in rich grassland with available water, Abilene benefited when the legislature repealed sections of the quarantine laws which barred Texas cattle from Kansas during certain times of the year, and cattle could now be driven up "McCoy's extension" to the Union Pacific railhead in Abilene. Of course, many of the longhorns needed to have their horns sawed off before they could be loaded. The first cars of Texas cattle went to Chicago in 1867, although it was rumored that the owners lost money on their first venture. Nevertheless, a spirit of optimism and expectation of economic opportunity ran through the state.

Half a continent away from Washington, where political decisions were made, I had to peruse newspapers and magazines in an attempt to discover federal land and Indian policy in the West. With Reconstruction foundering and Andrew Johnson under unrelenting attack in Congress from Radical Republicans, it seemed that peace with the Indian tribes was a dish too long left on the stove, when, quite by chance, the man I most respected in town, former Governor Charles Robinson drove up to me as I walked toward the telegraph office, hoping for a wire from Russell Downing about a writing assignment.

"Out early today, Ezra?" he asked, touching the reins to stop his horse, a dappled gray. I had indeed started out early on an unusually warm spring day, as had the governor, known to take a daily drive to survey grazing land he owned on Mount Oread. Kansas was already in drought, and grasshoppers were said to be eating their frenzied way across the state. Something in his voice suggested, however, that he might be interested in a topic other than the weather or the grasshoppers. "Hop in and we can ride together." I did not ask him where we might go, pleased to be with him. I had long admired Robinson for his vision of Kansas as the New Jerusalem, the state we were building with great travail in a rich but desolate land, still, in the West, a land of the buffalo and the howling coyote. I mumbled my assent. He clucked to his horse, and we were off in a walk. "We talked some time ago about the Indians in Kansas, did we not?"

"The Indian raids continue in the West, sir," I replied. "And the Indians mistrust the white man because of the Chivington Massacre. Even though it occurred in Colorado Territory and not in Kansas."

"Yes, of course." He lifted his head and gave me a long look to see if he had my attention. "I think you will be interested in this then," he said,

his voice rising. "A friend in the office of Thomas Murphy, superintendent of Indian affairs, writes that there is to be a pow-wow in Medicine
Lodge in south-central Kansas, and most of the tribes will attend. A train
of wagons and ambulances is already on its way under the convoy of
companies of the Seventh Cavalry . . . with clothing and food for the
Indians. Bribes—something Indians like."

"Will there be another attempt at a peace treaty then?" I asked.

"All of the Plains Indians will be there—the five major Plains tribes,
all represented. We have promised lots of presents to get them to come.
And I forgot to mention, Nathaniel Taylor, Commissioner of Indian
Affairs, will be there too. So, this is a chance for a treaty, Ezra, for all the
tribes to sign."

"But will we have support in Congress?" I asked.

"The Commission is already in Kansas, and it includes Kit Carson,
whom the Indians trust, and the half-breed Cherokee Jesse Chisholm,
and others. This is the time, Ezra. The pow-wow begins in mid-October
after all the complaints and claims by the Indians have been presented.
Then they will get down to terms—I hope." He gave a grim smile and
lightly touched the reins; the horse obeyed, and the buggy came to a stop.

It was no coincidence that Governor Robinson had stopped at South
Park, the place where Quantrill's raiders had paused on that stifling
morning four years ago, separating into three columns to race down the
three main streets of Lawrence, the middle band down Massachusetts
toward the Eldridge House Hotel, killing every man they saw and burning every building they came across. Was Robinson here now in an act
of expiation?

Why *had* he brought us here, to a place which must have held painful
memories for the man who from Mount Oread had seen everything that
had transpired on Black Friday? My mind was already racing ahead to
the meeting that was to be held in Medicine Lodge. Would there finally
be peace in Kansas? Peace with all the Plains Indians: the Comanche, the
Arapahoe, the Kiowa, the Apache, and the Cheyenne, headed by Chief
Black Kettle, the renowned warrior whom I longed to see. For almost six
months, in fact, I had not written a word for the *Globe Democrat*. Had
Russell Downing forgotten about me or found another correspondent
for western Missouri and the state of Kansas? The governor clucked and
lifted the reins, and the horse slowly moved forward.

To be far out on the plains was exactly what I wanted: to see tribes of Indians, to renew my friendship with Jim Hickok, who had just been featured in a "dime novel" by R. M. de Witt, *Wild Bill, the Indian Slayer,* with a violent woodcut on the cover. If I were lucky, I might also hear some of the vivid stories of Bill Cody, whom I had last heard of as an Indian scout working out of Fort Dodge.

"Let you know what I hear about Medicine Lodge," I said as Robinson pulled up on Massachusetts Street to let me out of the buggy. "Perhaps I can get out there to see for myself." He shook my hand, always one to observe the proprieties, and I smiled to myself. "Good day, sir."

Filled with enthusiasm, I hurried home to discuss my scheme with Hannah. My plan was simple: I would offer to report on the Peace Treaty at Medicine Lodge, and Russell could use as much of my story as he wanted, and I could save the fat and bones for something I might send to one of the magazines.

Although the sun was hot, I did not pay mind to the heat in my excitement about Medicine Lodge and the pow-wow. I already knew how I would get there: the west-bound train to Salina and from there travel with a unit of the Seventh Cavalry heading due south to the Medicine River, where troopers might even now be readying the meeting place and unpacking supplies. I ran by the sunflowers which grew behind our barn, so withered now by the drought that the huge, black-seeded heads hung down in surrender. The crops in the vegetable garden and our bushes and trees had been kept alive by Phoebe and me, carrying well water in buckets.

"Did you hear from Downing?" Hannah asked, surprised to see me running on such a hot day.

"No, but listen to this, my dear," I said, breathing heavily. "There is a pow-wow with all the Plains Indians . . . to end the raids . . . across western Kansas."

Hannah raised her hands in mock surprise and laughed. "And *you* intend to be part of it?" she asked.

"Well, yes, since you put it that way," I answered, trying to hide my chagrin. "I intend to ask Downing to send me out for a day or two."

"A *week* or two more likely," Hannah replied with what I hoped was a laugh as she shook her head and put a pitcher of milk on the table with bread and cheese.

After dinner, I made my way to the Western Union Telegraph office with the message I intended to send to Downing.

"Have a telegram to send," I said to Orville Roden.

"Well, I happen to have one for *you*," the telegrapher said, handing me an envelope with my name on it.

I tore open the envelope. The message was brief: *Need you to go to Richmond, MO 40 miles from KC. Bank robbery mayor and two others killed. James gang? -Downing.*

CHAPTER FIFTEEN

LOATH AS I was to abandon my hope of attending the pow-wow in Medicine Lodge between the Plains tribes and the United States Commissioner of Indian Affairs and instead travel to Richmond, Missouri, to report on the killing of a small-town mayor, I said with Shakespeare's Coriolanus, "Thus I turn my back. There is a world elsewhere," and prepared to leave for Missouri. The *Globe Democrat* was, after all, a St. Louis paper. Stories about Kansas were of little interest now that the war had ended, and most of our subscribers lived in Missouri. Besides, I owed my allegiance to Downing, who had offered me a position in 1856 when I possessed no credentials but a willingness to travel to a raw and dangerous territory to establish a legal practice. It was a debt I could repay only with absolute loyalty.

Anticipating an early departure on the west-bound train to Salina—before learning I would not be sent west—I had sketched out a beginning for my story of the Kansas Indians. When Andrew Jackson took office in 1829, succumbing to pressure from settlers in Georgia and Appalachia, he implemented the Indian Removal Act, passed by Congress a year earlier, making unwanted land west of the state of Arkansas a permanent home for the "Five Civilized Tribes"—the Cherokee, Creek, Choctaw, Chickasaw, and Seminole—pushed from their homes and forcibly resettled (except for the Seminoles) one thousand miles away on land west of the state of Arkansas, now called Indian Territory. The largest of these tribes was the Cherokee, who suffered most from the coerced relocation, but greed overcame equity, as it often does, and despite protests, in the Territory, the resettled Cherokee would abide.

Indian Reservations had also been assigned in Kansas Territory for Indians removed earlier from the new states north of the Ohio River. In fact, federal policy in the 1820s seemed to make Kansas a permanent Indian territory, like the land west of Arkansas. As a small boy, I recall my father having arguments about federal land policy, although to be honest, I remembered little besides a phrase he had used: "Indian dumping ground." Whatever it was, he did not favor it.

By the time I was born in Saint Louis in 1834, the Delaware Indians had arrived in their new home in Kansas, but they did not stay long, being forced to sell their land and move on. My father roared about that too. "Move On!" He had yelled to anyone who would listen. "We should make that into an amendment to our constitution: Indians, Move On!" Indian land was already up for sale in Kansas Territory, and settlers from Missouri, with no legitimate claim, had already established themselves along the west bank of the Missouri River.

Then, in 1854, the Kansas and Nebraska Territories were thrown open to settlement, and the Indians were told to move again. By the time I entered the Kansas Territory in 1856, the Indian question had been replaced by the slavery question, and Kansas became the chosen battleground. Neighboring Missouri was southern in outlook and habits; the "cotton culture" controlled the federal administration, the economy, and the courts, so in order to keep slavery out of the territories, a new political party had formed in Ripon, Wisconsin, the Republican Party. Texas had already been admitted to the Union as a slave state, increasing the power of the "slavery" lobby in Washington. The use of unpaid labor, the sale of cotton cloth, and the enslaved Negroes themselves as commodities increased the enormous wealth and influence of the South. But a bloody war had been fought to address the conditions that divided us into "slave" and "free."

All this, I told myself, was now water under the bridge. Despite the use of Indian troops by both sides during the war, however, the question of an Indian Nation had still not been addressed, but perhaps it would be at Medicine Lodge.

Before my departure for Wyandotte, the Missouri River, and Richmond, I walked to the haberdashery on Massachusetts Avenue to purchase a new shirt or two for the journey I could not avoid. Hearing a noise as I stepped up on the board sidewalk where Eighth crosses Massachusetts, I turned to see a buggy coming like a prairie tornado, skidding into a turn in front of me, kicking up a cloud of dust as the driver hit a mule-drawn freight wagon traveling north.

In an instant I saw that the drivers were the two young men in town whose friendship I most valued: Isaac Worthy, the young Negro who had helped carry the dead and dying to the Congregational Church after Quantrill's Raid, the male citizens of Lawrence having been shot as they came from their beds, and Jeremiah Whitman, the rip-snorting young militiaman who fought with the Kansas citizen-soldiers at the Battle of Westport in Missouri, forcing Confederate General Price to flee to safe haven in Arkansas.

Quickly, I jumped into the street to assist the drivers. Isaac was the eldest by about five years, but Jeremiah was bigger and had already reached into his boot for a knife. Since I knew Isaac would step back from a conflict, I ran to Jeremiah and his buggy, which had been damaged. Both the buggy and wagon were mule-drawn, and none of the animals seemed injured. Splintered pieces of the buggy's wheel lay in the street, but the heavier Sonnet freight wagon seemed sound.

"We were going at a spanking pace," Jeremiah said loudly, glancing at me to see if I would support his story, since, if a Negro and a white man had a dispute on the frontier, the white man was assumed to be in the right and the Black man would usually lower his glance, never looking the white man in the eye. Indeed, trouble had occasionally erupted in Lawrence between whites and Blacks wearing Union uniforms, even though tens of thousands of Negroes had fought for the North in the war, and Negroes in uniform were a common sight.

"That should wake up the rats that live under the sidewalks," I said, stepping between the two young men. Isaac brushed dust from off the sleeve of his jacket and began to examine one of his two mules.

"I swear those rats have learned to count so they know how long they got to cross the street," Jeremiah said, ignoring Isaac and continuing to address his remarks to me.

"Maybe they've learned to dig tunnels. Can escape from the rat-catchers that way too," I joked. Isaac nodded but did not smile.

"Guess I got to get what's left of this buggy down to Big Ears King. See what can be done to the wheel," Jeremiah said, still looking at me.

Then he paused and I thought he might be looking for a jest and, as it happened, he was. "Or maybe rats got a pocket time piece to see how long they got to cross the street," Jeremiah continued, patting the head of his mule. "Well, rats got no pockets for a watch, so they must just count off the time and then run across like I said before."

"Let me help with your buggy, Jeremiah," I remarked. Isaac was already in his wagon. Neither of the young men had spoken to each other, exchanging only menacing stares before Jeremiah smirked and smiled at me.

After Jeremiah and I had dragged his buggy to the wheelwright who worked for Big Ears, I bought my two shirts and walked home to sit in the shade with Hannah, who was eager to learn what had transpired on Massachusetts. The spring rains had not come, but the heat had; it was already very hot for the beginning of June. "Isaac was driving one of the Sonnet wagons," I said, "and Jeremiah Whitman was larking about—driving too fast."

"Desmond's the steady one in that family, sweetheart," Hannah mused aloud.

"I reckon Ed Whitman thinks so too," I replied. We sat in companionable silence, watching the songbirds who came to the bird bath that Samantha and I filled every morning during the drought. Although many men have stiff, formal relations with their wives and children, I had been taught by my father to prize familial ties—the ties that bind, he used to say—because the death of our mother had left him with an unusually tender heart. Many widowers married again, but my father did not.

"I shall miss you in our bed tonight," Hannah whispered to me, although no one was close at hand to overhear her. "Now, go get your bag, and the children and I will drive you down to catch your train to Wyandotte."

"If you see Jeremiah coming, drive up on the sidewalk," I said, laughing, and Hannah hooted with glee, her red hair flying as she shook her head.

Later, on the train to Wyandotte, traveling through the parched countryside, I dozed, half-awake, half-asleep, and, lulled by the rocking of the car, I thought I was being carried by a rolling thunderstorm. Then, as the train came to a stop, I jerked awake. Even in my sleep, the rain did not come. As I left the train, I noticed a dry wind which blew down from the bluffs on which the stone and brick buildings of Kansas City stood, well above the confluence of the two rivers which joined together to crawl eastward toward the Mississippi like a muddy serpent.

My journey on the steam ferry was downriver to Lexington, except that this time I was landing on the north bank in order to make the short ride to Richmond. I was happy enough not to revisit Lexington where I had seen Little Archie Clement killed six months earlier, in December of 1866, especially since I still wondered if my friend Colonel Benjamin Maypole might be implicated in Clement's death.

Western Missouri was as dry as Kansas. The spring leaves on trees, which lacked deep roots, had already withered, showing edges curled from lack of water. The lawns in Richmond were already as brown as grass in August, and, for a second, I wondered about Medicine Lodge and the pow-wow: had there been enough spring rain on the High Plains to nourish the bluestem there? After I saw my horse stabled behind the boarding house where I was stopping, I walked through the quiet town; since the bank robbery had occurred almost two weeks before, the excitement had faded. As I went into the boarding house, there—surprisingly—before me stood Colonel Maypole, as though he had been conjured up by my thoughts, like a fairy-tale character in one of the bedtime stories I read to my children.

"Ezra," he said, less surprised by our meeting than I was. "Thought Downing might send you over here for a story about a mayor who got in the way of a bullet." He paused for a moment and wiped his face with his kerchief before he spoke. In his tweed suit, he was too warmly dressed for the hot weather. "Not a big story unless the mayor happens to be a friend of Russell Downing and Governor Fletcher." My face must have shown surprise at my ignorance of the connection between Downing to the mayor. Now I understood why my publisher wanted me to write about the death of a banker and small-town mayor, who seemed of little consequence in Missouri politics.

"Let's get ourselves some whiskey before dinner. Seems I have a lot to tell you, Ezra," he said, taking me by the elbow. The sun was already setting and peach-colored clouds streaked low across the western horizon.

In front of us, a dog wandered wearily down the street, looking for shade or perhaps water.

"I received no instruction from Downing except to get over to Richmond," I replied defensively, letting the Colonel lead me out onto the dirt street. All these little Missouri towns looked alike to me, sleepy, dry, and dusty. As in Lawrence, the inhabitants seemed to be waiting for spring rains, which had not come as they were wont to. Nothing about their demeanor suggested that three people had been killed in a robbery two weeks before. If outsiders—news correspondents, for instance—had come to town as a result of the incident, they seemed to have already moved on, finding no other story here. Moved on—as the Indians had been told to do.

The sun was falling below the horizon, but the evening was stifling and unpleasant with a heat that made one's shirt stick to one's back. The Colonel wiped his face and neck again, but did not remove his coat. "So Downing and the governor were friends of the mayor?" I asked, realizing I did not even know his name.

"Mayor Brewer, who also owned the bank," Colonel Maypole said, like a bored schoolmaster trying to coax an answer from a dull student.

"Never heard the name before," I said. "But what ties these men together then?"

"All strong Unionists during the war," the Colonel answered. "Look, many of the Unionists own banks or hold stock in the express companies and so are targets of the bushwhackers. Some people in town think killing Brewer was behind their choosing to rob *this* bank. Can I prove it? Well, no, but people believe it."

"Should I not have proof of some kind before writing the story, Colonel?" I asked him. He was shrewd, but now I wondered if perhaps he was more devious than I had imagined.

"I suggest you write the story and let Downing find your proof, but talk to the sheriff first," Maypole replied with a smile and a grim laugh. "His name's Barngrover. Don't let me steer you wrong, young man." The Colonel stood up and took off his jacket in the June heat. At last, even his stubborn nature had succumbed to common sense.

"Let's round up some supper, and we can talk about the James gang." This he said in a whisper, knowing a story about Frank and Jesse James would please Downing because it would sell papers in Missouri, as John Brown, Old Osawatomie, had sold papers before the war. Perhaps after all, I thought, this might make up for missing the pow-wow in Medicine Lodge. The Colonel had a disconcerting way of throwing a baited line into the water and waiting for a strike. "I can introduce you to Barngrover if you like."

When undertaking an assignment, whether as a news correspondent or as an attorney, I prided myself on being prepared for the task at hand. I usually learned as much as possible about the history and politics of an area before entering it and about the persons I would be likely to meet. Thus, I had prepared for the US Seventh Cavalry and the Great Plains Indians only to be sent east to Missouri to come face to face with the resentments and grievances of the Missouri Bushwhackers. So, I would start with Barngrover until I could find my footing. "Is the James gang behind the robbery?" The Colonel silently scrutinized me. "And are the Younger brothers with the James gang now?" I asked, but again, the Colonel did not answer.

I still had my old commonplace book with the names of the Quantrill Raiders: Bloody Bill Anderson, Little Archie Clement, Frank James, and all the others. As they were killed, I ticked them off the list, and now only a few were left. William Quantrill had been killed in Kentucky; Dave Poole, according to the report, had fled to Texas following the debacle of Little Archie's death, whether fleeing Missouri authorities or the remaining members of the Clement gang, I did not know, but Frank James and Cole Younger were still in the state and were perhaps implicated in some of the recent robberies.

Now that railroads had spread across the Missouri River Valley, members of a gang could arrive at a town one by one, get horses from livery stables in a nearby town, and attack a bank without alerting anyone. All this the Colonel explained at supper in a hot dining room. "I thought after Clement was killed, we might see fewer robberies—and we have—but this was one of the most ruthless killings we have seen yet: three dead. I suggested we bring in the Pinkertons. Broke up a ring of train robbers on the Adams Express earlier this year, but the governor quashed that, said it would show we can't deal with our own problems." Maypole had a disgusted look on his long, angular face and shook his head. "Railroads, freight lines, express companies: everything has changed since the war, except the violence."

As we finished our meal, Colonel Maypole seemed distracted and remote. "What do you know about fraud laws, Ezra? Is fraud the same in Kansas as in Missouri?"

"Much the same, I should think," I answered. "But as an attorney, I deal mostly with wills, contracts, property. Not the criminal law. Why do you ask, sir?"

"No reason," he said. "Just curious. I certainly look forward to reading your story." We shook hands, not knowing whether we would work together again.

The next morning, needing to patch something together for Downing, I went to look for Sheriff Barngrover. A little man with a squint in one eye, he had no time for me. "Told this over and over," he growled. "You can read it in any of the papers." I appreciated the irony in his utterance, although I did not think it was so intended.

Every person I talked to was equally unhelpful. One man simply shook his head, grunted, and walked away. It seemed obvious that Downing had waited too long to send me to Richmond. The robbery had taken place two weeks before, and, as we say with a hunt, the trail had gone cold: even the best coonhounds could not have picked it up. Moreover, accounts of witnesses could have been compromised by contamination with other testimony or dimmed by the passage of time.

I could discover nothing trustworthy about the identity of the murderers, certainly nothing that could be used in a court of law. Names were mentioned about identities, then immediately followed by equivocation or retraction. For every person who thought the James brothers were involved, an equal number believed they were not. It was an utter waste of time, and, except for the amount of money taken in the robbery, I had no information for Downing.

The next morning, a rising wind suggested that the weather might be about to change. Hoping that rains were coming, I galloped to the river to catch the ferry bound for Kansas City and then the train west into Kansas.

At the livery stable north of the river, I returned my horse to wait for the steam ferry, which would carry me upstream to Kansas City. Since

Barney Appleyard was now piloting the big sternwheelers, I expected an uneventful voyage, but I was mistaken. Canvas was being placed over boxes on the platform and tied down in anticipation of a storm, neighing horses were being stabled, and dogs ran for cover as the sky darkened, and thunder began to rumble in the distance.

As the big milk cans were loaded on the ferry, I sat down next to a man in simple working clothes, and I could infer from his hands that he was accustomed to hard labor. His dark hair was mingled with gray. He was bearded, and his teeth were bad. "Rain coming," he said, "and cooler weather. Name's Zeke Hallett. Where you from, pardner?" He sucked his teeth. "I'm bound for Kansas City."

"Lawrence in Kansas," I replied, waiting to see if he would provide more information about himself. "I'm Ezra Middleton."

"Lived there long?" he asked, exhibiting an air of easy insouciance. He took a chew from a plug of tobacco and offered the cake to me, which I politely refused.

"Since before the war," I said, adopting an equal indifference, since Missourians and Kansans had a history of mistrust that went back many years. With Missourians, you never know.

"Heading home then?" He asked and, without waiting for my reply, added, looking up at me, since I stood above the bench on which he sat. "I was with Quantrill during the raid—with the Clay County boys. No hard feelings, I hope. It were a time of *war on the border*."

It was not war, of course, that killing of unarmed men and boys in Lawrence, but flat-out murder. I wanted to scream those words to feel better, but it was long ago, that day when my friend Henry Sonnet and two hundred others were murdered in the streets and in their homes. "At least you weren't killed, pardner." He pronounced the word *kilt*. He grinned maliciously, or so I thought. This was not the fantasy of a storybook where feelings were romanticized, but the brutal world of time and space and motion, guns and death. Old grudges and grievances, still settled with a gun. My heart was beating excitedly. I forced a question through dry lips.

"Clay County, eh? So you rode with Frank James?" I asked, and he responded warily, like a turkey tiptoeing from the woods.

"Like Frank, lots of our riders were tough 'cause they had to be," my interlocutor replied. I was hoping he might show remorse about the murders, but he seemed to be growing more arrogant. "Border war was bloody, and it went on and on." I nodded, hoping he would continue talking. When he did not, I asked a question I wanted answered.

"Was Jesse with you in the raid?" He shook his head.

"Too young, so he was kept home. Mad as a wet hen he couldn't go. Not like Frank. Always talking about books, was Frank, like a schoolmaster! Only thing he loved was Shakespeare!" Then, to show his disdain for books, Zeke leaned forward so he could reach the spittoon and spit his wad of tobacco. Most it went in. "Shakespeare! Imagine that!"

He seemed more concerned about the changing weather than an event four years in the past, and try as I might, I could not get him to return to the Raid, which seemed not to trouble his conscience. "I'm looking for work in Kansas City. What's your profession, if I can ask?"

"I work for a Missouri paper. Been to Richmond to write about a bank robbery there," I replied, hoping he might know something about the robbers. Perhaps he thought he had said too much already, so, giving me a hard look, he scurried away to sit by himself. Something I said had scared him off. He did not look at me again on the ferry and disappeared at the quay in Kansas City, where I hailed a hansom cab to get out of the rain and so rode across the state line into Kansas. I was pleased that once on the train in Wyandotte, I would ride dry and comfortable, now that the rain had arrived and the drought seemed to be finally coming to an end.

When I ran to the passenger car, huge raindrops splattered on the platform, spotting my coat and bag and striking the train with force. Within seconds, the "wrathful skies" described in *King Lear* had opened above our heads, and a pelting gale rocked the car. For this scene on the deserted heath, Shakespeare borrows a line earlier sung by the Fool to end *Twelfth Night*, suggesting that sorrow is part of our condition as humans, and again in *Lear* it is sung by a half-wit.

I thought on the words during the ride to Lawrence, "the wind and the rain," the companions on my journey. Our life, despite what religion may tell us, is ruled by time, chance, and fortune—especially fortune. Although *Twelfth Night* ends joyously for most of the characters, the song always haunted my recollection of the play: "Hey ho, the wind and the rain . . . For the rain, it raineth every day."

When the train from Wyandotte arrived in Lawrence, the rain was still falling, but the wind had diminished. Heavy clouds stretched overhead, and light from lanterns in the depot was reflected in large puddles near the railroad tracks. Beneath the dark clouds, which hung overhead, a thin rose band of light now shone on the horizon. Cool weather followed the rain, and even though it was June, I shivered in my jacket, remembering the oppressive Missouri heat of the previous evening. Larby Jones yelled to me and waved his lantern.

"Over here, Ezra!" He shouted. "Hannah thought you would be on the train." Since it was the last train of the day, it was, of course, a good guess. He handed me a rubberized cape to pull over my coat. "Rain's about to stop, I think. Sure was a bodacious storm," he chuckled.

I took his lantern and, after we found the wooden boxes for Leona's wholesale company on the platform, we quickly loaded the wagon in the rain. With his bad leg, Larby had trouble lifting heavy boxes, so I was glad to help him whenever I could. "I can drop you home on my way to the warehouse . . . less we bog down in the mud somewheres," he said with a laugh.

As we pulled up in front of our house, the dogs barked from the barn. Even without instructions, Larby knew not to drive up the alley where water pooled after every rain, despite my attempts to improve the drainage. As I crossed the sodden turf, Phoebe appeared at the door, light from the open door spilling into the darkness, a cheery sight to welcome me home.

Hannah had a pot of coffee waiting for me, and Phoebe filled a mug for me and one for Larby, who stood by the mules. "Be careful. It's hot!" she warned. I knew my supper was waiting on the stove; on occasion, Larby would join us, but not tonight. He gulped down his coffee, eager to be on his way to the warehouse, and off he drove, the wagon throwing mud behind it. Because the days had gotten longer after the vernal equinox, the sun was still providing light in the evenings, and to the west, the heavy clouds behind Mount Oread were now tinted a lemony pink. Hannah, at the door, opened her arms to me.

In my eyes, Hannah had always been a beautiful woman, even though on first meeting her in St. Louis, I mistakenly believed her proud and contemptuous. Now I thought her even lovelier than when, a decade earlier, I courted her, a mere girl. Her hair was darker now, more auburn than red, but men on the street still watched her as she walked, especially when she wore her riding costume as she did that evening, apparently having ridden out during the day.

Although most women her age dressed in long skirts and went out in buggies, Hannah insisted on riding her pony or walking on errands. Some people called her headstrong—or, if they were not fond of her, obstinate or shrewish, or other terms even less polite—but my pride in her was unbounded. She insisted on a woman's right to vote and to manage her own financial affairs. Hannah also cared for those in need and did not gossip or scorn the poor, mixed breeds, or colored persons.

"I rode out to see Tabby today," Hannah said. Tabitha had been left a widow by Quantrill's Raid, one of the few women who had not taken a second husband, and, like my copyist Molly Garnett, Tabby supported herself and helped other women in distress. Indeed, the women of Lawrence had been heroic since the day of the Raid, when they saved husbands and brothers from Quantrill's murderous wrath, and cared for the injured or the dying.

Eager to tell Hannah about my meeting with the Quantrill raider on the train, I warmed my hands on the coffee mug as I waited for her to put my supper on the table: a thick slice of bacon, some fresh bread from the oven, and butter, freshly churned. "I've been thinking about the song which ends *Twelfth Night* . . . because of the storm, I guess." She laughed. "A comedy for everybody, except poor Malvolio," I said. We had spoken that phrase on the evening of our first meeting, and, ever since, the sentiment had brought smiles to our faces as well as laughter. "I had something remarkable happen to me today, my dear," I began, but she stopped me.

"I saw Isaac yesterday," she said.

"Jeremiah ran into the freight wagon again?"

"No, listen to me," she exclaimed. "You need to hear this. Isaac is waiting to ask you for Phoebe's hand in marriage. He's all nervous about it. Afraid you may object." I took a deep breath. All fathers with marriageable daughters probably do. My news about Frank James would have to wait.

"What would you have me do?" I asked her, following that question with a second one before she could answer. "Is she ready for marriage?"

"She is about the age I was when I married you, sweetheart," she replied with a smile.

I smiled at her, but I could not get Zeke Hallett out of my mind, or Frank James, who had once been only a name, but had become a whole person once I knew he loved Shakespeare and was as bookish as I was. Hallett had dislike for literary persons like me. So, I was not surprised he would denigrate literature and Shakespeare, but what did trouble me was Frank James's love for Shakespeare.

Were we—Frank James and I—more alike than I would admit? And what about other writers like Emerson and Melville? Did James read them too? Had he read Melville's collection of poetry published the previous year? How could he read such writings and not be moved to virtuous actions? Was not that the purpose of poetry? And had he ever read the great new poet Walt Whitman, whose elegy on Lincoln had moved the country? Would he have mourned the martyred president as did I?

CHAPTER SIXTEEN

WHEN I RETURNED from Missouri, my mind was a tangle of thoughts and recollections, like the bag of colorful pieces of fabric which Hannah collected to use in braiding rugs. The rain had cooled the air, softened the baked ground, and left shallow lakes in the streets of Lawrence. After supper, Phoebe brought out a freshly baked cake and offered me a slice and another cup of coffee. Before their bedtime, our three children approached, all smiles, as I finished my cake. I remembered the scene in *Julius Caesar*, when the conspirators, with murderous thoughts, surrounded Caesar before beginning their bloody ritual, and I was amused to think my fate—like Caesar's—had already been decided when my three young assassins, all giggles, circled me, their hapless victim.

"Have you made up *my* mind for me already, Phoebe?" I asked with a laugh as I pushed my chair back from the table. "You know how much I care for Isaac, and—yes—I know he is waiting to ask my permission for you to marry him." My oldest child giggled again and twisted the towel in her hands as though she were beginning to break a chicken's neck—not a good omen, if one were to believe in them. I gently took the towel away, hugged my leggy and beautiful child, and raised her face so I could examine her closely. In two years, she had grown half a foot and was now almost as tall as I. Since I could sense disappointment in her face, I winked at her and left my hand on her shoulder for a moment.

In bed that night, Hannah and I quickly came to an agreement that our daughter *was* ready for marriage and that I would notify Isaac before Hannah and I talked to our daughter. My joy was increased when

Hannah informed me that Leona had a small house to the east of us, in an area where Black families were now living, and she would give it to the newlyweds as a wedding gift. Before I drifted off to sleep, I realized that although my trip to Richmond had been a bust, Hannah and Leona had saved the day.

The next morning, the world seemed fresh and new as I rode into town, thinking riding was better than walking in the muddy streets. On my way to the newsagent, I noticed Big Ears outside his livery stable in his waistcoat, since the morning was a bit chilly, even though it was the end of June. I had not seen much of Ears recently, so I was surprised that he now looked a bit different, still with his freckles, of course, and ears that stuck out like unclosed doors, but he seemed heavier, with a round face and a belly, when examined closely, which looked like a full sack of meal.

"How have you been keeping?" I asked Big Ears, who stood in a shallow puddle, which spread out before his establishment. Water dripped from the stable's roof, causing me to think of a favorite line from *The Tempest*, when Ariel speaks to Prospero about the honest councilor, Gonzalo: "His tears ran down his beard like winter's drops from eaves of reeds." I do not wish to dwell on the "beauties" of Shakespeare as many commentators do, but instead address the purpose of Ariel's speech. Prospero's enemies continue to threaten him—the bestial Caliban and the scheming politicians, Antonio and Sebastian, unnatural betrayers of brothers. Only the spirit, Ariel, had remained loyal. Prospero must not only defeat his enemies but, when all is said and done, he must also be able to forgive them for their evil.

Ariel tells Prospero that if *he* had seen the suffering of his enemies, "your affections would have become tender." Questioned by Prospero, Ariel responds, "Mine would, sir, were I human." Here, I believe, in this trope, Shakespeare characterizes the essence of humanity: not just to forgive one's foes but the ability to weep for their suffering. This was the sentiment I took from the play and, given the opportunity, I would have written about it. The scene is better than a sermon on forgiveness or even a paraphrase from the Bible, although I would not have expressed that view to the Reverend Cordley.

"Least we didn't get washed away," Big Ears said to himself, a rare dyspeptic sentiment from the normally cheerful liveryman.

"With the sun out, most of the puddles will be gone by tonight," I replied, leaning down from my horse to shake his hand. "But as for the mud—" I broke off my question and both of us laughed, knowing that unpaved streets and poor drainage were problems that Lawrence had not successfully addressed despite many attempts to do so.

"Been hearing that joke about the rider whose horse was pulled from the mud. 'Don't leave me yet,' he said. 'Another horse is beneath mine.'"

King was laughing heartily at his own joke when we noticed Davey Weekly in his wagon coming down Rhode Island toward us, splashing through the puddles. "Got dry hay for you, Ears," he announced before pulling on the reins and shouting "whoa" to his mule.

"How's things at Blanton's bridge?" Big Ears asked. "Flooding on the Wakarusa?"

"Well, maybe a little, I guess. The river left her banks in places," Davey answered, "but not much." He eased the wagon into the stable and jumped down. "Glad to see *you*, Ezra," he called out, "thought you might be at Medicine Lodge for the big pow-wow with the Indians." He paused, but I did not answer immediately since the pow-wow was a sore spot with me. "Bet there were more Indians than you can shake a stick at."

"Well, I was ready to go there, but got sent to Missouri instead. Mayor of Richmond was killed when his bank was robbed." I had dismounted but still held the reins. "Hostile Indians don't mean much to Missourians, you see. They don't want to read about Indians. They're hundreds of miles away out on the open plains—western Kansas, Wyoming, Dakota."

"Indian raids still a problem along the railroads in Kansas, I hear," Davey observed quietly. "On the rail lines . . . on occasion attacking trains. Gotta get rid of the Redskins in Kansas somehow."

"Treaties keep collapsing because everybody violates them—and I mean white men as well as Indians," I said and waited to see if someone would disagree with me since I had a little speech ready for anyone who might do so. "I mean white men *and* Indians," I tried to begin again. This was what I was ready to say in the story I had *not* been asked to write. "Our country has gone mad with expansion. The whole country wants to make money now that the war is over." No one spoke, and my companions looked at me as though I had uttered sentiments in an unknown tongue. "The factories that used to make shoes and uniforms and guns."

"Heard those shoes didn't last through the first rain in the war," Big Ears interjected.

"Well, Kansas *is* a new state," Davey interrupted. "We got to catch up with the East. Build more railroads. Make better shoes, for that matter. Repair our roads. String more telegraphs. Open colleges in Kansas. Build dams on our rivers." Davey gave a little snort and shook his head as if exhausted merely by the effort of listing the tasks that needed to be undertaken.

"I suppose that means Kansas needs to expand to the Colorado border or the mountains, eh?" I replied, pausing for rhetorical effect, a trick I had learned from my father. "So what happens to the Indians then? The Plains Indians hunt buffalo. Once we exterminate the buffalo, do we just exterminate the Comanche and Cheyenne as well?" I did not say this out loud and did not intend to insult my friend by blaming him for a view many people held.

"Guess they might be talking about that right now in Medicine Lodge," Davey said, apparently annoyed by the direction the conversation had taken. "*Treaties* must carry out our understanding of America's destiny—the vision for our country."

"The white man's vision?" I asked, hoping someone would suggest the need to compromise and work together: the different people, different parts of the country, men and women, all religions or none at all, working together, white men and Indians and Black men too. "The nobility of shared effort for a common purpose, I mean. Whitman's been writing about that for a while now. The brotherhood of man. In his poetry before the war and *since* the war too."

"'I am the hounded slave: I wince at the bite of the dogs,'" I said, quoting a line I remembered. "Whitman sees with the eyes of a Black slave. And he wants us to see with those eyes too," I added. No one responded to my comment, so I tried again, addressing Davey.

"Have you *read* the writings of Walt Whitman? He writes about America, a land of promise, of optimism, with room for everyone, all occupations, beliefs, and religions. 'Song of Myself,' Whitman's poem is called." I paused briefly and then continued. "His is not the kind of poetry we studied in school. At least, not in the school *I* went to. His is the poetry of our *new* age. He even uses the voice of an escaping slave—before emancipation." My audience of two watched me intently, but without comprehension, the kind of look a cow gives you.

"Well, we all want progress, Ezra," Big Ears said, and I wondered what was different about him. Was he growing a beard? I tried to imagine him with mutton chop whiskers. Before I could steer the conversation back to Whitman, Ears was ready to ask a question. I don't think Big Ears took poetry as seriously as I did—few of my townsmen did—but I wager Frank James over in Missouri did. Perhaps *he* alone considered such matters as I did—poetry and the Bard.

"Say, what *is* Bird up to, Davey?" Big Ears asked, returning to a subject which had been a matter of speculation. "Just more of his malarky?" No one seemed to want to hazard an answer, so I waited for my chance, hoping I had not missed it.

"Goats!" Davey answered, and the group guffawed. "Lots of goats on his place. More goats than all get out! Will eat the grass and then all the weeds." Everyone waited for Davey to continue. "Maybe Bird eats *them*—the goats, I mean. I don't know, but he sure ain't running beeves or breeding horses on his place. Waste of good land. Still lying fallow." Big Ears was shaking his head in frustration since the land where the Wakarusa flooded each spring was prime farmland. No one could figure Bird out, and most folks had quit trying. Davey had gone to see if the hay had been unloaded, and Big Ears followed him into the stables.

"Wonder about the rain upstream on the Medicine," I said aloud, not expecting an answer. There was one thing, however, which bothered me like an itch in a place where I could not reach to scratch—to get relief—and that was the notion that Frank James did love literature and greatly admired Shakespeare. How, I wondered, did that comport with his vicious actions? Like discovering that a Bible-reading Christian worshiped Satan or scalped foes like a heathen, as Little Arch had done.

I had, of course, seen heavy fog in my travels around the country and knew that when cold air met warm, wet air along a river or lake, a bank of fog formed and spread across the water. I was in such a moral quandary now that I wished for a wind to come and sweep away the fog in my mind to give me clear vision.

Days earlier, when I realized I would not go to Medicine Lodge, I had asked Hiram Boyle, the newsagent, to get papers which might have accounts of the pow-wow on the Medicine River, and he had done so: *The New York Tribune, Herald Times, Cincinnati Commercial, Gazette,* and the local Medicine Lodge paper, *The Barber County Index.*

Now, from the papers spread out on my desk, I learned much, especially the account by the news correspondent and adventurer Henry M. Stanley, who had arrived in Medicine Lodge under the convoy of three companies of the 4th Artillery of the U.S. Seventh Cavalry in ten ambulances and a train of 30 wagons containing presents for the Indians, as well as miscellaneous stores. In his accounts, Stanley exhibited an inquiring mind and a felicitous style.

Stanley described the crossing of the Arkansas River south of Fort Larned. Even though the Arkansas had not flooded, the crossing had been difficult because of the several herds of cattle being driven to the site of the pow-wow and the bales of surplus military clothing, tied in huge bundles, which, it turned out, the Indians disdained and ignored

After the crossing of the river had been affected, the surplus clothing could not be re-baled and was left in heaps on the ground. I could not understand why the army thought the Indians would want old uniforms anyway, since the Indians were still furious about the Chivington Massacre, which, of course, had been carried out by the Colorado militia, not the army, but nevertheless by *white men* who had slaughtered Indian women and children.

After the first night, the train was joined by 60 more wagons and two companies of infantry, so the train had now grown to about two miles in length. The government had spared no effort or expense to provide the resources to ensure a successful peace conference. Thomas Murphy, Superintendent of Indian Affairs, had earlier hauled in, by six-mule teams, additional stores from Fort Larned, 60 miles to the north. It seemed to me that this was one of the biggest operations since the end of the war and exactly what people in the Missouri River Valley and the High Plains had been demanding for years to address the Indian problem.

All of the five major Plains Indian Nations were represented at the pow-wow. The Comanche, with Young Bear as Head Chief, were represented with 201 lodges (large communal tents); the Arapahoe with Little Raven, 171 lodges; the Kiowa, with Chief Satanta, 150 lodges; the Apaches led by Wolf Sleeve, 85 lodges; and the Cheyenne led by Chief

Black Kettle, the largest and the most feared of all the tribes, with 250 lodges. It was the Cheyenne who were the key to peace, people in Kansas believed.

According to the news accounts, the federal party contained a number of the West's best known white men: Kit Carson, the famous scout; Jesse Chisholm, the half-breed Cherokee who opened the Chisholm Trail; William Bent, founder of Bent's Fort on the Arkansas, and A. B. Boone, grandson of Daniel Boone, all men whom the Indians trusted, as well as other officials and at least four generals.

Then, according to Stanley, the speeches began—the chiefs and U. S. officials seated on a large canvas in the shade, everyone dressed in such a way as to impress the other participants. Commissioner Nathaniel Taylor welcomed and recognized each tribe, and interpreters explained Taylor's words to each tribe in the language of that particular tribe.

The chiefs all expressed a desire for peace, and testimony was taken to justify the payment of compensation for the Chivington Massacre. Henry Stanley was impressed with the picturesque beauty of the setting, although his description of the smell of dog stew prepared by the squaws raised questions about how to take his word "delectable." Nevertheless, the federal officials promised that all annuities would be paid and that the terms of the treaty would be kept by the white men.

The main terms of the treaty were agreed to by twenty Indian leaders and by the seven whites who represented the settlers and the federal government. Stanley found it curious that each Indian chief touched the top of the pen as their names were recorded, before each placed an X beside his name.

The treaty's terms were as follows:

That the Indians never capture or carry off from the settlements white women and children.

That the Indians permit the peaceable construction of any railroad not passing over their reservations as herein defined.

That they never kill or scalp white men or attempt to do them harm.

That they not attack any wagon trains, coaches, mules, or cattle belonging to the people of the United States.

That they agree to withdraw all opposition to the military posts now being established in the Western Territories.

In return, the United States government agreed to erect various buildings, such as schools, warehouses, houses, mills, and provide annuities of clothing and small amounts of money to the Indians. These seemed to be terms that the statesmen, politicians, and generals in Washington thought would bring peace to the plains, and one correspondent wrote that the treaty "opened a path for the civilization and transformation of a savage race into peaceful citizens." There was even an official photographer for the event. Of course, the Indians did not see themselves as a *savage race*, but as a nation whose land was being taken from them piece by piece. If asked for an opinion about the new peace treaty, I would have expressed some doubt about its success.

When I looked in the newspapers for the names of my friends Jim Hickok and Bill Cody—and others, like Custer, who knew the Plains—I became aware that they did not appear in the news accounts because they were not politicians or makers of policy. Had the wrong persons been sent to Medicine Lodge to negotiate with the Indians? Things might look very different out there on the prairie than they do in Washington.

To begin with, the Plains are different from the American East. Kansas is flat—flat as a flapjack, some had said—although that is an exaggeration since hilly areas like the Flint Hills occur in the southeastern part of our state, as well as in the state's western part, where the foothills of the mountains seem quietly to swell up as the land rises, as though God's creation were still incomplete and had not yet been finished at the end of the sixth day.

Moreover, much of the soil in our state is sand prairie, easier to work than the heavy clay soil of western Missouri, once the sod has been *busted* (as men say), and there are not many changes in elevation, so Kansas rivers are sluggish and without strong currents except in time of flood, when sand bars reach out to snag whatever is washed downstream. After a heavy rain, even the Kaw River outside Lawrence carves new and often surprising channels in the landscape.

The terms of the Medicine Lodge Treaty did not have many incentives for good behavior by the Indians. I saw that one correspondent had written that "the treaty not only later ensured the entrance of Colorado into the nation, but it also opened up New Mexico and Arizona to the white man."

That view seemed to be founded on hope or ignorance rather than experience on the frontier. What kind of future did the West have if it did not also include the welfare of the Indians? In times of drought, what could the Indians do to survive except raid farms, steal cattle, or attack the railroads? One thing I did know, if nothing else: this treaty was not good news for the Indians because no resources would be provided when the big bluestem and switchgrass were plowed up for crops, the last woods cut down, and the land that the Indians considered sacred fenced off for settlers, their crops, and sheep.

CHAPTER SEVENTEEN

WHEN I CROSSED into the Kansas Territory at the end of May in 1856, I felt as if I had been born again—not in the religious sense, of course, but because I thought I would be beginning a new life in the West. I have always been skeptical of religious conversion because I have seen men who confess to a profound spiritual change after church or a revival meeting, but continue to pursue their vain or vicious practices while claiming that baptism had washed them white as snow. This skepticism came from a father who was of a forgiving nature but also had a sharp eye for the shyster or hypocrite. He claimed he could detect a cheat by the tone of his voice or manner of his speech. Habitual liars are often jittery, he insisted, even when telling the truth. He also said that, above all else, a liar needed to have a good memory so as not to contradict himself.

During Territorial Days and later, I was well served by the careful habits of my father because much of the land west of the rude border town of Westport, Missouri, seemed to be inhabited by those left behind and forgotten by polite society—often the cheats and the indolent, the flotsam and jetsam of the country.

From my father too, I had learned about the principle of fairness, which I first thought of as a pagan virtue but which seemed, as I grew wiser, much like the Golden Rule I had heard about in church as a boy. From my father, I also learned to love and respect the law—not a particular law, of course, but that body of principles established by authority, society, or custom which governs the affairs of men.

In the 1860s we had fought a terrible Civil War and then dealt with an imperfect Reconstruction, since several groups of people had yet to be accommodated in this "reconstructed" nation—more than three million or so former slaves and that nation-within-a-nation, hundreds of thousands of Indians, spread across the southwest of our country and into Canada, a population subject to our laws only as formal treaty would allow. The Indians, our courts had determined, were not full citizens and therefore could not vote in federal elections, nor could they seek justice in the courts of a land which they believed was rightfully theirs.

If the difficult questions about Negroes and the Indians had not yet been addressed, a third group—white women of voting age—had been completely overlooked or perhaps cynically ignored by the white men who make our laws: wives, daughters, sisters, unmarried women of mature years, widows. How the rights of women and questions of female suffrage would be handled by the men in Congress, the courts (federal and state), and the legislative bodies of the states I could not hazard a guess.

After statehood in 1861, Kansas had recovered from a recession which was the aftermath of the war, as well as severe drought, leaving the state with little cash or capital for building or hiring, but settlers nevertheless continued to arrive, and competition for new institutions became fiercer and fiercer as the population of the state grew westward along the two major east/west rail lines: the Union Pacific, Eastern Division, and the Atchison, Topeka, and the Santa Fe, running parallel to the UP, about fifty miles to the south, following the old Santa Fe Trail out of Westport into Kansas.

In 1861, Topeka had been chosen as the capital in a state-wide election by white male property owners, and competition for the location of state institutions became even more frenzied as towns politicked and often cheated and bribed to acquire a public or private college. Additionally from June 1860 to November 1861, no rain at all fell in Kansas and a less propitious time to charter a state university could scarcely have been found than 1863, when the town of Lawrence, led by the former governor, Charles Robinson, and Manhattan were locked in a struggle for a state educational institution, along with a third town, Emporia, also in the eastern part of the state. Given the circumstances, Leavenworth was pleased to acquire the state penitentiary and leave the location of a college to the other bidders.

After more bribing and politicking, "the University of Kansas,'—not yet a physical entity but already divided into three parts like Caesar's Gaul—the agricultural college going to Manhattan, the state normal school to Emporia, with Lawrence receiving "the university," although what would be taught in Lawrence was not specified.

Perhaps "the university" was what Shakespeare calls the *remainder viands,* the uneaten food left on the plate when the meal is over. Moreover, the original charter for the university absolved the legislature from providing the financial support that an educational institution needed to develop and prosper, especially with a handful of denominational schools in Kansas also seeking what little money was left in people's pocketbooks. So, where then would funding come from?

Behind the posturing and platitudes in the legislature, the citizens of Kansas now watched and waited to see whether the Indians would abide by the new treaty agreed to at Medicine Lodge, but I also kept an eye on the white men, whom I thought a greater threat to stability and peace on the plains than the Indians. I talked to Eli Foster to try to learn what was being said in the bank and to Charles Robinson, who owned land on the hill behind the town, which everyone now called by its new name, Mount Oread, although I preferred one of the earlier names like the Devil's Backbone.

Eli reported the gossip of the common folk in town while Governor Robinson looked at politics through the lenses of the investor, but by October, their views were pretty much the same, both cautiously optimistic but wary. Lawrence had been rebuilt following Quantrill's Raid, the new Eldridge House Hotel had opened on Massachusetts Street, and the first students had entered the single, recently completed stone building that comprised the University of Kansas. Having seen university buildings in New England, I thought the academic building in Lawrence a very modest beginning, but it did, in fact, exist, surrounded by treeless prairie and entered by sunbaked mud roads from town through fields of heavy-headed sunflowers.

I had to remind myself that it was little more than a decade since I had come to the Kansas Territory and witnessed—and wrote about—the Battle of Black Jack, where John Brown routed a company of Border Ruffians. Now, ten years on, the eastern part of the *State* was peacefully settled as far as Abilene and Salina in the central part.

Today, a single building stood on the campus, fifty feet square and three stories high, and now there was a faculty of three—all male—and fifty-five students, although not a single one of them was academically prepared for college study or qualified for admission. So, in the first year, students were nurtured in a Preparatory Department while the lone building was finished as the funds on hand allowed.

The three professors—Elial Rice, David H. Robinson, and Francis Snow—were hired after much disagreement and bargaining; Robinson's specialty was Latin, although he was competent in Greek and ancient culture, an excellent appointment. Francis H. Snow was proficient in ancient languages and culture, but also loved entomology, and if there was anything that Kansas could offer, it was a richness of insects, especially in late summer, around harvest time. Professor Snow took students on collecting trips around the state and quickly established himself as a favorite for his wit and enthusiasm.

I found him to be congenial and was impressed that, in our conversations, he made ancient civilization seem fresh and vital, as I am certain he did in the classroom. He delighted in telling anecdotes about the Chelsea Physic Garden, a teaching facility for apothecaries near London, England, where he had studied. He insisted that students learn the proper Latin names for common plants and insects, causing some people to mock him for pretentiousness but endearing him to his students.

Who knew there was so much to learn about the locusts that could strip a Kansas farmer's fields from reading about locusts in the Old Testament. Yet Snow was no stern materialist or pedant like Mr. Gradgrind from Charles Dickens' *Hard Times,* squeezing the life out of everything he touched. When students left Snow, they seemed to walk away with smiles on their faces.

If the university was fortunate in the employment of Professors Robinson and Snow, Elial Rice was another matter. Because Charles Robinson had assisted the university with several loans and land swaps, he carefully watched over what he regarded as *his* creation, perhaps in too paternalistic a way, in the opinion of his enemies. Professor Rice was said to exhibit "superior airs" and was accused of spending too much time and energy promoting his wife for a faculty position. Whether he was in the wrong or not, the question seemed to turn the faculty and perhaps some of the students against the dour, unfortunate Rice.

The curriculum for the preparatory students demanded two years of Latin (Caesar, Cicero, and Virgil) and one year of Greek (female students could substitute French for Greek). By the autumn of 1867 (as the great pow-wow was drawing the Plains Indians to Medicine Lodge), there had been a few dropouts, and the total number of students enrolled in the university had, in fact, declined.

Detractors in town, like Jeremiah Whitman, jested and jeered at the university's struggles, but there were flickers of hope, because the Board of Regents had begun transforming the barren hilltop above the town by planting five hundred trees and Osage hedges, and grading the grounds to beautify the campus. With ten rooms in the building for classes, offices, a library, a laboratory, and storage, all that was lacking was central heating; each room had its own stove for warmth. These were "hard times" indeed in Kansas, with few luxuries in the new university.

After one year, two students were succeeding in the college course, both girls. One was Henrietta Black, described as a "prodigy of scholarship" by the faculty, who, to everyone's surprise, suddenly married Professor David Robinson, thus in one act depriving the university of its entire junior class. Jeremiah suggested in jest that only women of mature years and past childbearing be admitted henceforth as "frosh." In spite of debt, drought, and female entanglements, the university in its second year seemed invigorated by its struggles, and Charles Robinson was even observed on occasion to smile.

Nevertheless, during that autumn most of us in Lawrence felt that the university badly needed to increase enrollments, a goal that could only be reached by enlarging the faculty before the new academic year began, but now, surprisingly, the disaffected Professor Rice assisted the university by accepting a job at Baker University, a small denominational university nearby in Baldwin, Kansas, taking his contentious wife with him. The university moved quickly to offer the vacant position of chancellor to John Fraser, and the faculty and the inhabitants of the town celebrated his selection.

While Lawrence was abuzz with the announcement of the new chancellor's plans to address the university's many needs—a larger budget, better instructional space, and more faculty—the golden feet of autumn had silently stolen through the woods and across the farmland of eastern Kansas. The sumac began to turn scarlet (as it had done in 1864 on that bitterly cold Sunday morning during the Battle of Westport, when ice glazed the water barrels, and the Kansas militia, poorly equipped, fearful, and untested in combat, trotted into battle against the invading Confederate cavalry of General Sterling Price).

Ever since I was a boy in St. Louis, I have liked the change of seasons, with new smells and sounds as nature itself turns like the works of a clock, and mankind studies how the fruits of human enterprise can be used for the advancement of society. In rural areas the diurnal changes are deeply felt: patterned frost on window panes, the squawks of chickens as a farmer's wife steals into the henhouse to gather eggs, the heady smell of wood fires across town, the calls of wild ducks flying south, and the barking of dogs when the men from the abattoir arrive to carry the domestic animals to slaughter. Other sounds joined the rural chorus: trees being felled for fuel, animals shod at the farrier, and teams of horses or mules carrying the products of the farms to town.

With the coming of cold weather at the end of October, Big Ears King had lighted the potbellied stove in the tack room of his livery stable, and the aroma of freshly brewed coffee filled the air each morning, mixing with the familiar odors of horses and manure. In the morning chill, Little Joe Oscar and Davey Weekly, in town from the horse farm, warmed their hands near the stove and blew on their fingers for good measure.

"Nip in the air today," Joe Oscar proclaimed to his small group of auditors, who nodded and grunted in agreement. "One of the earliest freezes in years." Like many Indians, Joe Oscar—a half-breed—was known to be laconic, as though he were trying out the white man's language to see whether it suited him, before speaking at length.

"Isn't it about time for Prudence to produce a pup?" Jeremiah inquired. Something about Jeremiah's question told me it was meant to be jocular, not insulting. "Looks like one is about to pop out any minute now, and cry for his supper."

"Come sit a spell in front of the stove," Big Ears said to me. "Thaw out your bones." He smiled and pointed to the empty chair beside him, but I shook my head because I wanted to stand so I could feel the warmth of the stove on my back.

"It's been an anxious time for Eli," I said, "But Prudence is healthier now than she was before." Everyone knew what I meant when I said *before*, some of them probably thinking it bad luck to mention the death of the other baby, but, of course, I knew that was only superstition. "Hannah has made her walk out every day as Doc Gafney insisted she should. He says the baby could come at any time."

"Well, that *is* good to know then. Should be just like caring for a sow whose time has come," Weekly exclaimed, "but I would not put it that way to Eli," Weekly let out a hearty laugh, and the others joined him, for Ed Whitman had joined the circle in the tack room moments before, along with Jeremiah and his older brother, Desmond, both of whom had grown up in Lawrence.

"So how are you finding Colorado?" Big Ears asked Desmond, who had poured himself a cup of coffee. "Guess you got plenty of snow already."

"Already snowing in the mountains, I 'speck. Winter comes early out there, you know, but maybe I'm just used to it now. Some of the highest peaks keep their snow even in the summer." After speaking, Desmond loosened his cravat and took the empty chair. We had heard much about Desmond's success as an outfitter for gold miners—some of them still called "fifty-niners"—even though the Colorado gold rush of 1858 and '59 had lasted only about two years, and far more prospectors had gone bust than became millionaires.

No need to question Ed Whitman about his older son because we had known Desmond and his brother Jeremiah since they were boys, the older brother cautious and steady, the younger, Jeremiah, rash and headstrong, often improvident. Since he had missed the time when a fortune could be made by taking risks and speculating, Desmond had instead invested in a partnership with a friend in an outfitting business and put his profits back into the business, which he expanded through contracts he had signed with the Colorado militia during the war.

Now Desmond was a merchant in Golden City in the foothills of the rugged pine-covered, mountain chain which was now crossed by telegraph lines and railroads that connected the Great Plains to California and the states of the Pacific Coast, hundreds of miles in distance, once part of what the newspapers called the Great American Desert, but now filling up with roads, towns, and farms of all kinds and sizes. "Finished my business here yesterday," Desmond said. "Taking the evening train

to Denver. Just came by to bid you adieu," he declared, shaking hands
with his friends from the past. Many of the men had known him since
he was a boy.

As it happened, selling supplies to prospectors was far more lucrative
than *being* a prospector, as Desmond quickly figured out, for in a short
time he had made himself a wealthy man, based on his knowledge of that
stubborn but indefatigable pack animal—the mule—which I believed
had been instrumental in settling the West and possibly even in helping
us to win the war of the Rebellion. Long-eared soldiers, many people had
called them jocularly. I had heard or read that Ben Franklin had wanted
to put the wild turkey on U.S. currency instead of the American Eagle,
and probably on the Great Seal of our country as well. In fact, I liked
the symbolism and the symmetry of both the mule and the turkey on a
twenty-dollar gold piece, the mule winking at the turkey conspiratorially.

Suddenly, there was commotion in the streets, too early for the arrival
of the morning mail or for the sheriff to be arresting a drunk who had
gotten a second wind with the dawn. Dogs were barking, and several
people had noticed the activity. Immediately, I thought of the earlier
birth at the Foster home and the dead baby, a tragic mischance. This
time, Eli, Prudence, Doc Gafney, and the midwife were prepared for the
baby. What could possibly go wrong with such a common occurrence as
a birth? Well, especially on the frontier—pretty much anything, as we
had seen the year before.

"You and Eli go way back, do you not?" Davey Weekly asked, the
pitch of his voice making the utterance into a question, supplementing
the syntax.

"Partners since the Westport campaign. Well, I also had a squad of
young militiamen entrusted to my care since I was ten or so years older
than the boys who joined up with me. Hid behind rail fences in the
cornfields and pastures 'til they learned soldiering. Tried to stay dry and
warm and find food for ourselves . . . and the mules and the officers'
horses. Officers rode and militiamen marched." The commotion had
died down, but my listeners still kept an eye on me. "You see, Eli was the
quartermaster, so I was eager to make friends with him."

"What about Hickok?" Ed Whitman asked. "He wasn't in the militia
with you, was he?"

"No, not in the militia," I quickly responded. "An old friend. Did see him after the battle, though. He was a Union spy, you know, though how he could employ disguises never made much sense to me, given his size and his distinctive drooping mustache."

"Stealthy as an Indian too," said Little Joe Oscar, the half-breed, mimicking an Indian sneaking about on tiptoes. All the listeners were seized with laughter, especially Jeremiah, but Joe's poker face remained expressionless. He missed his calling, I thought; he could have been on the stage in a farce. Since I was present, Big Ears could not claim to have intimate knowledge of Hickok's whereabouts, so he asked a question instead.

"Where *is* Hickok and his sidekick, Cody?" Big Ears asked with nonchalance.

"Well, Hickok is a U.S. deputy marshal now," I answered. "Captures deserters and mule thieves—wanted for theft of government property." This was all I knew about Hickok at present, and *who* knew where Cody was. And so, I followed the others outside into a bright and frosty morning. The telegrapher's boy, Orville, waved to me from the board sidewalk in front of the Western Union office.

"This one's for you, sir!" he shouted as he handed me the envelope. Expecting a message from Russell Downing, I tore it open and unfolded the slip of paper to see that it was not from Downing but from Colonel Maypole.

Need your help, the message read. *Will arrive Thursday. Staying Eldridge House. -BM*

CHAPTER EIGHTEEN

ON THE APPOINTED day, as I awaited the arrival of Colonel Benjamin Maypole, I paced the lobby of the new Eldridge House—as fine a hotel as any in Chicago, the locals said—and wished the town could settle on a scheme to complete the drainage and paving of Massachusetts Avenue. Wooden blocks had been tried, but they had sunk into the mud and disintegrated, the mud having gained another triumph. Despite the elegance of the lobby and the furnishings, the Eldridge House still seemed to me more like a hostelry in a frontier town with its dirt street and board sidewalks.

My mind was troubled by the urgency of the telegram: what assistance did the Colonel need, and what could he expect me to provide? Clouds stretched over Massachusetts like unbleached wool waiting to be washed and carded. This slate-gray day did not show off Lawrence as the hot, bright sunshine of summer would have done, since the November light seemed not to draw colors from objects, but to leave them like balls of laundry pulled from the washtub. I longed for a fluffy cloud bank on the western horizon, which the sun could set aflame in red and vermilion.

Standing in the lobby, I looked around to determine whether the Colonel might already have registered, there now being three rail lines serving Lawrence: the Union Pacific from St. Louis, the Atchison, Topeka, and Santa Fe from Chicago, and the Leavenworth, Lawrence, and Galveston (Jim Lane's old railroad, a north-south line which had recently completed a wooden bridge across the Kaw). He could be on either of the east-west lines, so instead of flipping a coin, I asked Big Ears whether he would meet one train while I continued to wait at the hotel for passengers from the other.

The train whistle was now as common a feature of life in Kansas and Missouri as were the church bells, which on Sunday mornings called the faithful to worship, and people in Lawrence set their pocket watches by the train whistles. Now, metallic noises from the Santa Fe depot several blocks from the hotel indicated the arrival of the two o'clock train from St. Louis and the East.

Thus far, the year had been eventful, and I wondered if the Colonel would bring news that we would remember as equally significant. Two days before, we had witnessed the wedding of our daughter Phoebe Brown to Isaac Worthy. Hannah and I had hoped that this young couple would be married in our church, but Phoebe insisted that they take their vows in the Negro church in East Lawrence, which had welcomed them into their fellowship. Hannah and I were happy to accede to their wishes because we believed the white congregation of our church might have raised objections to its use for a Negro nuptial.

After the ceremony, Hannah and I had stood in the street to cheer the newlywed couple as they began life together. As it happened, we were among the few white persons at the ceremony. The night before the wedding, Prudence had given birth to a son—Thomas Ezra Foster—and Hannah had stood beside Phoebe as one of the matrons of honor, Leona Sonnet, the other.

Two momentous events at the same time, and I wondered whether the Colonel might provide the third, since superstitious persons thought significant events often happened in threes. I, of course, did not believe this, any more than I believed the old wives' tales that the new science was disproving about the age and geological history of the Earth, matters which should be subject to observation, testing, and analysis.

Currently under debate in our town was the geological nature of petrified bones of ancient animals now turned to stone that lie beneath the earth in Kansas. I knew from my studies in college that in its account of the earth's age, the Bible is neither a comprehensive book of science nor a reliable chronicle of history. Many people, of course, disagree with me.

Now I stood in the street outside the Eldridge House, awaiting the Colonel's arrival. The marriage of Phoebe and Isaac—in which I had had a small role as father of the bride—had filled me with joy and pride, but now I wanted to know why the Colonel had come to Kansas and what help he needed or expected from me.

As I examined these questions, a train whistle sounded, announcing an arrival at the new Santa Fe depot several blocks away in East Lawrence. In a matter of minutes, my wait would be over, since Colonel Maypole and a finely dressed lady had already appeared in King's buggy. Did the Colonel have a wife? I had assumed he was unmarried, although I could not remember what had given me this belief. Nodding to me, the Colonel helped his companion from the buggy as a member of the hotel's staff snatched up the bags and whisked them inside.

"Welcome to Lawrence," I said, addressing both persons as I made a slight bow because it seemed the thing to do. I immediately felt a sense of embarrassment, as though I were playing a minor role in a melodrama on stage and had forgotten my lines.

"So, *this* is the renowned news writer and friend of Russell Downing," the woman remarked in a cultivated accent. "I am happy to meet you, sir," she said formally.

"Allow me to introduce my sister, Ezra," the Colonel announced. "This is Verity Maypole Boyle!" As the Colonel lifted his head, the family resemblance became obvious. Verity had the same angular face as her brother, the same whitish-blonde hair, an attractive lady about my own age—that is, about thirty or so, perhaps ten or twelve years younger than her brother, but sterner of countenance than he.

"Shall we have a cup of tea or a sherry while we get acquainted?" I stammered as the Colonel looked to the reception desk.

"Later," he quickly answered. I began to suspect that he was as embarrassed at the awkwardness of our meeting as I was. When he took her cloak, I saw that Verity wore a silk dress of so deep a blue that it appeared almost black under the gas light which burned in the hotel lobby on an overcast day, regardless of the time.

"I believe I notice the family resemblance," I commented with a smile, and the visitors seemed to take my observation as the compliment it was intended to be. "Sometimes we have clear, crisp days in November, but we shall *not* have such today, I am afraid." In the street, the commercial activities of the town continued under darkening skies as the workday began to make way for evening. In the failing light, the cold chilled my bones.

"A lovely hotel, Mr. Middleton," she said, "and it must be rather new because Lawrence was burned to the ground in Quantrill's raid in '63, was it not? I know a bit of Kansas history, you see."

"It was, madam," I hastened to reply. "And Mr. Shalor Eldridge rebuilt on the site of his earlier hotel. In fact, this is the *third* hotel to occupy this spot. Kansans are stubborn folk. Like the Missouri mules of legend," I added with a laugh. "Of course, I am myself a man of Missouri, so I may be allowed the jest, I hope."

Her manner seemed stiff and haughty, and I tried to think of some noble person with whom to compare her, and could think only of Queen Victoria of England, perhaps alike in haughtiness, but utterly different, the Queen being short, dumpy, and dour in photographs or etchings in the newspapers, nothing like the slim and elegant Verity Maypole.

Of course, good manners forbade me from asking questions of the Colonel's sister. All would be explained in due course, I assumed, perhaps when Hannah joined the Missourians and me for supper at the hotel. I was now even more curious about Verity than I had been about the Colonel when I first came to know him.

"A man is known by the company he keeps," Verity said uncertainly. After a pause, she quickly looked at me. "I understand that you are a student of literature as well as a news correspondent and an attorney. Do you also write about the stage?"

"When I do, my friend—*your* friend too, I believe—Russell strikes out the reference, although I can on occasion slip in an allusion. Homer nods, they say, and, yes, on occasion, even Downing does!" I laughed, but the lady ignored my attempt at humor, perhaps misunderstanding my jest.

"The long and short of it is, we need your legal advice and common sense, Ezra," the Colonel said suddenly. "It seems Verity is in a bit of a pickle, not of her making, by the way, and our attorney has thrown up his hands. She received some very bad advice from her husband, the late Mr. Boyle."

I attempted to offer my condolences, which she accepted without indicating whether the loss was recent, although I noticed that she twisted the handkerchief she held and averted her gaze.

"I believe she is still in some distress," the Colonel explained. "Let us continue our discussion at supper, if doing so would not bore or upset your wife." I assured him that it would not and said that Hannah's presence might make Mrs. Boyle less uncomfortable, and so we parted to meet again in several hours in the dining room.

Later, when we came down for supper, the last light had long since vanished from the western sky. As I knew she would, Hannah had prepared dinner with her usual care. Indeed, her red-blonde hair was tied back with a magenta scarf, the reddish purple bringing out a subtle shade in her dress. Her life out of doors gave her complexion a healthy freshness which Mrs. Boyle did not possess. Of course, I have always taken pride in Hannah's physical beauty as well as her character and intelligence.

When we met for dinner, our Missouri visitors seemed eager to learn more about Kansas and why Hannah had chosen to leave Missouri for a state so recently admitted to the Union. "I am led to believe you are also a Missourian," Mrs. Boyle said to Hannah when we were all seated at the table in the paneled dining room. The table was beautifully laid, cut flowers, even in winter, were at the center of the table in a glass vase, the color of the juice of cherries.

"Yes, but when I came up the river with my new husband, I became a Kansan in an instant," Hannah said, "a woman of the prairie. Although the same could be said of many pioneer wives who journeyed west with husbands." She smiled graciously at the Colonel's wife. "I admire the spirit and sacrifice of the women who came west."

"You must have known Mr. Middleton well . . . to undertake such a perilous adventure with him?"

"I had known him only a matter of minutes when I made the decision to follow him to Kansas." Hannah paused for a moment, still looking across the table. "I was a schoolgirl, you see, but we did not come to know each other at a school dinner or at dances." Hannah paused again, and I perceived the Colonel and his sister leaning forward a bit. "We met briefly and then immediately parted. I wondered if I would ever see him again, although I hoped I would. Travel was difficult in those days. Not only distance, but often violence on the Kansas Border too. Ezra wrote about twenty letters to me over many months expressing his love." She paused again. "With the twenty-first letter, I said 'Yes,' and so Ezra came back to St. Louis for me, we were married, and I journeyed to Lawrence to begin life with him."

"With no regrets, I assume?" Mrs. Boyle asked with a smile. At last, a genuine smile from this reserved lady, I thought. Would there be more?

"No regrets at all," Hannah said. "None at all, except that now I have many projects to attend to—suffrage for women and protection of their rights, a homeland for the Indians, land for landless former slaves, and better education for all Kansans. The list goes on and on." She shook her head and laughed, and her fiery hair fell across her shoulders. "So many things that need to be undertaken. I am breathless listening to this rehearsal of the things I wish to do."

"Perhaps we could take these one by one," the Colonel said, breaking into a smile. "Are you always in such a hurry, Mrs. Middleton? All of these matters are of interest to me too."

"Yes, and it's Hannah, please," my wife said. "I hope to be your friend, Colonel, not a commercial associate. You need not be so formal with me." Her smile took away any impropriety or rudeness, and the Colonel seemed won over by my wife's candor. "Perhaps you think me forward. If so, I apologize for my lack of manners. Perhaps Kansans are simply bolder in society than Missourians. And I am fully a Kansan now."

"Hannah is accustomed to speaking her mind," I explained. "One always knows where he—or she—stands in conversation with her. Candor has always been at the heart of our marriage too."

More travelers had entered the Eldridge, and some waited to be seated in the dining room. Along with the new patrons came a breath or two of cold air, causing the candles on the tables to flicker whenever a waiter entered the room. It seemed as though ghosts from the time of war and destruction still lurked in the shadows, even though the hotel was sparkling new.

After the wine had been poured and our supper ordered, I was eager to turn to what had brought the Missourians to Lawrence. "What is the nature of your difficulty, Mrs. Boyle?" I inquired, "And how may I assist you?"

"Well, Ezra, it's flat-out fraud, if I may be blunt . . . and the treachery of a villain," the Colonel said forcefully, his voice a harsh whisper. I remembered that *villain* was a favorite word of the Colonel's to describe an opponent of *any* kind, and I listened carefully while wondering if Verity would be allowed to speak for herself. She seemed languid, which I believed to be the result of her journey from Missouri. Even speedy travel by train can be wearisome.

We waited until the waiter who had served us had moved away from our table. At the earliest opportunity, the Colonel quickly took the floor while I waited to see whether the lady would speak for herself or defer to her brother, inhibited perhaps by his presence. I was determined to hear the story in the sister's own words if I could—as in the courtroom, we want to allow the defendant to tell his story and hear that story told in his own voice.

Thus, I addressed my question to Verity, for the first time calling her by her Christian name. "Who is the villain, Verity, and *what* has he done?" She glanced at her brother, took a deep breath, and began her tale. Three other tables in the large room were occupied, but those diners were far enough removed to allow us some privacy.

"Someone you may know," she said quickly to me. "He lives in Lawrence, although is often in St. Louis, it seems." Her voice was strong, sharpened by her anger, as though she had been waiting to be asked to tell her story. "His name is Vitruvius Bird!" Now there was fire in her voice and in her eyes too! "I have not met him, though I wish to do so."

The question seemed to have encouraged Hannah, although, if truth be told, she was always ready with an opinion on some controversial question and eager to voice it. "Of all the matters that need to be addressed by modern society, the *chief* one is suffrage for women," she said. "Even more than land for Negroes or a permanent home for Indians! But I am truly sorry for interrupting you, Verity." I shot a look at Hannah, and she nodded to me. I hoped that she would hold her tongue so that I could hear more from Verity.

"Since the Fourteenth Amendment, which enfranchised the Negroes included only men, *white* women have continued to be denied their full rights as citizens," Hannah declared and put a finger to her lips to show that she intended to stop talking, but she continued like a runaway carriage. "I know there is deep religious and social concern about giving women the vote, and the Bible is often cited to support denying suffrage to women. Even reasonable men may not admit their own reluctance to question the matter—but to *my* mind it is actually a pigheaded refusal to admit their own prejudices." Those of us at the table seemed surprised at Hannah's frankness in the expression of her views—except, of course, for me.

"Perhaps if we lived in western Kansas, where renegade warriors still raided on occasion—despite the treaty signed at Medicine Lodge—we would think the Indian question the most pressing," the Colonel said in his deep voice, his hand resting on the table beside his plate.

"Women simply want the rights given to *all* citizens by our Constitution!" Verity said in the kind of whisper used on stage, which does not seem to carry beyond a small group, although the theater audience, of course, can hear it. I was surprised that Verity had spoken so bravely on a controversial matter and expressed a view which would have shocked many. Hannah, it seems, had encouraged Verity to speak her mind.

"Shakespeare's women—some of them—insist they be allowed to speak for themselves. And *choose* for themselves too!" I commented, hoping to entice Verity into speaking her mind, but fearing it would also encourage Hannah.

"Well, how long will it take? As long as the Negroes had to wait for freedom?" Hannah waited, but no one attempted to answer her rhetorical question. There was now a line from a play floating around in my mind. It came from one of my favorite comedies, one of Hannah's too. On our first meeting years before, I had identified Hannah as "Lady Disdain," the outspoken and loquacious Beatrice in *Much Ado about Nothing*, that witty comedy of deception and mistaken identity. In intimate moments, I would even now refer to her in jest as Lady Disdain.

For what stayed in my mind was not a clever rejoinder by Beatrice but a single line from a song sung by a minor character called Balthazar: "the fraud of men was ever so." The fraud of men!

"Fraud" was also the word the Colonel had used to describe Bird's actions and, of course, I remembered how Bird had attempted to cheat the Widow Cornish in the sale of her farm. Now he seemed to be at it again . . . or worse, unless someone could stop him.

"What was the fraud precisely?" I addressed the question to Verity since I had now put myself in the role of her attorney. "Please tell me the whole story. Leave nothing out."

I bent forward and gave her what I hoped was a reassuring smile as I pulled out my commonplace book—what might have been called a diary by more fashionable people in the East. I motioned to my dinner companions to begin to eat and took a morsel or two from my own plate while keeping my eyes locked on Verity. I felt she trusted me, but I needed her to tell me everything so I could record it for possible use later. Hannah and the Colonel did not speak but politely consumed what was on their plates and smiled at Verity from time to time.

"This was a time of swapping or buying land while the counties were being organized," Verity said, choosing her words carefully. "Although we were Missourians, my husband thought money could be made on land speculation in Kansas. Towns were looking to raise money to build rail lines because railroads promoted growth and prosperity for towns. It was like another gold rush—except the commodity now was land, and there was intense competition, even though, paradoxically, there was land in abundance."

Verity smiled and continued to address me, although her listeners at the table hung on her every word as though each of them had money invested in some risky or questionable land scheme. I remembered that in the past, Governor Charles Robinson had said to me on several occasions, "It's always about the land, Ezra!" And I am still sure that he was right.

"So, who owned the land?" Hannah asked, taking a bit of potato on her fork. "The Indians?"

"Well, much of it was public land once, I guess," Verity responded to her as I wrote notes in my commonplace book. "Just empty land, but most now privately owned, often by a railroad. The war was recently over, and, as people said, it was the 'Wild West.' Counties were being organized in the western half of the state, and every little town wanted its own rail line to pursue prosperity, because more people meant more commerce and more jobs."

I remembered the years after peace came as a time of fluctuating prices and expansion. Towns could vote taxes, which went directly to the railroad, or buy shares in the railroad, or purchase its bonds. Sometimes, a railroad official would plot out a new town and sell lots to raise money. It transpired that whenever land changed hands, somebody made a profit, often a large one.

Of course, I did not speculate myself any more than I would have gambled my savings at poker—like my friend Jim Hickok, who frequently won vast amounts of money at the gaming table and just as often lost everything. With a family to feed, one becomes more conservative, more careful in his actions. Almost everyone was gambling ther—and not just with cards; men would bet on anything. If they lost today, they would win tomorrow! Or so they believed.

"Poker and whiskey were the loves of my late husband's life, as is the case with many men." Verity paused for a moment before speaking again. "He was an Irishman, of course." I found it difficult to keep from laughing, but, as we say, it was no laughing matter for Verity. "He was much given to drink," she said succinctly, and the Colonel nodded at the sentiment and reached out to take his sister's hand.

"He was sold bonds by Vitruvius Bird, altogether worth at least twenty thousand dollars," the Colonel said, obviously impatient to conclude the story.

"Well, worth nothing!" Verity interrupted. "We paid more than twenty thousand dollars for those pieces of worthless paper." In the telling, I had expected Verity to break down in tears, but I had misjudged the depth of her passion and strength of her character. "Damn him to Hell! Bird!" She cried out in an angry voice, and the other diners reacted in shock to this breach of decorum, as did the waiters and a person whom I assumed had come from the reception desk.

After Verity's outburst, the four of us moved to a small room with a fire burning in the hearth, and with a pot of tea to restore her, Verity continued her tale. "Vitruvius Bird and three other men had sold fraudulent county bonds in Comanche County, a county just then being organized, and populated only by jackrabbits, coyotes, and prairie dogs. For the election, the names of *bona fide* inhabitants who wished to organize the county were not, in fact, collected according to statute, but were merely copied from a hotel register in St Joseph, Missouri, and one of the four, Charlie Vertue, was thus fraudulently elected to the Kansas legislature. He was then foreman on Bird's farm and still works for Bird, I believe."

Verity continued, "In the legislature, he got a law passed authorizing the County to issue twenty thousand dollars in bonds, and these bonds were then sold to a speculator, one Alexander Falmouth of London,

England. Since objections had been made to the bonds, my foolish husband was convinced to buy them at a discount to keep the price from falling. So, we owned worthless bonds and were now in debt more than twenty thousand dollars."

On Verity's face, the wrath had been replaced by a look of despair, while the Colonel's red face revealed the depth of his choler. "In those days, there were no state or national banking laws governing a private institution like the one Mr. Boyle patronized," Verity explained, "and Kansas as yet had no bank examiners to ensure that financial institutions were solvent."

Of course, the cheats could be taken to court, I assumed, but there would be costs, and it seemed unlikely to me that the Boyles could ever recover any of the $20,000 they now owed to Falmouth since he had not behaved unethically or illegally in any way. These cheats had operated within the law and had used Boyle's desire for quick profit against him. Some men steal with the wave of a revolver, others with the flourish of a pen.

I believed that the Maypoles could have attempted to sue Bird, but I could find no grounds to sue the Englishman. I promised to go to Charles Robinson for advice and assistance, but my friend was no longer part of the Kansas government, and since he was not an attorney, I did not see how he could be helpful. I apologized to the Maypoles that I could not relieve their financial distress, but assured them that I would represent them at no charge if they wished to pursue some further legal action. I felt that I had failed them, but what recourse did I have? As an attorney, I had promised to uphold the law. My hands were tied. Bird and Vertue seemed to have the law on their side.

After putting the two Missourians on the afternoon train the next day, I was relieved to return to the subject Hannah and I had discussed the previous evening, *The Merchant of Venice*, a play about bonds and debt, disguise, trickery, and vengeance. Hannah and I had exchanged looks during our dinner with the Maypoles, but Lawrence had little in common with the Venice of the play, and, in any case, I was no Portia, whose legal knowledge could defeat a bloodthirsty opponent, nor was my clever wife someone who could trap a villainous Shylock by turning his own legal terms against him.

Not all the Jews in the play are presented as diabolical, of course, and I do not feel that Shakespeare necessarily wants the audience to side with the Christians against the Jews. In our discussion, Hannah expressed sympathy for Shylock, but I stopped short of seeing the Jew as entirely sympathetic.

In the play, of course, Shylock is a moneylender and a usurer—not a merchant like Antonio—and I agreed that the Christians are as morally reprehensible as the vengeful Shylock. Shakespeare has turned the expected morality upside-down, as he occasionally does. I have, however, always thought *The Merchant of Venice* to be a good play for a fallen and imperfect world like our own.

When I argued about the play with my father many years ago, I had not yet experienced or understood the guile, treachery, and deceit of those in power. Of course, at that time, I did not yet know about the evil of Bloody Bill Anderson or Little Archie Clement, *real* villains who scalped and cut off the noses and ears of their dead enemies.

CHAPTER NINETEEN

ON THE NIGHT after the Maypoles left Lawrence, I slept soundly beside Hannah, disappointed that I had been of so little assistance, but still believing I had done everything I could for them within the law. I was again reminded how little control we often have over events in our lives. At the end of Shakespeare's most painful tragedy, after killing his wife, Othello asks: "Who can control his fate?" The noblest and most powerful character in the play, called "all in all sufficient," has been with ease destroyed by his trusted subordinate, the evil Iago.

Toward morning, I awoke, our bedroom still and cold as a tomb, not certain whether it was the smell of burning wood or the noise in the streets that had roused me from sleep. In the dozen or so years I had lived in Kansas, knocks on the door at night, the calls of the watch, border guard, or militia often were an unwelcome aubade, although after the bloody conflict of 1861 ended, the unexpected night noises declined sharply in frequency.

As my mind cleared, I became certain a fire had occurred—not in Lawrence but somewhere in the farmland which surrounded the town. Once I threw open the front door and, covered only by a quilt fashioned by Hannah, walked barefoot over our dried lawn, I could feel snow or sleet beneath my feet: the winter's first dusting covered the ground. I could see riders and wagons rushing toward the Wakarusa, which flowed quietly to its juncture with the Kaw downriver around the shoulder of Mount Oread.

"Where's the fire?" I yelled at two of the riders. "Not in town, is it?"

"Out by Blanton's bridge!" a voice from the darkness called in response. "Along the Wakarusa!" Blanton's bridge, of course, was the old wooden bridge over the tributary of the Kaw, dating from Territorial Days, the time which had been called "Bleeding Kansas" in the newspapers, when Free-State settlers and bushwhackers began the conflict that quickly developed into open warfare.

Near the shallow river was the horse farm of Captain Dan Cornish, now owned by Davey Weekly, who bred the finest riding horses in Douglas County. I was immediately concerned that some of the buildings on his farm might have gone up in flames. A conflagration could endanger lives, but it would also ruin Weekly if it reached his horse barns.

Rushing back inside, I snatched up my trousers and put my bare feet in the boots where Hannah had placed them—ready for me to "throw on" quickly, as we say. Everyone on the frontier had such a drill for an emergency, and all members of a family knew their parts in the drill. Our eldest child, Phoebe, was recently married, but I thought our new son-in-law, Isaac Worthy, probably would have heard the ruckus and run to help, coming from their home in East Lawrence.

When I neared the Wakarusa, I realized that men were assembling to fight the fire in the lane that ran toward the bridge—a lane too narrow, rough, and uneven to bring fire equipment from Lawrence—so they carried axes, shovels, and buckets to contain the fire. In the firelight, I now saw many men I knew—Davey Weekly, Little Joe Oscar, Big Ears King—and also farm hands whose faces I recognized. The fire seemed not to have spread to the Weekly buildings, but Vitruvius Bird's house was heavily damaged, probably lost, and his other buildings threatened by the ravenous flames, which ate through the dry grass and weeds that took over Bird's farm each summer. A few grains of sleet hissed on glowing embers on Bird's property.

Horses that had carried men from town as well as nearby farms whinnied in fear and excitement as riders struggled to control them. Goats and a sheep or two scampered back from the fire to sound angry bleats, before standing in stupid defiance in a spot they had vacated only minutes before.

Then one wall of Bird's house collapsed, throwing bits of scorched wood and embers into the air, the embers a glowing fountain of gold.

Luckily, there was no wind to spread the flames into the dry woods, and most of the burning weeds had already been stamped out by men from Weekly's farm, working under the direction of Lawrence's new sheriff, Chet Oatman, who was fighting his first fire in town and seemed uncertain about what to do.

"How'd this get going?" I asked Davey, pulling him by the arm.

"Couldn't say," Davey replied, wiping his brow with the dirty sleeve of his shirt. "Bird's never around when things need to get done. Haven't seen Charlie Vertue either."

"Think Bird's around someplace?" I asked and got only an exhausted grunt from Weekly. Although the fire seemed under control, several men continued to carry buckets of water from the Wakarusa to douse the smoldering and crackling wood as the fire finally burned itself out. I hoped the sleet would assist us in extinguishing the last of the fire.

"Anybody know *how* it got started?" Big Ears King asked loudly as though he might have an answer to his own question or at least a theory about how the fire had started. Big Ears had a theory about everything that happened, and it was often fanciful or flat-out wrong. "Maybe our new sheriff got an idea." King had pronounced the noun as "idee" as he usually did, and I am certain I smiled, but, of course, we all understood his meaning.

"Look like it start in barn!" Little Joe said, "then spread to house." That was my supposition as well, for I had been watching the half-breed carefully, once the fire was out, kneeling in the ashes for a closer look and holding up pieces of wood for inspection. "Nothing left of house or barn. Where Bird? Where Vertue?" He shook his head and, throwing down the charred wood in disgust, held out his empty hands. "And just where were all the goats, which usually scampered through the weeds?" I asked myself. Most of them seemed to have disappeared.

"Excitement's over now," Weekly called out, "but Little Joe and I will stay till dawn just to make sure it don't flare up again." Everyone seemed to agree the fire was out, but several were in no hurry to depart. Now the last of the clouds had finally split up, the sky clearing.

"We need to find Vertue," Big Ears said. "Nobody's seen him at all." Big Ears pulled a flask from his coat, passing it around the small knot of firefighters who stayed to watch over the cooling embers, which now gave a final crackle or two. Little Joe took a swig from the flask and turned to the others, not that anyone dared contradict the half-breed, regarded as the best tracker and scout in the state of Kansas.

"Think I will try to get home and back to bed," I announced. The crowd had thinned out, and, although I could have gotten a ride home, I decided to walk since the moonlight was now bright as day in the silvery, leafless woods, which I would need to traverse to get back to town.

Hannah was waiting for me by our fireplace, in which a small but cheery fire now burned, illuminating the room. "Tell me all the news, husband," she said. "Our bed is still warm, and you must be cold. Or I can heat some bath water for you, if you wish me to."

"My feet feel like ice, in truth." I could see from the clock on our mantle that the time was just after five, even though the sun was not yet above the horizon. I had pulled off my boots and lay on the bed fully clothed under the quilt as Hannah began to rub my feet. "Luckily, no damage to the Weekly farm. But Bird lost his house and barn, though, as usual, he is nowhere to be seen. All his buildings lost, I think."

"How did the fire get started?" Hannah asked, keeping her voice low, although I thought there was little chance our children, heavy sleepers, would hear us.

"Don't know that. And no sign of Charlie Vertue either. Little Joe told me he looked for him." Then I joked that perhaps Charlie was curled up in the woods with Bird's goats, but Hannah, probably weary of stories about the goats, ignored me. I had no notion where the pockmarked, vulpine little man would be, of course, although I was sure Verity Maypole, if she could have found him, would have provided a swift and violent end for Vertue, given half a chance—and an end to Bird as well.

Although I thought I would not fall asleep, I must have done so, since I rolled over, and suddenly the sky was bright and Hannah had left the room. When I got out of bed, I heard our dogs barking and saw that Eli was approaching our front door, perhaps to re-establish his practice of dropping in on his way to the bank.

"Come in and warm yourself, Eli," I said, opening the door. "Like the old days." Eli put his collar down and rubbed his hands together. "How's baby Thomas? Getting you up early, is he?"

"Couldn't come out to the fire last night," Eli replied. "Thomas was screaming, and I had to help Prudence calm him down. Wouldn't go back to sleep, and *that* didn't happen 'til after the sun came up." Eli laughed.

"You didn't miss much," I said. "Haven't talked to Little Joe yet this morning." Eli nodded his head. "We couldn't find Vertue last night, and Joe thinks he might be under the burned-up timbers of the house— or even the barn. Coals too hot to look last night." Eli nodded again. "Joe thought the fire might have started in the barn since it had already burned down by the time we got out there. Anyway, Vertue seems to have burned to death."

"Seems likely," Eli said, before looking at the clock which ticked on our mantle. "Well, I'm in charge at the bank. Got to go and open up." He took a final sip of the coffee which Hannah had poured him and put down his cup. "Tell Hannah goodbye and thanks," he mumbled, pulling up his collar as he opened the door, allowing the cold morning air to stream in. The sleet from last night had already begun to melt where the sun had touched it. "Do have a bit of a bone to pick with Hannah, though," Eli added softly.

I looked at Eli, but he looked away. "How so?" I asked.

"Well, sometimes she gets a bee in her bonnet," Eli said, not meeting my eye. "Rather big bee in this case," he mumbled, clearly embarrassed.

"Sometimes she pushes too hard, Eli. I know that," I said and chuckled. "What is it now?"

"The vote for women! Suffrage!" He seemed annoyed, but not angry, as one might respond to a pesky horsefly that, despite all efforts, could not be shooed away. Suffrage was a subject which, as a news reporter, I knew something about, although I had never written about it, and besides, I thought suffrage a misleading term because the real issue was not just about the vote for women but rather the legal status of half the inhabitants of our country, as Hannah was always prepared to point out to me.

The suffrage movement seemed to have its origins in the debate over the rights of women in the 1840s, especially at the convention in Seneca Falls, New York, in 1848. For many women—and some men—it was now "the cause." Everyone knew about Susan B. Anthony and Elizabeth Cady Stanton; even Frederick Douglass had been enlisted in ratification campaigns in some states. But it seemed not yet to be "the cause" in Kansas, to Hannah's disgust.

"Prudence and I think women are too delicate, too emotional to be involved in politics," Eli said after some hesitation. "Politics and war are not for women. They need to be protected." Of course, I wanted to remind Eli how it was the *women* of Lawrence who protected their husbands and brothers and extinguished their burning homes during Quantrill's Massacre in '63, but I held my tongue because Eli's mind was fixed on the bank, the keys already in his hand.

"Well, guess I must be late too," I said. "Want to talk to some folks this morning, starting with Robinson. And Little Joe about the fire, of course." Robinson was my friend, Charles Robinson, the former governor of the state, accused of fiscal malfeasance in his first term, and driven from office, and Little Joe Oscar, a Dakota mixed blood, was Weekly's foreman, a man I trusted as much as any white man.

I pulled on my coat, kissed Hannah goodbye, caught up with Eli in the street, and hurried with him toward the Watkins bank. Although no longer a news correspondent, I maintained a keen interest in partisan politics and enjoyed chatting with Robinson, the man who had led Lawrence since Territorial Days, although many people in town now considered his views to be old-fashioned.

On my way to find the governor at the site of the fire, I descried Little Joe Oscar tiptoeing through the ashes and charred timbers of Bird's house and barn. Since we are friends and had shared confidences, I knew that Joe would speak his mind freely to me, and I desperately wanted to know his opinion about the cause of the fire. "Do you know how it started, Joe?" I asked him when no one else was around. If anyone could provide answers, it would be Joe.

"You ask right Indian, Ezra," responded Little Joe, a big smile revealing his white teeth. "Here, answer for your question. Sheriff might figure out by tomorrow." He laughed and his eyes shone with delight. "Or maybe not."

"Don't leave me in doubt, Joe," I said, shaking the hand he offered me.

"Simple as a pie," he said. "Someone set fire to barn, and barn set fire to house. On purpose! *Not accident.*" I shook his hand again and thanked him. "*Not accident,*" he repeated. Now, however, I had another question or two, but this time I could not get answers from Little Joe.

Someone had settled a score with Vitruvius Bird, and I hoped to find an answer or two before I talked to the governor, even if the answers might reveal an unpleasant truth when we had assembled all the facts. Someone had torched the barn of Vitruvius Bird, and Charlie Vertue appeared to have died in the fire. Although there were plenty of people who disliked Bird, I could think of only two who would have wanted to kill him, and they were people I liked.

Months before, I had struggled with questions about Colonel Maypole's actions when Little Archie Clement was killed, and now, I was faced with the same dilemma. I am not, however, a Peace Officer, and I reminded myself that although I possessed no evidence that a crime had occurred, I thought I knew how one *might* have been committed and *who* could have done it.

If the Maypoles, brother and sister, had planned to seek vengeance on Bird, Verity could have continued on the rail trip to St. Louis alone with their luggage, while her brother left the train in Wyandotte or at some other stop, hired a horse and ridden back to the Wakarusa River under cover of darkness, set the fire in the barn, ridden back to Wyandotte, and crossed safely into Missouri.

I trusted that Sheriff Oatman would continue his investigation and assemble all the evidence to present at a hearing. *Suspicions* are not evidence of criminal intent, and *wanting* to kill someone is not a crime, I told myself. Perhaps a Pinkerton police detective was needed to build a case, but I was not certain that there was interest in pursuing a further search for truth, although I would share all my suspicions with Oatman.

The cold morning air was still heavy with the caustic smell of charred timbers, and a few people, driven by curiosity, on foot or horseback, were heading toward Blanton's bridge to view the burned buildings. As Governor Robinson drove up, Chet Oatman watched over the ashes like a hen guarding newly laid eggs. Robinson, newly arrived at the site, studied us from the pony-drawn trap in which he took his morning drive to inspect his grazing land on Mount Oread. I chose to talk next to Robinson, knowing I could later find out more about the fire from one of the others, and I gave a sort of salute to the Sheriff as I climbed into the trap.

"Yes, do hop in, Ezra," Robinson said. As soon as I was seated beside him, he loosened the reins and the pony trotted off, the trap bouncing down the rutted road. "You must have questions for me," he said with a laugh. "You always do."

"Well, you always answer them, sir, which encourages me to ask more. But I don't write for the newspaper anymore, as you know," I quickly added. "Yes, I do have questions for you, but not about this fire. First off, will the Republicans nominate Grant for president at their upcoming convention in Chicago?" Robinson guffawed and took a deep breath.

"Here is the question you should have asked instead: Will Grant accept the Republican nomination *when* it is offered to him? Everyone loves Grant now, even though he took heavy casualties toward the end of the war. But he is a hero because he *won* the war. Well, there were two heroes, I suppose: Grant and Lincoln!" I waited to see if the governor would continue, but he glanced at me and fell silent, intent on his driving.

"I know Grant has said in print he would rather just stay a general. Spend time with his horses. Not get involved in politics at all." Robinson watched me as I spoke, and he nodded.

"Well, everybody says *that*," Robinson responded with a mirthless laugh. "But when you get close to power, you find you cannot say no. I know that only too well."

"I apologize for bringing up a subject that may cause distress, sir," I said, "but the newspapers maintain that Johnson is still trying to restore—maybe I mean revive—the old political system in the South." I paused because my mouth had gone dry in the cold air. "Even though the Negroes have been emancipated, many of the old Confederate office holders seem to be back in power—or back in office—in those states that left the Union." The governor shifted his weight on the seat and adjusted his coat.

"Although a few things may be different, little actually seems to have changed in the South. The President has ignored the Republican Moderates, with whom he might have worked, and now has quarreled with the Radical Republicans, as everybody knew he eventually would. So now—from what I read—he has no support in Congress at all."

"I think Johnson's first mistake was vetoing the Freedmen's Bureau Bill," Robinson said dryly. "Then he made an even greater one by rejecting the Civil Rights Bill. He never learned to compromise." I thought Robinson was going to shout, but instead he lowered his voice and whispered harshly. "Compromise! As Lincoln did on more than one occasion. Yes, to be sure, Lincoln was a man of principle, but he also understood human nature." He paused for a moment. "Well, you know that, Ezra. Compromise is hard for a politician." He gave me a long, enigmatic glance and quickly looked away.

"His veto of the Freedmen's Bureau Bill, when he needed support from Republican moderates in Congress, was a strategic error," I said. "Or so I thought, and his inflammatory comments about Negroes! Johnson even raised the specter of racial intermarriage. He has shown himself to be a pigheaded buffoon. So why did we fight the war, if not to end slavery throughout the country? Lincoln should never have put him on the ticket. I *do* blame Lincoln for that."

"Remember, Ezra, at the time the Republicans thought we needed the electoral votes from the Border States, from states like Johnson's Tennessee. You think things can't get worse," Robinson said as he scrutinized my face. "I suppose you think we need another Lincoln." I must have nodded because a smile crossed his face. "I agree with you, but we don't *have* another Lincoln. Just a lot of mortal men. Some more mortal than others."

We had traveled up the long slope of the California Road as it climbed the escarpment of Mount Oread, and at the top, we passed Ed Whitman in his wagon, coming toward town from the west. Ed, who had been an outspoken abolitionist before the war, was a supporter of Lincoln and the Republicans. He now doffed his hat to us and seemed ready to stop, but Robinson only touched the brim of *his* hat and did not slow down.

"Ed's been complaining about all the Negroes who have come into Kansas," I said. "Many disillusioned former slaves believe they were promised forty acres and a mule, and are certain that farmland awaits them in Kansas, *the promised land*! In fact, it was reported Sherman had said those very words to the thousands of freed slaves who followed him as the Union army was marching on Atlanta," I suggested. "Maybe Sherman did say them. Maybe not! But the Blacks believed he had said them. That is what counts!"

Robinson pulled on the reins and said, "Whoa," in a soft voice; the pony stopped, and we could see Lawrence laid out below us to the east. The governor gave me a quizzical look. "Probably will turn out the Negroes only heard it secondhand from someone who heard it third-hand," Robinson said, nodded at me, and laughed.

"But will you look at it, Ezra! As beautiful a landscape as any in America." Robinson pointed toward the distant horizon. "Even in winter with all the trees bare." In front of us was the sweep of the Kaw and the Wakarusa, Blue Mound in the distance, cleared fields and pasture, cross-hatched with stone walls and rail fences, houses and barns anchoring the low hills, and, above us, clouds a gray like the feathers of the wood pigeon. "Clouds so low today you feel you can touch them," he said. The sleet had melted, the day was brisk, and sunlight made the land sparkle. "Makes you feel insignificant," he said.

"We shall never have industry here," I said, choosing my words care-fully, for it was a question, and he smiled because we both knew what his answer would be.

"We don't have raw materials for industry, but we have land and can grow crops and raise animals to feed people and move animals to market, but the people want to see factories and manufacturing and men being hired to operate the machines."

At the foot of the long hill waited Sheriff Oatman. "Need to know how to get word to Vitruvius Bird," the Sheriff said, raising his hand. "You know how to reach him, Ezra?" Oatman asked. "Little Joe found a body and says it's Charlie Vertue. Guess he burned to death. Found him in the barn under a ridge pole. Burned to a crisp!"

Neither Robinson nor I could offer Oatman information on Bird's whereabouts. It had been more than a year since I had laid eyes on Bird, and the governor could provide no assistance either. "How come nobody knows nothing about him?" the sheriff asked in frustration.

"Bird kept to himself," I answered. "Speculators bought land when the railroads first came to Kansas, and people said Bird paid top dollar for his land because he thought the railroad wanted it. Except, of course, the *direct* line from Chicago never came *here*. Went to Kansas City instead! The rail line we got in Lawrence came through Atchison, not direct from Chicago at all." Oatman shook his head again, disgust and confusion on his face.

"Well, Bird was no farmer anyway," Robinson said slowly.

"Most people think he was just a 'confidence man,' a swindler!" I said emphatically. "I was fortunate never to have had commerce with him, but I do know of people he cheated. *Caveat emptor*! Always good advice on the frontier." I stepped from the buggy and looked at the Sheriff and then at the governor.

"Good day!" Governor Robinson said with a wry smile, and Oatman spat in the road and scowled in frustration as the buggy pulled past him. "May be the last we see of Vitruvius Bird in Lawrence," the governor said. A smile may have crossed his face, but I could not swear one did. At the top of the hill was the pasture belonging to Robinson, except for the tiny parcel where the university's lone building stood. It could have been a scene from the English moors, I thought, so bleak and lonely. Despite Robinson's opinion, it was still empty prairie.

"Think Bird will be able to sell his land?" I shouted as the governor touched the pony with his whip, and the buggy began to move slowly down Mount Oread.

"Certainly," he called out in his familiar manner, tipping his hat, "but I guess Bird will be forced to sell his land at a considerable loss. Well, a pleasant Thanksgiving to you, Ezra."

Robinson had dropped me around the corner from the livery stable, near the smithy. Now, in Lawrence, if one wanted to know about mules, the person who could give the best information was Ed Whitman or his son Jeremiah; if about horses, Davey Weekly, and, if one sought humorous gossip, particularly of the scurrilous kind, Big Ears King or Larby Jones.

In front of the livery stable this morning here many of them were, like a flock of roosting grackles at sundown: there was Big Ears and, sitting in a Sonnet wagon like an oriental potentate on his throne, Larby, who had done well with only one leg, and, for good measure, to provide comic embellishment to every story, was Jeremiah, the court jester.

"Heard they found Vertue in the ashes this morning," I said, and my listeners smirked. The smell of burned wood was still in the air, carried by the cold wind, which had come up with the dawn. The bitterness of the charred smell was made sharper by the water that had been thrown on the coals the previous evening. "Anything new today?" I asked.

I thought I could see Jeremiah searching his mind for a comic reply which might elicit laughter from this pack of idlers, but his wit seemed to have gone dry. As I watched him, I heard a train whistle and pulled out my pocket watch to check the time of day, when I noticed excitement on a street near us. I knew what the idlers were waiting for.

What had caught everyone's eye were the riders coming down Massachusetts: my wife, Hannah, in her riding habit, and our thirteen-year-old daughter, Samantha, who was already developing into an attractive young woman, although I continued to tell myself she was still a mere girl. Both were outfitted for riding. Hannah's red-blonde hair had darkened to auburn, but she still attracted the male observers' attention as the riders raced down Massachusetts toward the center of town. Samantha, hair redder than her mother's, flaring behind her as she streaked by on her Indian pony, was already a skilled rider. On occasion, Davey Weekly would join them.

The two, mother and daughter, rode out almost every day in good weather, generally taking a route that traversed Mount Oread, came down Massachusetts Street, and ended on Rhode Island at Eighth Street, close to where our house stood. The last leg of the ride was covered at full speed and involved dodging through the commercial traffic from the nearby Sonnet warehouse, thus carrying a slight risk for a novice, but an opportunity for a skilled rider of either sex or any age to demonstrate riding ability.

For several reasons, our son Henley, who was ten years of age in October, did not accompany his mother and sister on their morning ride. Like most boys, he was happy enough to throw rocks at squirrels, and, in the spring, carried home baby birds and rabbits whose nests had been disturbed and attempted to nurse them to health. Henley fished, caught lizards, frogs, and tadpoles, and he loved, above all else, to chase the spring piglets and wrestle them to the ground, occupying himself in his own world of imagination and play.

Turning my back on the riders and their diurnal exercise, I sought out John Speer, publisher of the *Kansas Tribune*, the successor to the Free-State paper burned down in Quantrill's Raid in '63. Speer had lost two of his three sons in that cowardly Confederate massacre of Lawrence's men and boys and had, in addition, lost his peace of mind and ebullient nature. "Got a question or two for you this morning, John," I said, greeting him on the board sidewalk.

"You still writing for the *Globe Democrat*, Ezra?" he asked with a solemn look on his face.

"No. No. Just an attorney now," I replied. "But I do miss it, the writing, I mean. So, here's the question, John. What do you know about the editor of the news daily in Kansas City?"

The portly Speer ran his hand up his forehead and over his bald head, perhaps a remembered gesture from the time he had locks to push back, although I did not remember him with a full head of hair. "How much you want to know?"

"Whatever you can tell me about John Newman Edwards, the founder of the *Kansas City Times*." Before I could get another word out, Speer frowned at me, his brow furrowed in confusion or perhaps anger. "Seems like Edwards wants to fight the war over again, from what I hear," I speculated, and one of his eyebrows moved almost imperceptibly.

"Well, maybe he does," Speer said, biting off the words, as though they left an acerbic taste in his mouth. "He seems determined to be an apologist for the old Confederates in Missouri," Speer growled. "More troubling to me is his defense in some editorials of the bushwhacker bands—the James brothers and the Youngers—all bad actors who started out in Clay County, Little Dixie, as we used to call it."

"Well, Cole Younger rode with Quantrill, as both of us know," I added quickly. "And Frank James rode with them too, and probably killed men here in Lawrence." Speer was nodding. Although I no longer wrote for the St. Louis paper, I continued to follow the track of the Quantrill Bushwhackers like a coon hound on a scent, recording the deaths of the leaders in my commonplace book, which I carried at all times, and I suspected John Speer did much the same, refusing to close any account until the last of Quantrill's raiders was in prison or dead. "Now Edwards is writing editorials and even promises to print letters from Jesse James himself, asserting *his* innocence in the many robberies and murders in which he has been accused," I said quietly.

"I do not ordinarily read his newspaper, but what Edwards might say is of interest to me," Speer said slowly. "Perhaps what Jesse—or Edwards—says in print could incriminate at least one of the James brothers, and an arrest can at last be made. Might be easier now that Jesse's been labeled an outlaw in Missouri by Governor Crittenden."

"A little surprised Jesse never tried to rob a bank in Kansas," I said. "I know Frank James has spent time close by in St. Joe since he turned himself in and was paroled." I had hoped the Missouri militia had also set a watch on him, or perhaps Colonel Maypole had done so, if he had finally given up trying to recover money from Vitruvius Bird.

"It *is* curious he never did, with only the one river to cross to get to Kansas," Speer responded, perhaps speaking to himself rather than to me.

"Yes, easy to do." I said as Speer cocked his head like a chicken about to peck. "Why does this border stuff never seem to end, Ezra? Do you know? Goes on and on like the Big Muddy River."

I must have shaken my head because he smiled and shook my hand in parting. I wondered about the proper way to acknowledge the upcoming Thanksgiving holiday for a man whose sons had been brutally murdered, and since I possessed no answer, I merely said, "God bless you, John." How do you wish a still-grieving man a happy holiday?

Thanksgiving Day, the holiday begun by President Lincoln after the Battle of Gettysburg, was approaching in two days, and I knew that Hannah was already preparing the traditional meal, but the thought of empty chairs at the tables in Lawrence and across the Missouri River Valley as well filled me with sadness and regret. Eli and Prudence and the baby would be our guests at dinner, and, of course, Isaac and Phoebe—newlyweds and part of our family—would be there as well, with Leona Sonnet, whom our children had called "Grandma" all their lives.

With Johnson needing to be cast from office, I reckoned the year ahead could be the most contentious one since the Confederate surrender and peace in 1865. In Kansas, we were fortunate that the struggles to gain statehood had brought our new state together in common purpose: winning the war and settling the state, although there had been a dear price to pay. The Medicine Lodge peace treaty had already ended *some* of the Indian raids in western Kansas, but the buffalo were now gone for good, and, along with them, for the Indians, the loss of an ancient way of life.

Hannah and I may have been among those who were sorry to see it disappear, but Manifest Destiny was the watchword now in our country, enterprise and expansion, and like one of the new horse-drawn agricultural machines which could do the work of twenty men—clearing, plowing, planting, or harvesting—everything fell before it. The industry that had helped us win the war would now enable us to conquer the wilderness and perhaps, in the future, even illness and disease, just as distance was being overcome by railroads, the telegraph, and other products of human ingenuity, or so people hoped.

If Kansas had been unified by conflict and struggle, Missouri was another matter. Missouri had teetered on the edge of succession for much of the War, supported by a federal army and determined Unionists, and even though the Confederates had put a star on their flag for the "Confederate State of Missouri," the Rebel State had been a complete chimera since Missouri never left the Union.

Confederate values were, however, still alive in Missouri in the Peace Democrats (or Copperheads) as well as in some committed Secessionists, who desired to turn back the clock if they could. But no one wanted another civil war, and all our dinner guests and most of the country would agree with Hannah and me about that.

Where we would probably disagree was the looming question of female suffrage, a subject that Hannah was sure to raise, as she had often done before. And this matter might come up since the Fifteenth Amendment to our Constitution was about to receive final approval from Congress, giving the vote to Black men but *not* to women, either Black or white.

Hannah had always been outspoken about female suffrage, but it was an issue that had not found widespread support in Kansas or in the country at large. She told Samantha that someday *she* would vote, although Hannah believed she herself would not live to cast a vote in a national election. Kansas had held an election to give women the vote, but the measure had been soundly defeated by the all-male electorate.

In one year, in fact, the federal election of 1868 would take place, and the Republicans were already preparing for their December convention, at which Ulysses Grant would be nominated for the Presidency of the United States, with no serious opposition for the Party's nomination. The incumbent, Andrew Johnson, who had taken to calling himself "the White South's champion," would now run as the standard-bearer of the new National Union Party, a coalition of the old Peace Democrats, cobbled together with offshoots of the Republican Party.

I believed that in the days ahead, we in Kansas would do well to keep an eye on a militant movement called the Ku Klux Klan, which had originated in Tennessee and had quickly and violently spread across the South and now, like an insidious and deadly weed, had even invaded Missouri.

In addition to accounts in the papers, stories had reached me of widespread violence and oppression in the Deep South, of masked men in hoods and white robes, the burning of crosses, houses, and barns, and the beating and lynching of Black men, instituting a reign of terror in parts of the South as bad as the horrors of the French Revolution.

Barn burning was, in fact, the way the Border War in Kansas had started back in May of 1856, which the newspapers took to calling "The Wakarusa War," even though the fighting had involved only two small groups of settlers, each one trying to drive the other out of Kansas, the Free-State pioneers opposing the Border Ruffians or bushwhackers, who sought to establish slavery in the Territory.

Although much had transpired in the past eleven years—including our Civil War, the deaths of more than 600, 000 combatants, the assassination of a well-loved president, and the manumission of the slaves—the torching of Bird's barn brought back bitter memories for me since this latest barn-burning had happened exactly where the earlier ones had taken place—here in eastern Kansas.

Nevertheless, I felt our state was ready for anything that might occur, having survived a dozen years of turmoil from the time the Territory was legally open to settlement in 1854. I had passed my first night, not in the Territory, but in the village of Westport in the State of Missouri, a mile from the Kansas border, before crossing the next morning in the mule-drawn freight wagon of Henry Sonnet.

Westport—in my mind—was the true gateway to the West, the point of origin of both the Santa Fe Road and the California (or Oregon) Road, which separated about twenty miles away at Gardner, in Kansas, one highway following the old Spanish trade route southwest, the other heading due west to Topeka and beyond, across the vast prairie and through the towering mountains before eventually reaching the waters of the Pacific Ocean.

CHAPTER TWENTY

TO BE HONEST, I have not been fulfilled by the small accomplishments of my life—if accomplishments they be—since much of the time I have only observed and chronicled the deeds of others. Now, at the end of the old year, it seemed a time of beginnings for each person as well as for a country whose ruinous missteps in the three years since Lincoln's death could be rectified in November by the election of a new president. To me, the electoral choice seemed clear: Ulysses S. Grant of Ohio.

Grant had been a reluctant candidate, and he did not seem dangerously ambitious; he had humane plans for the hostile Indians in the West as well as the new Negro citizens, and above all else, he was *not* Andrew Johnson. There were, to be sure, reservations in my mind about a military man as President, but I believed Grant had a history of getting things done. And so, as 1868 was about to begin, I examined the choice I would have to make in the election that autumn and realized that it was Hobson's choice—taking what was available or nothing at all. Most of the men in Lawrence, I hoped, could also be counted on to vote against the buffoonish and incompetent Johnson.

During the summer, I had been reading Shakespeare's history plays again, especially some I had nibbled at but had not consumed. One such play was *The Second Part of King Henry the Fourth*, which I had foolishly dismissed as a hotchpotch—that is, a mixture of dissimilar ingredients—but on careful re-examination, I now judged it to be a comic masterpiece as well as an astute dissection of human motives in politics.

Not only did it reprieve the Bard's masterful comic character Falstaff, but it presented a portrait of rural England, which in its vividness I took to limn the life of Shakespeare's own boyhood in Warwickshire, though the location of the play's rural scenes in my edition is given as the neighboring county of Gloucestershire. Moreover, the senescent country Justices Shallow and Silence existed in a timeless countryside which could be our own Kansas, with the rhythm of the seasons, the price of bullocks and ewes at market, and tropes of loss, old age, and death.

His history plays were favorites of mine, in part because they treated the lives of simple folk as well as the pomp and circumstance of the powerful and mighty—the monarchs and generals—and the rural characters spoke in the colloquial way a farmer or drover might speak, whatever century or country he inhabited. To my mind, when these characters left the stage, what remained behind was a trove of riches: gold coins and pearls, dazzling jewels which fell from their pockets as their exit lines were caught in the light of their timeless eloquence.

Having lived on the plains for a dozen years now, I was used to bleak days which were cold, gray, and windy, but one winter day, the twenty-ninth of January in 1861, was different, for on that day, Kansas had become a state. The arrival of snow-covered Daniel Anthony from Leavenworth had brought the news that Kansas, after years of waiting in frustration, had finally been admitted to the Union.

There had been no such deep, paralyzing snow in Kansas since that time, and, of course, no celebration like the one that first night of statehood, when delegates to the Territorial Legislature, then meeting in Lawrence, celebrated with the inebriated inhabitants of the town. In my memory, I can still feel the ground shake as Old Sacramento, the captured cannon, roared and roared again, and with every roar the jubilating townspeople answered with screams of joy and tears of relief.

Lawrence in '68 was preoccupied *not* with politics—despite its being an election year—but with speculation about the extensive property formerly owned by Vitruvius Bird. No buildings were left on his land after the mysterious fire, which had destroyed house and barn, an act for which no one had ever been held accountable. The reclusive Bird, through his agents, had cleaned up the property for sale, and a sign had been posted on the road to the Wakarusa, announcing that an attorney in Topeka was handling the sale of the land.

Davey Weekly, who owned the adjacent farm, knew no more of Bird's plans than did the rest of us. Even Eli at the Watkins Bank could not predict what might happen to the farm. Everyone agreed with Governor Robinson that it was a prime piece of land, although it had never been properly worked by Bird, whom the townsfolk believed had initially purchased the land hoping to sell it for railroad right of way. Officials at the other bank were also in the dark.

And so, we waited and speculated, and like Shakespeare's senescent Justices, we jested about our lives and those of our friends and neighbors. We seemed to have forgotten another subject which inevitably came up: whether any of Bird's goats still wandered the land. Since there were no longer panthers and wolves in the oak and hickory forest that covered much of Bird's land, a few survivors from the goat herds might still be around somewhere, but if so, they went unseen.

Although the land itself was valuable, some outlay of money would be required to make it ready for farming since much of the acreage was judged too hilly, steep, and irregular for the new mechanized agricultural equipment. During the winter, more people gossiped about the Bird farm than about the presidential election to come in November. At one point, I thought about making a bid on the farm myself, but Hannah stopped me in my tracks.

"My love," Hannah said calmly after I had explained my plan to purchase some of the land. "If you buy that farm, you will always be welcome to visit me in St. Louis because that is where I will be living with our children! The choice, of course, is yours."

It goes without saying that I did not make a bid on the Bird farm. I had been many things in my life, but farmer was not one of them. And even when the price on the farm dropped and dropped again, I was not tempted. It was Ed Whitman, however, who finally made me realize just how foolish I had been even to think of farming Bird's land.

I had seen Ed riding into town on one of his big mules, making a stop at the general store where he slid off the mule and loosely tied him up. If I could not say that my wife had forbidden me to make an offer on the Bird farm, what I *could* say was that I had been advised not to buy any farmland at present. I knew that Hannah and I would laugh at the supper table that night when I explained what I would say about the Bird farm.

"You got book learning, Ezra," Ed had whispered to me that morning. "More book learning than any man I've ever known." He cleared his throat, and I waited because I knew he had more to say. In Kansas, we politely wait until a man is done speaking before we yammer across his sentence.

"I know you listen to Robinson, and I don't know what he's been telling you, but if he is advising you to buy land to farm, hold onto them reins and continue to practice the law. That's what you're good at." Whitman stood beside his big mule, and I was astride my horse in front of Big Ears King's livery stable, across the dirt street from the store, which sold boots and shoes. We spoke with our voices lowered, as if we might have been talking commerce, which in a fashion we were. Fresh dung in the street steamed in the cold air, and a slight breeze made Whitman's mule snort and eye me with suspicion.

"Well, Ed, I don't go to the governor for advice," I said, and *did* hold the reins tightly as I smiled at him and nodded. "Buying land is a gamble unless you know what to do with it, and I am neither a farmer nor a gambler." I smiled at Ed again, and he nodded to me and gently kicked his mule, which began to walk away in that stubborn, stiff-legged way mules have.

Now, in my opinion, every season of the year in Kansas has its own character, regardless of what the calendar says. October is a time of golden days when the sunlight is like polished brass or copper; in November and December, the air is fresh and frigid, the light is silvery, the wind blows from the north, often under pewter-gray clouds, and the sun, if it does appear, seems to burn with a distant, ineffectual fire.

The farmer has long since picked his last crop and split wood for his winter fires, and every morning a lonely snowflake or two may drift from the heavy clouds to melt on hitting the earth. And, in fact, no one ever has much good to say about the first two months of the New Year: they are consistently cold, windy, and usually wet, except for the present dry spell. Nevertheless, we hoped for winter rain or snow, and devout people no doubt prayed fervently for rain throughout the state of Kansas.

When I stopped at Big Ears' livery stable to listen to the morning gossip, I anticipated complaints about the lack of rains or snow. Instead of moisture, this January, we had seen a constant wind that promised but did not deliver a changing weather pattern. Big Ears had a nose for profit, people say, and, fittingly, ears for the news. And somehow or other, King had been the one to discover that something momentous was about to happen—or perhaps was already happening—on the Bird property. Something as momentous as a winter rainstorm!

He had winked at me in a way that made me think he might have something to say in private. Taking me by the shoulder, he gave me a little tug so I would follow him to one of his corrals, away from the men slouching in the street, trying to keep their hands warm by blowing on them. "Man from Topeka is here," he whispered harshly. "Says he represents the attorney selling the Bird property. You interested in working together?" He looked at me like a boy planning to raid an apple orchard, and so I responded with a non-committal look, wondering what he needed or wanted from me. "I could share the commission with you if we work in tandem," he said with what I thought was a bit of desperation in his voice.

Although Big Ears gossiped like a washerwoman, he was neither greedy nor unscrupulous: in fact, he was one of the most generous men in Lawrence, but he did love secrets and elaborate plans, even if they did not in the end benefit him. "You can have the commission, Ears," I said, answering his whisper with a whisper of my own, even though no one was around to eavesdrop. "I just want to see the end of Bird in Lawrence and this state."

"Attorney from Topeka, name of Cottingham, who is stopping at the Eldridge House," King continued, still speaking in a whisper. "Hired a buggy from me. Want to meet him?" I said that I did, my curiosity growing. So, I accompanied King across the street to be introduced to the man called Cottingham, the agent of the new owner of the farm. As we walked, he declared that the Bird farm had been sold to one Abner McKenzie that very morning, but the attorney did not divulge plans about the intended use by the new owner, whom I now met.

Abner McKenzie was the new owner, prosperous-looking, florid, and were he not hairless as a turnip, probably once had a head of red or fair hair since his eyebrows and beard were ruddy. He was not forthcoming in conversation and offered no explanation of the future use of his land, which was a parcel of some size, one of the larger pieces of land to change hands that year.

As a matter of fact, I could discover nothing about McKenzie or his plans, although I realized that in our brief social intercourse I had probably revealed much about myself: I was amused to acknowledge that the new land owner and his attorney had played me like a trout, finding out whatever they wanted to know from me, which was not much at all.

"Your business at an end here?" I finally asked, scrutinizing McKenzie more carefully now than I had done before.

"All of us are here while I sign papers for the land," McKenzie said, meeting my glance. "Staying at Mrs. Killam's at present. Need to be about when the boys start to clear the scrub oak." He looked at me and smiled faintly. The "boys" were a Negro work crew that hung around the livery stable to be hired for odd jobs. He must have known that freed Negroes did not like to be referred to as "boys," but he seemed not to care, perhaps because he would be the one paying them.

Mrs. Killam's Eastern House, of course, was well known to me. I had, in fact, taken Hannah there to meet John Brown on his last trip to Lawrence—before he left for Harpers Ferry and his martyr's death. I wanted to tell McKenzie about that, but the words simply would not come from my mouth. "You care to tag along?" He asked, and I nodded but did not meet his eye.

If there was anything Lawrence needed, it was industry. The year before a paper factory was started, making paper from straw, but there had not been a market for their paper, and a foundry that made wire was only modestly successful. Lawrence needed industry that would produce iron goods like stoves, plows, and farm equipment, but the coal deposits in Osage County proved to be of such low quality that it could not even be used in the boilers of locomotives.

If Big Ears was loquacious, McKenzie was his complete opposite, so taciturn that he might have seemed to be walking in his sleep or mired in thought even when awake. He was, however, as attentive to the nuances of our discourse as to the features of the landscape we were inspecting, so that nothing we were discussing or seeing now seemed to escape his notice. "Bird seems not to have done any farming here," McKenzie mused, looking over his new land, and shook his head slowly. "What was he planning to do with it then?"

"No one ever knew with Bird," I replied with a laugh. "Everyone thought he was a speculator, but, if so, he never seemed to guess right. Bought land he thought the railroad wanted! But a depression and bank closures came along in Kansas after the war. Lots of folks lost money on land, and I reckon Bird did too!"

"Well, wife and I been putting money aside for a place to settle down. When I found out I inherited land after my father died, I knew it was time to move west and start over again." McKenzie smiled and spit in the street. "This looked a good place to settle."

"Well, I don't want to seem to tell you your business, sir, but your new land is hilly and rocky in places. Hard to use the new farm machinery here," I said with some hesitation, lest McKenzie think my comments impertinent or judge me to be a fool.

"Good gracious," he said. "I don't intend to till all this acreage," he added with a laugh. "I am *done* with plowing. This here will be pasture for my milk cows! And I got a German family coming to build me a large dairy barn and a milk house and also a house for the wife and our two boys," he said, exhibiting a wide, craggy smile, resulting from his several missing teeth. So, McKenzie was not a farmer at all but a dairyman! And I immediately wondered whether one could make a comfortable living here from just milking cows and peddling their milk. In my opinion, a dairy was not what Lawrence needed most.

In about a week, the whole town knew of Abner McKenzie and his milk cows (although we had so far *seen* no milk cows at all) and went back to complaining about the dry winter and speculating about the barn which was now rising on the McKenzie land. By early February, the dairy barn had been completed and McKenzie had begun to move furniture and farm equipment into it. He was sleeping there at night too, although the rest of the family was still abiding at Eastern House.

The roads were dry but still frozen by the time the Negroes had cleaned up the property, and Little Joe Oscar had gone back to attending to his work on Davey Weekly's horse farm, announcing to anyone in town who would listen that the dry weather was, at last, mercifully, about to change.

I, for one, was always ready to listen to Little Joe, whose knowledge of the natural world was unsurpassed, even if his evidence might be unconventional. "Rain crows been out at sunset last two nights," he explained to the skeptics. "Means big storm soon." I had learned to take Joe's predictions seriously, and, even though I did not know precisely what he meant by "rain crows"—taking them to be mourning doves—I acted accordingly, tying up our dog Brutus (our older dog, Caesar, had died during the autumn) and making certain that all our sheep and pigs, chickens and ducks, were safely penned or cooped up.

It was so cold that we might get snow or sleet rather than rain, but I made my whole family ready for storms and wind since Little Joe was seldom wrong about whatever capricious weather might be coming across the plains.

By the next day, the air seemed damper, and now even the most skeptical of the inhabitants of Lawrence believed the winter rain was finally about to arrive, when, after midday on a Tuesday, the sky to the north turned dark as night, and suddenly the wind began to howl like a coyote. The temperature had dropped, and anyone on the street who had not sought immediate shelter would have to struggle against a wind which roared like a steam engine straining under the weight of loaded cars. In the Bible, we read of Forty Days of rain in the time of Noah, when the Flood inundated the earth and all its creatures, an account I considered to be more poetic than factual, although possibly containing some grains of truth.

Only the storm that followed Quantrill's deadly raid on Lawrence in '63 had come with such a sudden fury, and at the time we called it a hurricane because that was the strongest force in the natural world we could compare it to. The afternoon had now become as dark as midnight, but because it was winter, there was no thunder to accompany the moaning wind and driving rain.

The dirt streets in town quickly became rivers of mud, and the skies were roiled with turbulence like that of the flooded creeks, and within minutes, the usually placid Kaw began to flow with a frightening force. Despite the pelting rain, I covered myself with a poncho and ran to the barn to calm and feed the animals, which would be frightened by the drumbeat of rain on the roof and the lightning. From the barn, I fetched in more dry firewood after quickly inspecting our fences. It was a noisy night with wind and pounding rain, and I held Hannah close until we drifted off to sleep.

Although no bright sunlight informed me that the new day had come, I could observe the moonlight that illuminated the leafless trees whereon sat birds, like those in Chaucer, which in early spring slept the night with "open eye." I stole from our bed so as not to disturb Hannah, but I could tell that she was already awake and watching me, waiting so we could begin the day together. The coals in the iron stove were now unbanked. I threw in kindling and small pieces of charcoal, and soon we had a fire big enough for Hannah to cook bacon and heat the coffee pot, while I splashed cold water on my face and trudged to the barn to feed our animals.

The cold day which awaited us reminded me of those mornings during the war with Eli and the militia, particularly that icy dawn among the dried cornfields at Westport, death beside us, waiting for the fighting to begin. The horrors of those days were now far behind us, but they would never be forgotten by those of us who fought there.

What surprised me was not the absence of storm damage in Lawrence, but the number of birds hopping from limb to limb and descending to feed on grain swept from stores onto the board sidewalk, sparrows and wrens and starlings, birds that had stayed with us during the long dry winter. Joining them on this morning was a flock of robins, migrating, I assumed, from warmer climes to a still-thawing Kansas; in fact, the robins were the first I ever recalled seeing in Lawrence, surely a welcome sign of spring.

I remembered the red-breasted robins from my boyhood in St. Louis, where with cocked heads they stalked the lawns, listening for worms beneath the turf. The robins now seemed to be spreading westward, and I knew I should question Little Joe since he, if anyone, might explain their presence this far out on the plains. The big migrating birds—ducks and geese—had long since returned in the noisy formations that marked the change of seasons as they honked and flapped their way north to unreachable heights above our heads where our shotguns could not touch them.

Such a bright day had greeted us that, except for the muddy lake where Massachusetts Street had been the day before and some branches broken off by the wind, there were few signs of the storm. Shop boys and clerks in boots were already picking up the refuse of branches and sweeping mud from the sidewalks, and sure enough, Big Ears King was already in the street to supervise the cleanup, if not to participate in it.

Joining the men that morning were the two boys of the McKenzie family, Abner's blond sons, Clyde and Clem, close enough in age and size they could have been twins, and twins, in fact, many people took them at first to be, saying they were as like as two peas in a pod.

In particular, I kept my eyes on the elder, Clyde, who seemed to be about the same age as my daughter, Samantha. For a week or so, I had watched him with more than normal interest when my daughter raced past with her mother on their morning ride. It seemed possible that Clyde might be scrutinizing her as intently as I watched *him*, and, remembering feelings from my own youth, I looked for signs of a secret passion in his face but could see none.

Indeed, I remembered from my study of Shakespeare that Juliet had been only fourteen when that tragedy began, slightly older than Samantha was now, and I thought I could still remember what it was like to be so young and burning with the urgent desires of youth.

"Wakarusa still out of its banks?" Davey Weekly shouted, as a question for anyone who wished to comment on the rain. It was young Clyde who put aside his shovel and answered him.

"A sod soaker and gully washer, for sure," he shouted and pulled at the cuffs of his muddy, rolled-up trousers and looked around to see how his exclamation had been received by the others. There were enough chuckles and snorts to draw a look of satisfaction from Clyde. To me, it seemed an odd phrase for a boy to use, one perhaps he had heard his father or grandpa use to describe a heavy rain.

The previous evening, as the storm raged, Hannah and I talked in bed about young love. Jaques in *As You Like It*, I had reminded her, describes a love-struck swain as "sighing like furnace" while composing a ballad "to his mistress' eyebrow." I had maintained that Jaques' speech about the Seven Ages of Man contained some of the Bard's finest sentiments, especially the portrait of "the whining schoolboy with his shining morning face, creeping like snail unwillingly to school."

Hannah had whispered back that her objection to the speech was that there were no *comparable* portraits of young women, and I realized we were about to return to a subject I had been trying to avoid: the education of girls, in particular, one for our daughter, Samantha, now approaching fourteen years of age.

I had been adamant about sending Samantha to the new university on Mount Oread, whereas Hannah had suggested we send her east for her higher education, schooling more like that which Hannah herself had received at her female seminary in St. Louis. Of course, I had the money to send her to a fine school where she could learn the proper manners she had not regularly been exposed to; here in Kansas she rode her pony like a boy, her only musical training was singing in the church choir, and her society was the local barn dances, but the cost of her education had never been the issue anyway.

Hannah and I had agreed before our marriage that we were to be equal partners, and so the word "obey" was absent from our wedding vows, a decision so radical that her father initially had threatened not to attend the nuptials at all, although he eventually relented and even provided a surprisingly large dowry. My jest to my new wife was that had I known how desperate *he* was to rid himself of the impediment of a daughter, he might have been willing to increase the amount twofold.

Our wedding took place without the term "obey," and Hannah and I promised only to resolve our disputes with love and respect for each other. We were, however, forced to call on Leona Sonnet to assist us in a decision about Samantha's schooling, and we finally decided to keep her at home for one more year, during which time she could concentrate her efforts on her Latin, as well as to read Dickens, Shakespeare, Stowe, and Frederick Douglass in the *North Star*, a paper he now published.

Although Samantha had hair as red as that of her mother, her temperament, fortunately, was not as volatile and fiery. Perhaps like her mother she would choose someone older than herself, perhaps even Clyde McKenzie or Jeremiah Whitman or one of the other older boys who occasionally raced about the town on horseback after the "Middleton women," often accompanied by a noisy but friendly pack of dogs and now accompanied on occasion by Davey Weekly, who ostentatiously showed off the horse he would have me buy. But who, I asked myself, could possibly be good enough for Samantha? Certainly not one of the local boys like Clyde! That was *my* answer.

I am not so naïve as to believe that men do not enjoy seeing an attractive woman in a snug-fitting riding habit galloping by on a horse or pony. Hannah, who had been slim most of her life, after bearing two children, had a more mature, but no less attractive figure, which had obviously caught the eyes of the men of Lawrence, and, with improving weather, she now rode her pony more frequently. I suspected the men of the town were pleased with that.

As Hannah and I continued to discuss Samantha's education, the seasons had begun to turn from the harshness of winter to the warmth of spring. Building on the McKenzie property moved steadily along, with stone troughs and a sloping floor for the cows in the barn, and a brick foundation for the large milk house.

The last structure to rise was a frame house for the human inhabitants. Local bricks were used for all the foundations on the McKenzie land, with "LAWRENCE" proudly stamped on each brick. Indeed, many of the houses going up around town were now being built of red Kansas brick, and there was even talk of covering the streets in the commercial district in the same fired brick being used in the new houses. It would be an expensive undertaking to pave the streets in brick, but the more progressive people thought it well worth the expenditure and turned their attention to raising funds to pave the streets of Lawrence, forever eliminating the detested mud on Massachusetts.

But as yet there were no milk cows on the McKenzie dairy farm, and speculation increased as the calendar showed that winter was ending and March had arrived, even though on some mornings it seemed winter had not entirely loosened its grip on the Missouri River Valley.

When are the cows coming? Abner was asked again and again. He coughed, cleared his throat, blew snot from his nose, scratched his head, or smiled serenely at the questioner, seeming to enjoy being the center of attention. Some of the farmers from the countryside and the townspeople began to wager on the date the cows would come, but Abner McKenzie was as quiet and secretive as the legendary Sphinx of Egypt with her riddles. And every day the tension increased and the mystery of the cows' arrival seemed to deepen.

Then, on a calm morning in early April when the air was filled with perfume from the blossoms of the fruit trees, Jeremiah Whitman rode through Lawrence shouting, "They're here!" Men ran from the livery stable, the apothecary, and the barbershop to witness the cows enter town like the victorious Legions of ancient Rome, but the sounds were not the cadences of legionnaires nor even the bellowing of cows, but the clanging of milk cans, as several Sonnet wagons loaded with empty milk cans and guided by Isaac Worthy on horseback came slowly up Massachusetts from the station, down the lane that led to Blanton's bridge, and finally to the McKenzie farm.

Isaac was imperturbable, ignoring the hoots and shouts of the crowd, except to announce in a steady voice, "Got orders here for steel milk cans for a Mr. McKenzie." At the end of the string of Sonnet wagons was Larby Jones, talking and singing to the mules that pulled the wagons and warning the boys in the street to give way. I discovered that numerous bets had been made on the day and time of the arrival of the cows, but, of course, since no cows had arrived, all bets were off.

A week later, the cows did arrive, huge black and white Holstein milk cows in prime condition—not the familiar tan Guernseys I expected. Thirty-eight by my count, and they came on the railroad from Kansas City. Many had recently calved, and the bellowing Missouri calves were letting everyone know they were not altogether pleased with their new Kansas home, but a milk-filled teat or two soon quieted them, and the McKenzie dairy farm was open and ready for business.

Strangely, once the cows arrived, many people seemed to lose interest in them, some complaining that McKenzie had tricked them and created hysteria about the cows, although I thought all the hysteria could be traced back to the men of Lawrence with their wagers. Since the "hysteria" of women had often been used to deny them the vote, I knew that Hannah would appreciate the irony of the men's reactions as much as I did.

And I thought it equally ironic that McKenzie seemed to have devoted more attention to the welfare of his cows than to his human family, who had spent much of the winter at Mrs. Killam's boarding house.

On this balmy morning—truly a halcyon day—many men had been drawn outdoors to breathe deeply of the April air, but I was surprised when Davey Weekly stood so close at my elbow that I bumped into him at least twice, wondering whether he intended to ask a personal favor of me. Since he was not a secretive man, I glanced at him until he met my eyes with a steady look, hoping he would speak his mind.

"Your daughter Samantha is turning out to be a fine-looking young woman," Davey Weekly said to me in a cautious voice, when everyone's attention was diverted by a dog which had caught a rat and was giving it a last shake or two before killing it. Davey paused and seemed to look at his feet. "I pay attention to her on her rides out with Mrs. Middleton almost every day. She is an accomplished horsewoman. Knows her horses too, she does."

I was now certain that Davey was still trying to sell me a horse for my daughter, and not doing a very good job of it, but, in any event, I was more concerned about my daughter's Latin and her education than about her horsemanship. Yes, she needed a bigger horse, and her pony would be perfect for Henley, and, yes, I probably would buy a horse from Davey, who would offer a fine animal at a fair price. The dickering and wheel-spinning and long silences were the way business was done on the prairie. It would get done when it got done. Davey reminded me of a boy at his first dance who could not select a partner even though the music had already begun and all of the pretty girls had long since been taken.

"She's a woman now, Ezra, not a girl no more . . . uh, anymore," Davey said, now looking me in the eye. For a moment, I felt annoyed that my friend, almost a decade younger than me, should give me advice about my own daughter, but I knew it would be impossible to harbor a grudge against this pleasant young man.

"Got something to say, Ezra, which cannot be put off." He seemed almost apologetic, and so I was more certain he was about to ask for a favor. We had discussed my buying a horse from him—one for my daughter, Samantha—but that would be a straightforward business transaction since he had already given me the price he had in mind for the horse.

"Not sure yet about the roan we discussed," I interjected, "although he *is* a fine horse. Reminds me of the horse Dan Cornish had, though, if I *do* buy him, everybody will think I intend to run for Congress!" Weekly smiled faintly and continued to scrutinize my face. "An exceptionally fine piece of horseflesh," I added, and Davey gave a polite but perfunctory nod.

Obviously, he had something that needed to be said, and he was trying to get around to saying it. Some things take time, and today Davey was obviously not one to be rushed. He was smart and industrious, and he had already made his horse farm well known in Douglas County and eastern Kansas, and he was being called a man of means in town, although I thought that might be a bit premature since he was not yet thirty, about the same age as Jeremiah Whitman or my new son-in-law, Isaac Worthy.

Of course, without question, Little Joe Oscar, as his foreman, had also played a role in Davey's success as a horse breeder, although Indians did not seem to have the kind of business sense that white men had. Everyone said that white men sucked it from their momma's teat with the milk. But Joe had knowledge that no white man had, and together Davey and Joe were a perfect pair.

"Here's what I got to ask of you, sir," Davey said, at last breaking the silence. "Probably not the way it would be done in Saint Louis or the East." He had a pained expression on his face and looked sick in the gut—the way a cow looks when she is about to swallow her tongue.

"What is it, Davey?" I asked of my young friend, taking him by the shoulder.

"Ezra . . . Sir. With great respect, I ask it." Then the words tumbled from his mouth. "This is a matter I have struggled with. Didn't know how to tell you. 'Ask' you, I mean. How to bring it up to you, sir. You and me, being friends, and all. Well, here is what I got to say. Sir, I am asking for the hand in marriage of your daughter . . . Samantha! Humbly ask, I mean, sir."

In an instant, my world had turned upside down. Now I was afraid Davey would feel he needed to kneel or bow to me. Certainly, he was a friend, and was he now to be my daughter's suitor as well? Had he not just asked if he could marry her? Could she *have* suitors already, my girl Samantha? And did *she* love him—my friend, Davey? Had they been courting, and I had not known? Well, in literature, the father is always the *last* to know and is often hoodwinked. Had I been hoodwinked? By my daughter and my friend? Deceived like the *senex* in a stage comedy, and I not even forty years of age yet! I wanted to laugh but could only gulp air. Of course, I *liked* him, young Davey, but that was not what I grappled with.

Marriage at *fourteen*? I had asked myself. Did Hannah know what Davey intended to do, and, if so, why had she not told *me*? Had I, in fact, entered the last of the Seven Ages of Man which the Bard describes, and not even known of it? I had smiled at Davey, although I saw little in my dilemma, which I thought amusing.

"Well, I need to talk to Hannah about this," I had said awkwardly as I gave Davy a friendly swat on the shoulder. No, this was *not* how we did things in St. Louis. Perhaps Hannah already knew or surmised what was afoot. Was I then the *last* one to know? Davey's expression had not changed, but I could not give him an answer even if I had known what to say. And if I were to be the buffoon in this domestic comedy, I needed to accustom myself to the role I had been assigned to play. Davey could wait for an answer until I found one for myself.

But despite the thoughts and actions of sweethearts and lovers—and the parents of lovers—partisan politics had not been entirely forgotten in this, the election year of '68, even on a perfect spring day.

Certainly, the Indian raids had never stopped after the signing of the treaty at Medicine Lodge in 1867 or later with the killing of the Cheyenne Chief Black Kettle. The Indian raids, however, were now confined to western Kansas and the Dakota Territory, while eastern and central Kansas were quiet as a blooming rose garden as the Union Pacific Railroad greedily and silently devoured its way westward toward the Colorado line in great gulps of rich prairie sod. Quickly, the open prairie had disappeared, and little towns now sprang up along the newly laid railroad tracks as settlers came in.

Now the buffalo had almost disappeared in the state but the summer daisies and sunflowers were already in bloom, with other wildflowers to follow, as the weather warmed toward summer and, after days of rain, new foliage had appeared on trees and bushes, making the new leaves seem to be made of green glass, many as delicate as insects' wings, almost too fragile for the winds which accompanied the prairie storms.

Yes, men on the Lawrence streets continued to talk about the approaching November election and the candidacy of Ulysses Grant, but there was also a Kansas state referendum on female suffrage, the first such referendum in the entire country and perhaps a harbinger of the national debate on the vote for women, which would require an amendment to the Federal Constitution to become law. Hannah and her political friends believed this vote could give momentum to the cause of female suffrage, and I told her I would also support her cause and even raise the question with some men to whom I could speak freely. What I heard from them was that none of them—*none*—would vote for suffrage for women or even consider a "yes" vote. Hannah's political "cause" seemed doomed to defeat before it even began.

But since only white men with property could vote in Kansas, as in most states, the voices of women, Indians, and the poor, no matter how impassioned, informed, or articulate, would not be heard and would continue to count for nothing. "Nothing will come of nothing," we learn from Shakespeare's *King Lear*. So, I was not surprised when the suffrage referendum in Kansas was badly defeated by the voters; Hannah's cause had suffered a humiliating setback.

We must now lick our wounds, I told her, but be ready for the next time, for surely another opportunity to advance female suffrage would come. For the present, I said that everyone's eyes should be on Grant and the defeat of President Johnson, and then we could return to the cause of suffrage for women. I realized that through my love for Hannah, I had been quickly converted to "the cause," as it was now being called by the women who supported it, and a few brave men like the Negro, Frederick Douglass.

So, Hannah and I consoled each other: she over an election lost and I over a daughter who had grown up too soon, although Hannah quickly convinced me how fortunate we were in Samantha's choice, since Davey was a personable young man with solid prospects. To be honest, Samantha had done very well, I told myself, and, in any event, a marriage might be years away. But, still, she did seem too young to be considering marriage to anyone. Perhaps there would still be a time to talk about her further education before a final decisions were made.

Since I was no longer being sent out from Lawrence by Downing and the *Globe Democrat,* now I had to be content with reports in the newspapers about the plainsmen, drovers, and military figures whom I knew, but I also looked for newcomers who might be won over to our cause—equal rights for women—as well as those who might need the services of an attorney for routine legal matters.

Among the topics of the men who gathered outside King's livery stable every morning to joke and chew and spit was the change of name by one of the railroads which served Lawrence: the Union Pacific

Railway, Eastern Division, had now had officially become the Kansas Pacific (which was what most folk had been calling it for years anyway, since the old name was a jawbreaker and difficult to articulate) and everyone thought that Kansas Pacific "rolled off the tongue" in a pleasing way.

Although it may seem foolish, when I viewed the fresh gold lettering on the side of a newly painted coach, I felt an unexpected glow of pride on seeing "KANSAS PACIFIC," pleased that our state would be honored in the railroad's new name. Now we had a second railroad with Kansas origins, the Atchison, Topeka, and the Santa Fe being the first, although many of us doubted whether *that* particular line would ever reach all the way from Kansas to the New Mexico town in the name. But no one would take Kansas for granted now with our own railroads.

Of course, many of the men who had been my companions *were* still featured in the newspapers: James Butler Hickok, Buffalo Bill Cody, Generals Sherman and Custer of the U.S. Army, and others who had served in the West. Many of the stories about Cody and Hickok were written by greenhorns or effete Easterners and featured outlandish and often excessively violent descriptions like the accounts written by J. W. Buel in *Heroes of the Plains* or R.M. DeWitt in the dime novels, which had made Hickok famous across the entire country as "Wild Bill."

His friends also basked in his reflected glory: Texas Jack Omohundro, Colorado Charley Utter, and Jack Harvey were names familiar to nearly everyone in the West. And now there were even women: Indian Annie from Hickok's days in Ellsworth and later Calamity Jane, whom, some said, could outshoot Wild Bill, although I thought that claim a gross exaggeration.

Several of the accounts obscured Hickok's selfless or heroic actions such as his rescue of a hapless wrangler from a lynch mob in Hays City or the grievous wound in the thigh he received at the hands of the Cheyenne, a wound which may have been what caused him to leave his position as a military scout at the end of February 1869 and become a lawman in western Kansas, although I had not yet discussed that matter with him.

I did see Hickok from time to time in Topeka or Kansas City, of course, and we talked about our families or horseflesh or speculated about local matters or the severe Kansas weather because Jim simply did not like to discuss partisan politics in the way many men did; in fact, his chief interests were gambling, guns, marksmanship, and—many joked—women. Hickok was, however, the most famous Kansan since John Brown, still a crack shot, and I was proud to call him my friend.

There was, I believed, something else in him that many others did not see. Despite his fame as a lawman and his outward exuberance, I felt, there abided a pensiveness which he carried within himself and would not share with anyone. Although he loved jokes and leg pulling, he had a private side that was revealed only to a tight circle of friends. On occasion, when I believed he was about to reveal his private thoughts to me, he invariably stepped back into the safety of silence.

Buffalo Bill Cody was equally famous—not as a lawman like Hickok—but as a buffalo hunter who supplied meat for the crews that pushed the railroad westward across the Kansas prairie. He believed his long hair and buckskin garments attracted attention, and he outfitted himself accordingly. He was an excellent horseman, looked splendid in the saddle, was not a gambler or a frequenter of the saloon or dance hall, and put his greenbacks in the bank. Brave and unsullied in opinion, he was, in short, a model for office in any small town, as welcome as a cold beer on a hot summer's day. My friend Big Ears King speculated that he was a man without a mean streak, of solid repute, and I admitted that I knew of no flaws in his character, although I still thought Hickok the better man.

The West in our century, not yet completed, had produced many noteworthy and famous men, some of whom I had known and written about, as well as evildoers of all kinds. To my mind, the greatest villain of all was William Quantrill, who betrayed the town of Lawrence and led the slaughter of almost two hundred unarmed men and boys in a hot Kansas dawn, a Machiavellian and Iago, and his followers, Bloody Bill Anderson and Little Archie Clement, who killed because they learned to love killing. Against them could be placed the heroes of early-day Kansas: the first governor, Charles Robinson, John Brown, and, of course, President Abraham Lincoln, who saved the Union.

Certainly, I was writing less and less for newspapers and magazines and was now attending to my profession as an attorney. It had been the law, of course, which I had promised my father I would follow in the new state of Kansas, and I had been successful in my vocation. I had made another promise too—to my wife, Hannah—so after fifteen years of marriage, it was now time to act and bring that thought to actuality. So,

I set out to build the two-story brick house she had always wanted, one with a proper garden which might keep her at home more of the time and perhaps out of Kansas politics, although that proved a vain hope.

And now it seemed we might need to see our daughter, Samantha, married and perhaps add even more children to the family. Our son Henley had—as people say—grown like a weed and was now as tall as his mother. He was full of new terms like "cowboy," by which he meant a wrangler or drover, terms which I had used since I was a boy, but which were now as old-fashioned as the term "palfrey." And so, I realized that while I was worrying about Samantha, who was now "walking out" with Davey, as people were calling courtship, the English that we spoke was changing too. It was not the language of Chaucer or Shakespeare anymore, or even the language of Melville or Dickens, but something different and new.

Of course, ever since I was a student, I had known that language and words changed over time, and that what was incorrect today might well be entirely proper tomorrow, although, of course, I did not intend to start using "cowboy" in my writing or even in conversation with my peers. In one of my grammar books, years before, I had written these lines from Chaucer: "In forme of speche is chaunge." I cannot remember what had prompted me to copy the lines in my lesson book, but they now served to remind me that our English language is not a dead tongue like Latin but is living and growing like everything else around us.

While I was musing on language, from out his livery stable came Big Ears, wiping his brow with a red bandana and collarless in the heat of the morning. I was pleased to see Ears because I hoped to avoid Davey, who seemed to turn up with a regularity that was now beginning to annoy me. When I complained to Hannah, she shook her head and laughed. "If we had had more daughters, you would have enough votes to be elected governor if you played your cards right! But don't count your chickens yet, my love!"

Big Ears was in an unusually expansive mood, and I wondered why. "Got big news, Ezra," he announced. "Man I know from Hays City come to town this morning and says our old friend Wild Bill got hisself elected sheriff at Hays a week or so ago. Even left me a newspaper to prove it!"

I found it amusing that Ears had used the phrase "our friend" for Hickok since, to the best of my knowledge, he had seen Hickok only once or twice in his life. Of course, I was delighted to know that Hickok was again a civilian after serving as a scout for the Seventh Cavalry. The last I heard of him was his intended journey back to Homer, his home in Illinois, to see his mother and recover from a wound in his thigh inflicted by Chief Black Kettle. Then in 1867, he turned up again in Hays City, Kansas, the terminus of the Kansas Pacific Railway Company.

Hays City, center of the buffalo hide business, had earned a dubious but seemingly well-deserved reputation because of the gamblers, pimps, prostitutes, and saloon keepers who served the greed and lust of the buffalo-hunters, skinners, and those who catered to their appetites. The town had grown up about a mile or so from Fort Hays in September of 1867. One newspaper writer in the Junction City *Weekly Union* declared that "we should call it the Sodom of the Plains," shortly after the town was founded.

Then, in August of 1869, Hickok was elected Sheriff of Ellis County. He was still known in the town from his days as a scout and guide when his constant companion was Jack Harvey of the old Buckskin Scouts; it was believed that Hickok earlier might have had a hand in a gambling establishment in Junction City when he scouted from Fort Riley.

Despite its dubious reputation, Hays City was thriving and bursting with activity, although many of its respectable citizens made immediate law and order the priority in Ellis County. As a deputy United States marshal and army scout, Hickok was well known, a familiar face in Hays, as Big Ears was quick to point out to me. By the time he began walking the dirt streets of Hays, he had replaced his buckskin suits for a Prince Albert frock coat and checkered trousers, but apparently, he still carried his two large Colt Navy revolvers in their "butts forward" position. From time to time, as sheriff, he handled deserters from the army or known ruffians by clubbing them with one of his revolvers or by relying on his fists alone.

Now I believed I could stay current with the deeds of my friend Hickok, from stories in the Junction City *Weekly Union,* when in September an account appeared under the following headline: *Particulars in the Killing of Stranhan at Hays City.* The article explained that an inquest had been held, which determined that the shooting of a troublemaker in Hays by the new sheriff was a justified homicide. According to the story, "Too much credit cannot be given to Wild Bill for his endeavor to rid this town of such dangerous characters as this 'Stranhan' was." The correct name of the dead man, I was able to determine, was Samuel Strawhun, a known ruffian in Hays. However his name was spelled, he was apparently a recognized troublemaker.

Pleased that Jim Hickok was again in the state, now out of the army, and in Hays at the other end of the Kansas Pacific line, I sent off a short telegram, inviting him for a visit when his official travels took him to Kansas City or Topeka. Since we had not heard from him for some time, I hurried home to tell Hannah the latest news about him.

We were hoping that with a permanent job again, he might begin to put down roots in Ellis County, although I was less hopeful of this than was Hannah. Our two-story brick house in West Lawrence was coming along fine, and since I no longer traveled out of town for stories for the *Globe Democrat,* I could devote more of my time to the building trades and began to nourish the hope that Hickok might in fact be the first guest in our new home, if we could find a bed long enough for him.

In the days that preceded the presidential election, as the nation had watched the attempt of the Radical Republicans in Congress to impeach and convict President Andrew Johnson, I also kept my eyes on events in Hays City far across the state. In any event, in the presidential election, Grant defeated Johnson and Grant's other opponents, although by far fewer electoral votes than had been expected. I duly voted for the slate of electors pledged to cast their votes for U. S. Grant, according to the election laws of our country and state, not directly for Grant.

Of course, Hannah was unable to exercise the franchise at all, but she was happy with my vote for Grant since she despised Johnson as much as I did. As the votes for the electors across the country began to come in, it was apparent that we were to have a new president: U.S. Grant of Ohio. I was gratified that through the telegraph and railroads, our huge nation, stretching across an entire continent, could conduct an election in so short a time and congratulated my countrymen that after a bleak period under Johnson, we had emerged sound and whole. Many of us now celebrated the election of Grant as we had celebrated the nation's choice of Lincoln before him.

As a Kansan for two decades, I thought it time to re-examine my life on the frontier. While our state was still a territory, I had wooed and wed a Missouri girl, had two children and adopted a third, and pursued two careers, one as a correspondent for a St. Louis newspaper, the other as an attorney in a raw prairie town. After the Lawrence massacre during the war, I served with the Kansas militia as a private and fought at the Battle of Westport, where we routed the Confederate Cavalry of General Sterling Price, saved Kansas for the Union, and, on a bitterly cold and icy day in November of 1864, ended the war in the West.

Many faces are still before me, drawn from the well of my memory. Here before me now are the faces of Dr. Charles Robinson and James Henry Lane, different in temperament and politics but both determined to impose their will on events, united only by their passionate hatred of slavery; Robinson a fine-looking man with a high forehead, who wore spectacles and seemed the dispassionate pedagogue while Lane, his unruly hair flying, was fiery and equally single-minded in his pursuit of power.

Another face from the Territorial Days was that of Old Osawatomie, weathered and wrinkled John Brown, who single-mindedly saw the events of early-day Kansas as a struggle between good and evil in Biblical terms. His co pper-gray eyes still burn in my memory above his white beard. I should mention too, Thomas Pidgeon, his plain face, unattractive, now dimmed by time, though not his melodious speaking voice; it was he who had sold me the Colt Dragoon revolver which I carried and used at Westport because I did not trust the Enfield rifle provided by the militia.

Other faces from the early days are those of Henry Sonnet and his clever wife Leona, and that of Captain Dan Cornish of the Kansas Militia, who died at the Battle of Westport, where the young militiamen had called me Uncle Ezra—and I remember each one of them too, along with Larby Jones, who lost his leg in the battle. There was Russell Downing of the *Globe Democrat*, who sent me to Kansas, and, of course, faces from more recent days, including especially my own family and friends in Lawrence. And I can never forget Eli, Big Ears King, Little Joe Oscar, or Colonel Frederick Maypole, but I especially remember my partner in life, my wife, Hannah. Her face will be the last one I see before I die.

These descriptions can never do justice to the men and women whom I knew on the Border as we doggedly pursued statehood through war and finally peace. So, year after year, Westport has been the lodestone that has drawn me back to this town on the border where Kansas and Missouri come together, once in bitter and bloody conflict, and now at last, I hope, in everlasting amity within the Union.

ABOUT THE AUTHOR

ALAN ELLIOTT CRAVEN is a retired Shakespeare scholar and former college dean residing with his wife, Janice, in San Antonio, Texas. He has three adult children. Born in Kansas City, Missouri, he lived in Lawrence, Kansas for a number of years and has three degrees from the University of Kansas. His family has deep Midwestern roots, the Cravens settling in Missouri before 1830. As boys, his father and uncle knew the outlaw Frank James in Kearney, Clay County, Missouri. His mother's family moved to Kansas in 1861, the year the state was admitted to the Union. They homesteaded at Dry Ridge, Bourbon County, Kansas. Nine boys in the family fought for the Union in the Civil War, including his great-grandfather. In the presidential election of 1860, his great- great- grandfather and two other men were the only ones in their precinct to cast votes for Abraham Lincoln.

www.ingramcontent.com/pod-product-compliance
Lightning Source LLC
Chambersburg PA
CBHW011354010726
47494CB00008B/2315

9798888193594